About the Author

GL lives in the Pacific Northwest near the rugged and beautiful Oregon Coast. An avid reader, writer, photographer, chef, and vocal visible advocate for the BLGTQ community, GL writes when not working a day job.

GL is currently working on a lesbian fantasy set in ancient Scotland just as the Vikings are beginning to invade Britain.

SHIELDMAIDEN

BOOK ONE:
Quest for the Jewel

GL ROBERTS

Bella
BOOKS

2016

Bella Books, Inc.
P.O. Box 10543
Tallahassee, FL 32302

Printed in the United States of America on acid-free paper.

First Bella Books Edition 2016

Editor: Janet Mehl
Cover Designer: Judith Fellows

ISBN: 978-1-59493-497-1

For the SDGS and their giggles before bed.

King Heardred heard the distant voices on the wind—an odd, unfamiliar sound that caused his breath to catch in his throat. A strange light glowed over the horizon where light should not shine. The sun does not rise in the west, he reminded himself; this must be an aberration. He dismissed the strange glow as another of the surreal lights that often lit up the skies of the far north and turned back to watch the boats. The foreboding wind behind him, the king watched as another sack of provisions was loaded onto one of the long boats.

Götaland will lose a favored son, he thought, and he did not understand how that was possible. King Heardred's people had not met resistance from the Albans for centuries. But Helstun was long overdue from the raiding trip to Alban and the families of the men that went west over the sea with his son wanted answers. They looked to their king for an explanation.

Legend told of the coming of a Druid warrior, and even though the thought made the king sneer, it also made him take pause. No Druid myth—or curse—could stop him from finding out what had happened to his son. No legend would be able to stop his fury if his son was dead. He would avenge his son's death to the last man, woman and child who inhabited the mystic, Druid-infested island.

Taken from the ancient texts of the Clann of Brae Writings and Teachings, as set down by the Arch Druid of Brae:

The pact between dragonkind and humankind, long a treasured and cherished union, began eons before the words were carved into the sacred stones or inked onto the ancient parchments. Once a union of equals, over the centuries the pact was gradually refashioned—to the continuing detriment of dragonkind—and the tenuous thread that held the two together began to slowly fray.

Bound to the ancient ways by honor, dragonkind adapted to the changing ways of humankind, albeit with reluctance. Obedience to the pact was the duty of every dragon. It had been so since humans had crouched behind rocks and dragons watched over them from both the earth and stars. Dragons that had remained true and pure of heart and thought were granted a spot in the night sky from which to spend eternity looking down upon their earthbound charges. Angels with hearts as big as their bodies, they lit up the night with a light from within their souls, causing the sky to blaze with nobility.

The magical relationship between a female dragon, directly descended from the first dragon to leave the stars and come to earth, and a Druid princess, lies at the heart of this story and is the reason that it can be told.

CHAPTER ONE

Royal celebrations always took on an air of urgency, from the moment they were declared to the moment they took place, right until the last guests were safely sent on their way afterward. All court attendants assumed a multitude of duties on such occasions: Waiting ladies became decorators, stable boys became porters, even nursemaids took on additional chores. No one was spared. Waiting Lady Bryn spent countless hours preparing for the celebration by helping her princess choose a dress, decide on a hairstyle, determine the color of rose petals to be used in the courtyard, and select the food to have on the table that would please both the princess and her guests.

"Will you not take a bite?" a young kitchen servant asked Bryn when she came into the kitchen. In Bryn's hand were a piece of parchment and a small stick of colored wax.

"A piece of fruit would be good," Bryn replied. "Have the melons from the south county arrived?" Bryn held the stick of wax over the word *melon* on the parchment.

"Yes," the young man replied.

Bryn rubbed the wax over the word. "One less item to worry about," she said and smiled at the young man as he handed her an apple. "Thank you, Pilan." Bryn yawned and Pilan chuckled.

"I've been catching myself sleeping standing up," Bryn said. "Perhaps a short nap would be in order."

"For a Waiting Lady you work too hard," Pilan said.

"Ah, but think of the rewards," Bryn said, touching Pilan's arm. "The Princess Thalynder is worth every effort. Her smile alone could melt the winter snows."

"True, Lady Bryn. True indeed."

"Just Bryn, my friend. I may be a Waiting Lady, but I remain a Druid like you, and we both know we have no titles unless given to us by our elders."

"You are a lady in my eyes," Pilan said and turned back to his own work preparing food for the great feast.

Bryn decided that what little sleep might come to her would be obtained in the antechamber of the rooms of Her Highness the Princess Thalynder. From there she could anticipate the princess's needs—as she had been doing for nearly seventeen years—and be one step ahead of the rest of the frayed staff. For Bryn, the upcoming celebration was one she and the princess had been discussing for six months. It was an important date and, if all went according to plan, a new beginning for both her and the princess. Accordingly, Bryn informed her parents that she would henceforth be sleeping in the keep to be closer to Her Highness. Bryn moved out of her parents' warm and comfortable home and into the fortress of King Thamen and his daughter.

※

On the day she turned twenty—the date that confirmed her loss of childhood to the rest of the realm—Princess Thalynder rose early and dressed in her riding clothes. She pulled the dark green stockings up over her knees and tied the ribbons around her legs to keep the stockings in place. She added a dark green underdress over the stockings. She did not want to wake anyone to lace up the back of her dress so Thalynder chose an overdress that tied in the front. She slipped on her ankle-high deerskin boots, grabbed her cloak, and left her room. Walking quietly through the inner rooms, she managed not to wake the other occupants. Unbeknownst to the princess, Bryn was already awake and tending to the day's events.

Bryn heard footsteps in the inner sanctum and hurried to peer around a wall. She quickly drew back when she saw it was Princess Thalynder walking toward the outer yard. Bryn quietly followed the princess out to the garden where the dragon slept.

As Thalynder neared the bower that marked the entrance to the dragon garden, Bryn moved to the trees and waited. She knew her presence would not go unnoticed—the princess's dragon had superior senses—but she didn't want to intrude on this special moment between the princess and her companion. Bryn sat down on the soft, damp grass with her back against a tree where she could watch and listen as Thalynder greeted her dragon in the early morning light.

"Are you awake?" the princess asked. The dragon was still, her head resting on her forearm and her tail curled up under her back legs, much the way the cat in the halls of the keep slept.

"I am, Princess," the dragon replied.

"Today I am of age, Meydra." Thalynder turned her face toward the eastern horizon in anticipation of the sun and closed her eyes.

"You are," Meydra replied.

"After today, my father will expect me to wed," Thalynder said. She opened her eyes and placed her hand on Meydra's forehead. "I do not wish to wed."

"What do you wish, Princess?" Meydra asked.

"I wish to find true love," Thalynder said. "On this day when all childhood is shed, I have only one wish: to find a true love. How can I be so selfish?"

"It is not selfish to want to find a partner with whom to share your life," Meydra said and rose to a sitting position. "I too desire to find a mate."

"On this, the anniversary of my birth, I ask you, faithful Dragon Companion, to help me realize this dream." Thalynder wiped a single tear from her cheek. "It is known by all that dragons not only are born in truth but also can sense truth in the hearts of others. Help me find my true love, Meydra. In return, I will aid you in your search for a mate that is worthy of *your* love. We will make this our quest."

"If that is truly what you desire above all else, that will be my gift," Meydra said, bowing her head before Thalynder. Thalynder rubbed the dragon's head between her ears, causing Meydra to murmur softly.

"Come, take me to the hill." The princess grabbed the rope around Meydra's neck and climbed onto her back. "I wish to see the sun rise from the highest spot in the realm."

Meydra waited until the princess was secure on her back before standing up and walking out from under the trees. Bryn stood up and ducked behind the tree, and felt Meydra's tail brush the hem of her dress. She smiled and watched as the dragon lifted off the ground with an effortless beat of her wings and rose above the trees. Once they were out of sight, Bryn ran back to the keep, her bare feet sure and swift on the well-worn path.

Bryn of the Brae, daughter of Brymender and Arlendyl— Druid Elders of the Clann Brae—and attendant to the princess, left the cover of the trees and walked quickly back to the keep. Her thoughts whirled around Thalynder's words: *my father will expect me to wed*. Bryn knew Thalynder was expected to marry a prince or other noble-born man to secure the realm and continue the line. If only the realm felt as the Druids did about love and marriage, Bryn thought. Bryn believed that love was love, no matter where or how or who was involved. Love was not private or reserved, it was meant to be shared, open and celebrated. The realm of King Thamen planned and strategized over love and in the end, marriages were arranged and love was sometimes lost. For Thalynder to wish to find true love meant she understood what her fate would be if left in her father's hands. Bryn shook her head.

Since Princess Thalynder's fourth year, Bryn had been her constant companion. She was a scant six months older than the princess. Over the years, the two girls had become loyal friends. The princess had no other siblings and was hard on court-appointed attendants, but Bryn had won out over all the others. The court became Bryn's second home and over the years she shared in the riches the king bestowed upon his daughter.

By way of Thalynder, Bryn had the finest tutors. The art of warfare she learned from the captains of the king's army—when they were resting in the realm and not busy chasing bands of thieves or trying to stave off an invasion of the outer realms by the bloodthirsty Norsemen. She learned the art of sport from the hunters in the cool of autumn, when game was plentiful. Loyalty she learned by watching the captains, respect was learned in the subjects of the king's realm, and justice, as it had been taught from the beginning of time and practiced by all who imagined that fairness was the right of humankind, Bryn learned from her parents.

Though not born a royal herself, Bryn felt almost equal to the princess. She was a Druid, a race held in high esteem by the nobles as learned men and women. The Druids, with their tradition of oral history, taught Bryn ancient dragon lore and alchemy. She learned traditional uses for herbs and plants and the medicinal properties of each. Bryn had also been schooled in animal husbandry. She understood the intricacies of procreation long before the princess was taught them by her narrow-minded, court-appointed tutor.

Arlendyl, Bryn's mother, taught Bryn that sex was a sacred, intimate act between consenting partners and not to be taken lightly. Love, Arlendyl said, came unexpectedly. It didn't choose to wait for the right moment, or the right day or the right year. Love came and it never left. Love, Bryn came to understand, was exemplified by her parents' deep respect for each other and the sweet sounds of undiluted joy that came from their bedchamber at night.

Thalynder, Bryn knew from their many late-night conversations, found love to be something two-edged, much like the sword she wore at her belt. On one side was the love of her father, her dragon, and her friends. On the other side was an as-yet-undiscovered love, the one that occupied her dreams.

"If there was only someone like that in my realm," Thalynder once said after reading about a brave soul doing a daring deed to save a princess. Bryn wanted to be that brave soul and save her princess. She knew Thalynder longed for someone whose passion for adventure would match her own. The princess often told Bryn that she did not care about ruling her father's realm. Though she was schooled to rule, Thalynder longed for the day when her father would sire another heir. The chances of that happening remained remote because King Thamen was consumed with the raiders and the safety of his realm. He had little time for anything else.

"It is time we returned," Meydra said. The sun had risen above the horizon and the air was warming.

"Yes, I suppose it is," Thalynder said. "I can't wait to tell Bryn my plan."

"You will have to tell your father as well and he may not let you leave."

"He will if I can think of a way to make it seem important for the realm."

"Meaning what?"

"Oh, I don't know. Something beneficial like a prince for me to marry?"

"Even that may not sway the king," Meydra said and turned back to smile at Thalynder.

"It is past the time of the raiders. Most of the thieves have been forced out of the realm. What could my father be worried about?"

"He will find something. Are you ready to return?"

"Yes, take me to the courtyard. They are waiting, I am sure."

Meydra lifted into the sky and glided down toward the keep. She could see the courtyard clearly from the hill, and she saw Bryn waiting for their return. Meydra sent a silent greeting to Bryn, knowing she would not understand where the greeting had come from. Soon, Meydra thought. Very soon that will change.

Meydra landed in the middle of the courtyard, bowed her head, and lowered her shoulders for Thalynder to slide off her back. Bryn smiled at Thalynder as she came off Meydra's back.

Meydra saw the exchange between the two women and the blush that came to Bryn's cheeks. Her tail twitched. She bowed her head and gave one last smile to the princess, arched her back, and left the courtyard below, rising to fly back to her resting place in the Garden of Dragons. As she moved her giant wings silently to gain lift, she looked back down and watched Bryn follow Thalynder as she walked toward the doors of the residential section of the keep. Meydra's heart beat fast for a brief moment, then settled back down to a steady drumbeat. Her giant wings moved to momentarily block the sun and cast her shadow across the two young women, causing both to look up and smile at her. Another beat of her wings, and she was gone.

Bryn followed Thalynder into her chambers and helped her out of her riding clothes.

"Where is my party dress?" Thalynder asked and started humming.

"Hanging in the wardrobe where it won't get dirty or too wrinkled, Lynder."

Bryn always referred to Princess Thalynder as Lynder when her thoughts were warmly casual. In the presence of others, Bryn was careful to call Thalynder "Your Highness" or "Princess." But in the happy place where they were two young women, she thought of Thalynder in a softer light and the name Lynder tasted sweeter on her tongue. "You are humming and that means you are thinking of something not altogether *permitted*."

"I'll tell you after we greet some of the guests. My father is probably eager to get this day started."

"He is, and so is the realm. You know the significance of this day better than most and surely you see your father's subjects love you and consider you their next ruler."

"I do, but I've also told you I don't want the job. Enough," Thalynder said and chuckled. "Get me dressed and we'll go find my father."

Bryn followed the princess to the throne placed at the entrance to the inner keep, where King Thamen now sat. The king stood as his daughter approached, and when Thalynder was at his side, he raised his hand to the gathered crowd. Cued by his hand, servants released a shower of pale pink rose petals that drifted down from the windows and walls of the keep and decorated the courtyard. Bryn watched as the petals fell upon Thalynder's head and shoulders. Her heart quickened at the beautiful sight.

Thalynder took her father's hand and together they stood as the crowd cheered. The princess nodded in thanks and said, "Let the music begin."

Thalynder and the king moved into the Grand Hall where the noble lords and ladies waited for the princess's entrance. A rousing cheer went up when Thalynder appeared, and the air was charged with gaiety. Bryn recognized the tradition: the party outside for the subjects of the realm and the party inside for the nobility. The celebration would go on all day and into the night, capped off by a brilliant display of light and fire at midnight.

Bryn kept her distance behind Thalynder as usual. That was her place when in the company of the princess and others, a lesson she had acquired when she first arrived at court, and which was now as routine as breathing.

Letting go of her father's hand, Princess Thalynder walked among the guests, thanking them for attending her Day of Birth celebration. Thalynder turned to look for Bryn. She gently moved several nobles out of her way, grabbed at Bryn's sleeve, and gently tugged on it until Bryn was standing in front of her. Thalynder took Bryn's hand in hers and squeezed it.

"Do not leave me today."

Bryn looked into Thalynder's sparkling green eyes. "When will you tell me what is lurking in that pretty blond head?"

Thalynder giggled and pulled Bryn toward the long table laden with her favorite foods. "Come, let us grab some fruit, and I will tell you of the adventure we will embark upon come the morrow."

Before they could reach the table, however, they were intercepted by a group of nobles intent on toasting their princess. Thalynder quickly let go of Bryn's hand and greeted each man and woman by name. After accepting their compliments, she introduced them to Bryn, who in turn received her own share of gracious comments.

"Why do you scoff?" Thalynder asked after Bryn reacted to a particularly effusive compliment from a rotund and jolly nobleman. "You have your own beauty, Bryn."

"You, my princess, are the sky. Your hair is the color of the sun's rays. Your eyes are the green of new leaves that dot the arboreal canopy. You are like a sunrise."

"And how do you see yourself?"

Bryn held a lock of her hair and looked at it a moment. "I am the earth. Chestnut red hair, deep blue eyes. The nobles are only polite because I am the daughter of Druid elders. I am an oddity." Bryn's heritage was also a source of curiosity to most of the nobles, who couldn't understand the selfless way in which Druids conducted themselves.

"You are no oddity," Sir Arryn, captain of the King's Royal Guard, said as he passed the two women. "The princess is the dawn, bright and full of coming events. You, Lady Bryn, are the twilight, where all go to find peace."

Thalynder laughed as she turned to her other guests and never saw the blush that touched Bryn's cheeks.

Being in the company of Thalynder was always pleasant for Bryn. It also gave Bryn the opportunity to be of service to her. Thalynder did not like to be treated like a child, and pompous platitudes and comments about her obligations as heir and princess were almost guaranteed to provoke barbed retorts. When she heard Thalynder's voice taking on a tinge of contempt as she addressed certain of the highly adorned men and women, Bryn touched Thalynder's arm.

"Forgive me, Princess Thalynder, but I believe you mentioned you were hungry, having missed your breakfast this morning," Bryn said in an attempt to keep one of the men from falling victim to Thalynder's sharp tongue.

"Ah yes, Lady Bryn. Thank you for reminding me. Wouldn't do to fall away in a faint due to malnourishment in front of all these guests, would it? If you gentlefolk will excuse me, I will look over the table and satisfy my stomach with the cook's finest fare." Thalynder grabbed Bryn's hand, pulled her closer, and whispered into her ear. "You saved that man from having his tongue removed, boiled and placed on the table as a morsel for the dogs."

"Yes, Your Highness." Bryn tried not to laugh. "I believe you will find several dishes to your liking."

"Let's fill a plate and find a chair at my father's table," Thalynder said, dismissing the little crowd. As they walked along the table toward a large array of fruit, a flared note from a single trumpet called attention to the king.

"My father will speak," Thalynder said. "He is such a one for drama."

Bryn stood with her back to the table of food so she could see the king. Noticing that Thalynder was studying the food instead of paying attention, she cleared her throat and pulled on Thalynder's hand.

Thalynder raised her chin, looked at her father, and then—as he spoke about her coming of age and her need for a husband—gripped Bryn's hand hard enough to make her wince.

As the king congratulated his daughter on reaching the age of Consent and Commitment, Bryn heard Thalynder gasp. Fearing that Thalynder might be choking on something, Bryn turned to look at her. Thalynder's cheeks and neck were red, not from some obstructive morsel, Bryn realized, but from the king's words. As the crowd shouted their hosannas to the princess, Bryn offered her a cup of wine.

"Here, drink this to clear your head and cool your heat." She released Thalynder's hand, held the goblet before Thalynder and waited. The princess took the goblet and gulped the sweet wine.

"It is time to tell me what plan you have concocted, Princess. The one that has us leaving on the morrow."

Thalynder set the goblet on the table and grabbed two soft, ripe peaches. She led Bryn to the king's table, sat next to her father, and motioned Bryn into the chair beside her. She handed Bryn one of the peaches. King Thamen was speaking with Sir Arryn, their faces close together. The princess turned back to Bryn, smiling. She took a small knife from her belt and began to remove the skin from her peach, a small section at a time. "Why do you suppose the gods created peach fur?"

"To keep us from eating the fruit too quickly, allowing us to savor every bite," Bryn said and took a small bite of her peach. Juice ran off her lips and onto her chin, causing her to laugh. She started to wipe her mouth with her sleeve hem.

"Let me," Thalynder said and leaned toward Bryn to run her finger through the juice, then place the sweet nectar onto her tongue. "So sweet. Too sweet to wait another moment." She took a large bite out of her own fruit. "These are the best of the season!"

Bryn took a drink of wine from the goblet in front of her. She needed to distract the princess from the heat of a blush she could feel rising on her cheeks and to prevent herself from wondering if Thalynder meant to be so provocative. Bryn looked down at the platter before her and said, "Tell me your plan."

CHAPTER TWO

The two women spent the day talking with well-wishers, nibbling at the food on the table, walking outside among the gentlefolk, and huddling close together while they discussed how to put Thalynder's plan into action. They came to one early conclusion: the adventure would have to begin later than first hoped because preparation would take a day or two.

Thalynder was certain it would take weeks, if not months, to find true love. Bryn listened to Thalynder's plan, but believed Thalynder was not as serious as she sounded, hoping only to forestall her marriage.

At one point, when they decided that they would not take any men on the adventure, Bryn began to laugh so hard she found it difficult to breathe. Thalynder threw a handful of water from the fountain on Bryn, causing her to gasp and sputter, which in turn spurred Thalynder on into her own bout of laughter. As the giggles set in, the girls left the courtyard for the dragon garden, where Meydra rested in the cool of the darkened woods.

Thalynder approached the nest area ahead of Bryn. They walked onto the softly padded ground and Bryn noted Meydra's tail curled up under her belly. The dragon, when relaxed, resembled the cat that walked the halls of the keep. The cat always curled its tail up under its belly when it slept in the sun, its head resting on an outstretched paw. Thalynder began to walk around to face Meydra, when the dragon stirred.

"I am not asleep, Princess," Meydra said. "You may approach too, Bryn. You are always welcome."

Thalynder looked back at Bryn and nodded. The princess moved to stand in front of Meydra and reached out to touch her forehead, a gesture of recognition between Companions. Meydra lifted her head at Thalynder's touch.

"Have you told the king of your plan to leave?" Meydra asked.

"No. I will wait until the Asking Hour," Thalynder said and sat on a bench that was carved into the trunk of a fallen tree. "He cannot refuse me if I ask at that hour. He will be sitting in front of all his subjects and is bound by tradition to grant me my wish."

"That is not the time to ask," Bryn said, approaching Meydra. She gave Meydra's cheek an affectionate rub. "He will be shamed into letting you go and that will become a thorn to him."

"If I wait and ask him at another time, he will not allow me to leave," Thalynder said. Pulling her knees to her chest, she hugged them tightly. "I was going to use the opportunity of the Asking Hour."

"Perhaps if you ask for something else first, something that would be good for him, you, and all the gentlefolk of the realm, he will be more softhearted when you tell him of your true wish," Bryn said. "In any case, now that you are of age, you should not have to ask to leave. You should be able to tell him what you intend to do and why you wish to make the journey."

"That is an excellent observation, Bryn," Meydra said. "You will please your father, Princess, as he is already anxious at the thought of losing you to marriage. If you do not put him in an embarrassing situation in front of his subjects tonight, perhaps when the sun rises on the morrow, you can tell him of your plan and he will be in a much better mood."

Thalynder lowered her legs and stood up. She walked back to Meydra and stood next to Bryn. "He may be more accepting of my plan if I soften the blow. That is what the two of you believe?"

"Yes," Meydra replied.

"It will work," Bryn said. "He is a king, a father, but more important, he is a man. Think like a man, a father and a king, and you will know the right way to phrase your wish. You will not only be allowed to leave but he will send you off with a grand parade through the realm, complete with banners waving and subjects cheering. No one will know that you led the king to his decision."

Thalynder placed a quick kiss on Bryn's cheek and patted Meydra's nose. "This will be a great adventure!" A clear bell rang out from the inner keep and Thalynder took Bryn's hand in hers. "Come, Bryn. The Asking Hour is upon us."

Bryn rubbed the soft skin behind Meydra's ear and allowed Thalynder to pull her along by the hand. Bryn glanced back at Meydra and smiled. Meydra was going to be an ally to her, and that, Bryn thought, was a good thing. A dragon was best as your friend, dangerous and deadly as your enemy. Bryn was quite fond of Meydra. For as long as she could remember, Bryn had secretly wished Meydra belonged to her.

When they reached the outer wall of the keep, Thalynder released Bryn's hand and walked into the inner courtyard to stand next to her father. King Thamen addressed the crowd with a strong voice.

"My subjects," he began. "The sky will soon be ablaze with light and fire from the far lands of the east, but before we turn our eyes skyward, let us turn our ears here. Today we celebrate the anniversary of the birth of your beloved princess, Thalynder the Fair, of the Realm that Touches Two Seas. At this, the Asking Hour, we will hear now her anniversary wish." Thamen took his daughter's hand in his and leaned over to speak into her ear. "I do hope you have given this much thought."

Thalynder smiled up at her father. "Of course I have, Father."

"What is your wish, my daughter?" King Thamen said to the crowd. The crowd became silent. So silent that even the dragon out in the garden could hear the collective intake of breath of the crowd. All of the realm waited to hear the princess's birthday wish.

"It is always best for a kingdom to be ruled by a happy monarch, be it a king, a queen, a prince, or a princess," Thalynder said to the crowd. "A happy monarch, one who is loved not only by the loyal subjects of the realm but by his own family as well, is a truly great asset for any kingdom. For many years now, our king has been bereft of his own complement—a queen to sit beside him and bear his children and heirs. My mother died in the throes of childbirth and my father has been alone since that time." Thalynder squeezed her father's hand and took a deep breath. "Therefore, it is my wish before this year is out and I see another anniversary of my birth, that our king find and marry one who will fill the emptiness in his heart."

Thalynder turned to her father and placed a kiss upon his cheek. King Thamen stared at his daughter and in a rare public display of emotion, he gathered her in his arms and held her in a warm embrace. The crowd released its collective breath and let out a generous and hearty cheer.

Bryn smiled as she looked out at the crowd. It was the perfect wish—one that would benefit the king and his realm and, in no small part, Thalynder herself. Its big-heartedness would also pave the way for the king's granting of the princess's true wish. Thalynder had heeded Bryn's advice.

The sky lit up with the flash of fire that signaled the end of the day-long celebration of Thalynder's twentieth birthday. The crowd cheered each burst of fire. Thalynder sat on a stone bench, covered in a pelt of snow-white rabbit fur dotted with wilted rose petals and watched the display. Bryn started toward her and wondered aloud, "Where will she find true love?" The boom of the explosion echoed her own heartbeat, and when the brilliant display again cast a bright flash in the courtyard, she saw Thalynder's face light up with the spectral glow. Bryn sighed and made her way through the crowd toward the stone bench and Thalynder.

As Bryn approached, the princess made room for her on the bench. Bryn looked around to see who might be watching, and since no one was looking at them, she squeezed Thalynder's hand. Thalynder looked at Bryn and waited for the next explosion of light and sound. As the heart-stopping concussion hit their chests, she gasped and pulled Bryn close to her.

Bryn softly laughed at Thalynder's reaction and wrapped her free arm around Thalynder. She held her as the sky lit up and the man-made thunder pounded in their ears and chests. The last of the fiery display exploded in a flurry of miniature bright white blooms. The rapid-fire burst filled the air and the crowd clapped and cheered. Bryn began to remove her arm but felt Thalynder object by moving closer to her.

"You should try to get some sleep, Lynder," Bryn said. "When do you plan to tell your father that you are leaving on your journey?"

"*Our* journey," Thalynder said. "You have to come with me. I can't even get dressed without you. How can I go alone?"

"You wouldn't be alone, you know that."

"If I insist, you'll have to go."

"Would you insist?"

"No, but you know I need you. You've always been better at things than I. You can cook, I can't. You're the better swordsman. Being a Druid, you know all about the woods."

"So do the knights and captains of the guard. And you, Your Highness, are schooled in diplomacy and strategy. You are as capable as I in most things."

"Bryn, I need you with me. I'm lost without you."

"Our journey then. It will be our journey."

"Will your father allow it?"

"I don't have to obtain his permission, Thalynder," Bryn said. "I am, after all, nearly six months older than you. But I will tell my parents. They'll be concerned but they know me enough to trust me." Bryn removed her arm from Thalynder's shoulders. She started to rise from the bench and felt Thalynder grasp her hand and attempt to pull her back down. She resisted and said, "Come on, Lynder, you need to get some sleep, and you still have to check on Meydra."

"You're angry with me, Bryn. You cannot be angry. It is my birth day, and you are not allowed to be angry."

"I am not angry. No, not angry, just concerned. I do not need to ask my parents' permission, but traveling has always meant special plans for the Druids. Besides, it is no longer your birth day. The moon has risen and it is after midnight." Bryn pulled her hand from Thalynder's grasp and stepped back. She could not see Thalynder's face in the moonlight. "Do you want me to accompany you to see Meydra?"

"No, I will not be going out to her tonight," Thalynder said. "You're right, it is late and I have a task ahead of me that I anticipate will not be well received." She yawned. "I will send someone else to tend to Meydra's needs."

Bryn heard the sleep in Thalynder's voice and knew the princess would not be awake much longer. She pulled Thalynder up from the bench. "I will see to Meydra. You go on up to bed."

"Very well. Thank you again for your gift, Bryn." Thalynder touched the shell at her neck. "A perfect cowrie shell, and the silver filament is so delicate. Why didn't you want the others to see you give it to me?"

Bryn had scoured the shore of the East Sea for the perfect shell for Thalynder, one that was the right size for her neck and clear enough in color so as not to contrast with her skin tone. The silver filament that wrapped around the shell—inspired by the silver maple tree's lacy look—was Bryn's own design. She had fashioned the thread to look like a thin branch, giving the whole piece an earth and sea connection. When her father saw the finished piece, he had remarked that her ancestors would be extremely proud of her design. She had given the necklace to Thalynder earlier when they were walking back to the keep from the dragon garden. *You spoil me,* Thalynder had said to Bryn when she handed over the gift.

"We each now have the same piece to wear around our necks on special occasions," Bryn remarked, avoiding Thalynder's question.

"Why not wear it every day?" Thalynder asked. "Let us make a pact right now to wear these pieces every day of our journey and not to remove them until my true love has been found."

Bryn smiled. "As you wish, Lynder. We will not remove the necklaces until your true love replaces the shell with a pledge of undying devotion. Now, off you go to bed. I will go check on Meydra." She kissed Thalynder's cheek and waited until the princess walked under the archway that lead to the inner keep. The night breeze filled the air with the scent of roses. Bryn took a deep breath and headed for the garden where Meydra lay sleeping.

There was no need to check on Meydra. Dragons were not like horses or cattle. They did not need to have their troughs refilled or their buckets replenished with feed. They could fend for themselves. Dragons in the wild preferred caves, but when bound to humans, they slept in gardens of tall grass under high-canopied trees with deep green leaves and silver bark the same color as their skin, which made it hard for them to be easily seen by prying eyes.

Bryn knew all these things, though she did not let anyone know of the knowledge she possessed. Dragons were now reserved for the nobles and that law was strictly enforced, but her grandfather had once been bound to his own dragon. As far as Bryn knew, there was only the one dragon in the Realm that Touches Two Seas, and that was Meydra. There were others dragons on the island, of that she was certain. Her parents, in their extensive teachings about dragons, told her that several inhabited the island, and one of those was known to have descended from the first dragon to come to earth. The bond between dragon and human was a mystery one did not question. When a dragon chose to be one's Companion, that person was honor-bound to accept. Only upon death—the human's or the dragon's—would the bond be broken.

Bryn walked out through the back gates of the keep and looked at the night sky, which sparkled with a multitude of stars crowned by a slivered moon. The breeze stirred the grass around her as she walked the path that led to the dragon gardens. The deep sound of Meydra's breathing reached Bryn as she approached the entrance. Assured by the cadence that Meydra was still awake, Bryn stopped and touched two fingers to her lips and blew a kiss in the dragon's direction.

Meydra had felt the change in the air the moment Bryn stepped out from behind the walls of the keep. She lay quietly, her tail tucked under her and her head resting on her thigh, while Bryn walked toward her. She saw Bryn hesitate at the bower of linden trees that marked the entrance to the garden.

"I am not asleep, Bryn," Meydra said quietly.

Bryn walked under the linden tree arch, caressing the bark with her hand as she passed. She did not notice the shudder of the leaves in appreciation, but walked over to where Meydra lay. Bryn placed her hand on Meydra and ran it up and over the dragon's scales. The scales yielded to Bryn's touch and Meydra sighed.

"Lynder has gone to bed," Bryn whispered.

"She has had a long day," Meydra replied. "She was up quite early."

"Yes, I know. I was awake long before her and watched as the two of you left before sunrise." Bryn sat down in the hollow of Meydra's outstretched leg.

"You heard her speak of her quest to find true love."

"Yes." Bryn rested her head on her arm and curled closer to Meydra's warm body. "I believe she is under the impression the journey will take only a few weeks or perhaps a few months. Though I suspect Thalynder is really asking for time to think. She will be expected to assume a mantel of leadership in short order. She is expected to rule."

"The princess sees time as her enemy," Meydra said and moved her leg to protect and cover Bryn. "It would do no good for me to tell her that true love is already near. She would not believe me."

"You have already found him?" Bryn asked, yawning and closing her eyes. Meydra raised her body temperature to warm

Bryn, and adjusted her heartbeat and breathing to a pace she knew would lull Bryn to sleep.

"I know her true love is near."

Bryn's breathing deepened. "Is she…?" Bryn fell asleep before she could finish her thought.

"Sleep well, most treasured," Meydra whispered. Raising her head to listen to the sounds around her, the dragon was assured that all was well. Thalynder and the rest of the keep were asleep. Meydra made one last adjustment to her body temperature, then fell asleep with Bryn securely nestled against her chest.

CHAPTER THREE

Thalynder did not see Bryn outside her chambers as usual. She was flustered by Bryn's absence and nervously ran her hands over her dress several times. Thalynder wanted to discuss her speech with Bryn before going to her father, but now she would have to go to her father alone. She walked the long hall to her father's inner rooms and stopped outside his chambers. She took a deep breath as she lifted her hand to knock. Hearing voices inside, Thalynder hesitated. She leaned closer to the door and heard a voice she recognized. She tapped on the door and pushed it open.

Bryn and King Thamen were seated at a small table with Bryn's father, Brymender. Thalynder looked at Bryn, who stood and gave the princess a bow before sitting again. Thamen gestured to an empty chair at his side. Thalynder took it and waited for her father to speak.

"Your timing is perfect, Thalynder. Brymender has asked that I give Bryn permission to leave her court-appointed duties to fulfill a family obligation. Given that Bryn is now at the age of Consent and Commitment, I have granted the request." King Thamen reached across the table and took Bryn's hand in his. "You will need to take up with my daughter whether she wishes to accompany you on your journey, but as her father, I give my permission for Thalynder to go with you—provided you remember your promise to me."

Thalynder looked from Bryn to her father and frowned. Why did it now sound like the journey was Bryn's idea and not her own?

"My promise holds, my king," Bryn said. "If Thalynder goes with me, I pledge to have an escort of not less than three of your guardsmen accompany us. However, Your Highness, if Thalynder accompanies me, will not Meydra also be in our company? Would we still need the guardsmen?"

King Thamen shot a glance at Brymender before staring out the window for a moment. His shoulders raised and fell and he gave a nearly imperceptible shake of his head.

"Meydra will go only if Thalynder goes," he replied as he turned back to Bryn. "You will still need extra eyes and ears on the ground so I will insist on guardsmen. Here within the boundaries of my realm, my daughter is safe. Yet once you reach the highlands, you will be in the open and easy prey for any thief or pillager. We still do not know enough about the Picts or the lands they inhabit, and there is still concern about the raiders from over the sea. Though this is not their usual season of looting and murder, I am still apprehensive about you traveling with my daughter through their known areas of attack."

Thalynder had momentarily forgotten about the raiders. *This could be reason enough for Father to not grant his permission*, she thought. "Meydra can protect us," she said quickly. "She has always protected me from harm. She can raise the alarm quicker than any guardsman."

"Yes, Meydra's presence will be of great benefit to you," King Thamen said after a moment. He turned back to Bryn. "For my sake, as well as for your father's, you must hold to your promise, Bryn. However, I will reduce the number of men to one guardsman and one cook. That will give you an extra sword and an extra horse."

"Thank you, my king," Brymender said. "My daughter can be quite persuasive, and I am glad that you as a father can see through her. I agree to accept one guardsman on this journey so long as he is your best."

King Thamen chucked. "Only the best for our daughters. It is done," the king said. "Thalynder, you and Bryn have much to discuss. Return to me when Bryn has told you her plan, and we will discuss your place in the company of these travelers."

King Thamen stood, followed by Brymender, Bryn, and finally Thalynder. They all walked toward the door, and the women exited the room. They started down the hall when they heard the door of the king's room close behind them. Thalynder turned to see that her father and Brymender were not behind them and realized they had gone back inside her father's chambers. She clutched at Bryn's arm, causing Bryn to grimace.

"Why did it seem that the journey was your idea, and why did you go to my father without me? This was my idea and it was something *I* wanted to discuss with my father," Thalynder said. "You could have at least informed me of your intent."

Bryn put her hand over Thalynder's hand on her arm. "I am sorry I did not tell you that I was going to speak to the king, but when I awoke this morning, I remembered I would need the king's permission to leave. Knowing I would need my own father's help to obtain that, he agreed to intercede."

"You lied to your father?"

"Not really," Bryn replied. She gave Thalynder's hand a little squeeze. "I told him I wanted to see the Standing Stones. Since Staenis is not entirely out of reach of the king's realm I believed it possible that we could visit the Stones. Would you like to see the home of my ancestors with me?"

Thalynder glared at Bryn for a moment. "I should be angry. I looked for you in the library before coming to my father. I needed to go over my speech with you." Thalynder saw Bryn swallow hard and she released her grip on Bryn's arm. "I had the whole thing planned and knew exactly how I would broach the subject with my father. You should have told me. I am your princess, after all." At the entrance to the courtyard Thalynder smoothed her dress and walked out into the sunshine.

"I'm hungry. Let us eat now and after that we will go let Meydra know what has happened. I will go again to my father's chambers at the hour of midday, and he will ask if you and I have discussed your plan. Ha! *Your* plan," Thalynder said. After several moments of silence, she said, "I suppose it is better for him to think that you conjured all this up."

Bryn smiled. That had been her thought as well: if the king believed the plan was hers, no blame could be laid upon Thalynder should the quest fail. There was one piece of the conversation that Thalynder would not be pleased about: she would not like what the king had said about his plans for her marriage. Bryn had to tell Thalynder about the king's plans, but doing so before Thalynder met with her father might cause her to become angry or defensive when she spoke to him.

Bryn decided she would broach the subject while they were with Meydra. Better Thalynder be angered in the presence of her and Meydra and not with the king. He could withdraw his permission to allow Thalynder to accompany Bryn as easily as he had granted it. For now, Bryn needed to soothe Thalynder's bruised feelings.

After she and Thalynder ate a hearty breakfast of fresh bread, dried fish, and fruit, they left for the dragon garden. The day was warming quickly, and the heavy formal dress Thalynder had chosen to wear to meet with her father grew damp with perspiration. When they discovered that Meydra was away for the moment, Thalynder leaned against the cool bark of the linden, untied the string at her neck and opened her collar, sighing.

"I would like a swim before meeting again with my father," she said. "Let's run down to the falls and bathe."

Bryn's dress and overtunic were light and airy, a gauze woven by her mother for days like today, but she was warm too. Seeing the flush on Thalynder's neck and cheeks she said, "We should speak with Meydra before you see your father, but if we do not linger, we can cool you off first."

"I'll race you!" Thalynder said.

"And you will lose!" Bryn smiled and began to run. "You are wearing slippers—and more clothes than I own!" she called back over her shoulder. Already she was deep into the trees, her steps swift and sure, moving lightly over earth and stone. Emerging into the clearing by the water's edge with only the slightest change in her breathing, Bryn leaned back against a tree and listened for Thalynder's heavier gait. She heard a sound overhead and looked up to see Meydra coming to the clearing, and on her back rode Thalynder.

"Lynder, you cheat! I still arrived before you did," Bryn said. She unlaced the quilted bodice of her dress. "Remember: the rules still apply. I go in first, you do not enter until I have surfaced."

"I hear and I obey, O Mistress," Thalynder slid off Meydra's back. "Though you must help me undress first. This overtunic laces up the back and there are two other dresses beneath it. If you wait for me to undress myself, you will either burn in the sun or wrinkle up in the water."

Bryn laughed and stopped undressing. Her feet were bare; her overtunic lay in a heap on the ground. The laces of her underdress were undone, revealing the tops of her breasts. Exposed so, she could feel the heat rising in her neck, but knew she could easily blame the redness on the run through the woods. Bryn approached the princess, turned her around, and began to untie the many laces. "Whatever possessed you to wear this today?"

"I wanted to look like a woman and not a child when I went to see my father. If you had been around you would have known this." Thalynder attempted to remove her slippers while Bryn worked her laces. Losing her balance, the princess fell back against Bryn, who wrapped Thalynder in her arms to steady her. "Oh dear," Thalynder said through her giggles. "We'll never get in the water at this rate."

"There is no need to hurry now," Bryn said into Thalynder's ear. "Since Meydra is here, we can discuss your plan—I mean my plan—no, *our* plan as we cool ourselves in the water."

"True." Thalynder stood back up and Bryn resumed the unlacing. It was not the first time she had assisted the princess this way. Afraid they might hurt or injure Thalynder, the women of court who helped her dress and undress were slow and methodical, to the point that Thalynder often wiggled out of her clothes before they could finish unlacing them. The princess had told Bryn she appreciated that she was quick and sure and approached the task with a no-nonsense attitude.

"There, that is done," Bryn said. "Now for the inner dresses."

"This next one laces in the front." Thalynder turned to face Bryn. "The inner one slips off."

"Then you can finish undressing yourself," Bryn said, smiling at Thalynder. "I will finish unlacing myself and get in the water and wait for you."

Bryn unlaced her own bodice and her dress fell away from her shoulders and down her arms. Her breasts and waist were exposed as she let the dress drop to the ground. She stepped out of the dress and stooped to pick it up. As she stood up again, she glimpsed a slight blush on Thalynder's face. Seeing her blush caused Bryn to feel her own heat rise.

"You are pretty, Bryn," Thalynder said and kept undressing. "I especially like the color of your nipples. Rose, I would say, and your skin is fairer than I remember."

Bryn turned her back to Thalynder and laid her dress over a rock. She did not turn to Thalynder but said over her shoulder, "Of course I am paler. I have not been able to bathe in the sun since your father's edict to have an attendant or companion at the water's edge. I have not had the chance to lie naked under the sun for many months." She glanced up to see Meydra looking at her and saw the hint of a smile cross Meydra's mouth. Bryn felt the heat grow more intense. She took two quick steps toward the pool, leapt off the small rise, and dove into the water.

Gliding under the water, Bryn moved through the cool liquid like an otter, smooth and fluid. She reached the waterfall on the far side of the pool and came up behind it, using it to shield her eyes as she watched Thalynder remove the last of her clothing. Watching Thalynder stand and waiting for her to give the signal to enter, Bryn took a long look at her. Her pale alabaster skin was covered by her sun-colored hair that glinted in the daylight. She looked at Thalynder's breasts and her small, dark nipples, and felt a wave of desire build deep inside her stomach. She stepped through the waterfall and waved to

Thalynder. Thalynder's body penetrated the top of the water, and Bryn marveled as time slowed and she could see the water cover Thalynder inch by inch. A moan escaped her lips but was hidden by the sound of the water as it tumbled over the rocks overhead and fell into the pool. She sank back into the water and waited for Thalynder to rise to the surface.

The two women lazed about the pool's edge and spoke with Meydra about Bryn's meeting with the king and his desire to have a guardsman as a member of the company.

"There are several captains for Father to choose from," Thalynder said as she ran her hands through her hair.

"Yes, and several of them have been our tutors in hunting and warfare," Bryn said. "If I were your father, I would choose the captain who knows best how we would respond in the wild. Someone who could anticipate and work with us."

"You are too much the tactician," Thalynder said. "Leave the thinking to the captain."

Bryn gave a small frown that only Meydra saw. She liked to think ahead, to plan and calculate. She was good at it. *Well*, she thought, *I won't hesitate to be myself once we are away from the keep.*

"Sir Arryn was my favorite tutor," Bryn said. "He is also the best marksman."

"But he is so old," Thalynder chuckled.

"He's not even ten years older than you or I," Bryn reached out and pinched Thalynder's arm. "He is a good captain and loyal to the realm." He's also a good secret-keeper, Bryn thought. She remembered the few times Sir Arryn had commented on something she did better than the princess and he had promised to keep her secret. Like the time she found a wounded stag and nursed it back to health. Any other guardsman would have admonished Bryn and killed the stag.

"If he is the best, my father will choose him. Tell me, what did your father say when you told him you wanted to see the Stones?"

Bryn ran her hands lightly over the water's surface and watched the sun catch the little droplets, turning them to glittering jewels. She smiled at Thalynder's reflection in the ripples. The Standing Stones of Staenis, Bryn thought. "Not unlike the ring to the far south in Britannia, the Stones are a sacred place to Druids. It is believed that the Stones hold the knowledge of the ancient ways of the clanns. Knowledge of all life including how and why dragons came to be Companions of humans. My clann often makes pilgrimages to the Stones."

"And your father accepted that you would want to go now, without him or your mother?"

"It is a rite of passage for all Druids who have reached a certain age." Bryn moved to the edge of the pool and held onto a large rock. Meydra joined her at the edge, and Thalynder moved through the water and used another large rock to steady herself. Bryn slapped the pool and watched the water ripple away from her hand.

"I've wanted to make my own pilgrimage for several years now but was not allowed to do so because I was in service to the king." Bryn gave Meydra a conspiratorial glance and then looked back at Thalynder.

"To answer your question, no, my father did not question my wanting to go see the Stones," Bryn replied. "The only question he asked was whether you would be going all the way to Staenis as well." Bryn reached up from the pool to touch Meydra's tail.

"Yes," Meydra said softly. "He would want to know that."

"Why?" Thalynder asked. "Do you know Staenis, Meydra?"

"I do, Princess, and I will tell you about it one day. But it is a long story and now is not the time. It is the time to get you two fish out of the water. You, Princess, must meet with your father, and you, Bryn, will keep me company while she is away. Now, out of the water and dress."

Bryn got out of the water and stood on the bank. The sun felt warm on her skin and she would have liked to lie in the grass and dry completely before getting dressed. But Meydra was right: Thalynder needed to get back to her father before he found reason to change his mind, and Bryn still had to share with her the king's plan for Thalynder's marriage. She offered Thalynder her hand and pulled as Thalynder rose out of the water. Thalynder's wet body sparkled in the sunlight and Bryn felt a moan rise in her throat. She caught the moan before it left her mouth and turned away. Bryn handed Thalynder her underdress and grabbed for her own. She dressed quickly.

"Lynder, I must tell you something else," Bryn said as she handed Thalynder her tunic. She waited as Thalynder pulled the heavy outer dress over her head, then stepped up behind her to lace it up. "Hold your hair out of the way, please."

"What else, Bryn," Thalynder said as she pulled her hair over her right shoulder. "It must have something to do with my father."

Bryn paused a moment. She fingered the laces of the dress and found that the words she needed would not come.

"Why do you not speak?"

Bryn took a deep breath to clear her mind. She tied the laces and took a step back. She saw Meydra behind her and backed up another step to stand with her back firm against Meydra's scales, as if to draw courage from the dragon. "Your father will plan your marriage and wedding while we are away," Bryn said. "His plan is to be ready when we return."

"I must tell him the truth," Thalynder said, her face flushed scarlet. "He cannot do that if he is made to understand that I am on my own quest to find true love."

"No, Princess," Meydra said. "You cannot broach this subject with the king. It will anger him, it will anger you, and you will part badly. There is another way."

"What other way, Meydra? To let this happen and allow my father to seal my fate?" Thalynder asked and glared at Bryn. "Did my father swear *you* to secrecy?"

Bryn reached out to take Thalynder's hand, only to have Thalynder withdraw from her touch. Bryn sighed, knowing how all of this must appear to Thalynder. She stepped away from Meydra and toward Thalynder, and said, "I was not sworn to secrecy. Your father fully expected me to tell you of his plans. You are to be given the choice to go with me or stay and accept suitors and make a decision."

"If I go with you, a husband will be chosen for me. If I stay, I will be made to endure all manner of pompous behavior from men I do not wish to marry," Thalynder said. "The choice is no longer a choice. I cannot let my father choose. All my plans are for naught."

"There is a way to postpone the deed," Meydra said. "Will you listen to Bryn?"

Thalynder looked at Meydra and frowned. "Very well." She grabbed Bryn's hand and held it tightly. "Tell me, Bryn, how do I take the sting out of this bite?"

Bryn pulled Thalynder close to her and held her hand up to her heart. She wanted to wrap the princess in her arms and tell her not to worry. She longed to have the answer to all of Thalynder's questions. Bryn pushed a lock of hair from Thalynder's face.

"By telling your father that you look forward to his decision for your future," Bryn said. "Ask him to wait for you to return from the journey. Tell him how happy and relaxed you will be after a trip to the cooler regions, and that when you return you will be willing and ready to marry."

Bryn waited while Thalynder stood looking at her for a long time, not speaking. She watched Thalynder take deep breaths, letting the words sink in to help her make a decision. Thalynder moved a step closer to Bryn and kissed her cheek. Bryn squeezed her hand.

"You make a good speech, Bryn," Thalynder said. "Let us hope it works on my father."

"Go now to your father before you again become angry."

Thalynder spoke to Meydra while looking at Bryn. "Take me to the keep, Meydra. Bryn will walk back and meet you in the garden."

Meydra bowed her head and shoulders and waited as Thalynder climbed onto her back. In an instant Meydra was in the air and heading for the keep. Bryn watched as Meydra and Thalynder disappeared over the trees. Bryn set her bare feet on the path back to the dragon garden. "I hope she will keep her wits about her," she said to the trees. As she passed through the forest, the trees bowed ever so slightly and sighed when she absently brushed her hand against their bark.

Bryn arrived in the garden to find Meydra waiting for her. Meydra's tail flicked quickly, revealing her agitation. Bryn sensed the deep concern within Meydra's heart. She approached the dragon and, without thinking, ran her hands overs Meydra's exposed chest. Bryn felt the quickening of Meydra's heart under her hands and found her own heart wanting to keep time. Bryn traced the smooth scales up Meydra's chest to her chin and over to her cheek. Bryn rested her hand on the creature's cheek and looked into her eyes.

"What has you so concerned, Meydra?" Bryn asked as she gently stroked the dragon's cheek.

"I am torn between two resolves."

"Do you wish to elaborate?" Bryn asked and sat down. She rested her hand on Meydra's chest.

"Only as far as I am allowed," Meydra replied. "I am torn between my love for my mistress," and here she sighed heavily, "and my sworn oath to her father."

"You swore an oath to the king?" Bryn asked, believing Meydra was discussing King Thamen.

The dragon did not answer.

"Ah, you must not answer, Meydra. I too know things that must be left unsaid. I understand all too well the need for silence." Bryn moved her hand across Meydra's chest in a slow circular motion. She paused where she could feel Meydra's heart at its strongest and held her hand against the supple scales. She felt soothed by the steady beat. After a moment she realized that her own heart was beating with the same rhythm. Beat for beat their hearts kept time. Bryn did not understand why their hearts should be keeping time with each other. Maybe there were aspects of a dragon she had yet to understand. Nevertheless, she liked the feeling. She smiled. Perhaps, she thought, it was because of their shared love of Thalynder, or Bryn's own love of dragons—whatever the reason, it was another secret Bryn would keep locked away in silence.

CHAPTER FOUR

"Thalynder must have seen her father by now." Bryn rose up from the patch of grass she'd been lying on. "I should go back to the keep and see if everything is all right."

"I take the delay as a good sign," Meydra said as she arched and stretched her back. She lifted her head and smiled. "Would you like to go for a ride?"

"Oh, Meydra!" Bryn replied. "Is it allowed? Yes, yes. I would love to."

"Climb on my back, and we will soar for a while so that I may stretch my wings. And yes, it is allowed. After all, who argues with a dragon?"

Bryn laughed and climbed aboard Meydra's back. She hitched her dress up above her knees and slid forward to sit with her legs gently resting on either side of Meydra's neck. It seemed to Bryn the best position for comfort for both her and the dragon.

She leaned over and spoke into Meydra's ear, "Is this comfortable for you?"

Meydra purred. "It is the best way to ride a dragon. Though I don't seem to be able to convey that to the princess."

"I shall instruct her," Bryn said and laughed. "Take me soaring, Meydra."

"Yes, Bryn." Meydra smiled at the sound of Bryn's laughter. Meydra lifted up and with a slow beat moved high above the trees' canopy.

Bryn ran her hands gently over Meydra's outstretched wings and felt the muscles beneath the skin flex with each movement. She leaned forward and kissed the back of the dragon's head. Her laughter could not be contained; it floated in the air and its sweet sound caused the trees to raise their limbs overhead to feel the notes of pure pleasure fall from the sky and rest on their leaves like water after a long drought.

"Higher, Meydra," Bryn called out above the wind.

"As you wish, little sister," Meydra replied quietly enough that Bryn did not hear her.

"Now I see why the nobles claim dragons for their own. This is bliss," Bryn said and rubbed Meydra's neck.

"Nobles!" Meydra said and quickly began her descent back to the garden. "I am sorry, Bryn, but we must not be seen by the nobles. I must alight and do so quickly."

"I understand." Bryn looked around her and took in the world from where she sat. It was a treasured flight, one she would not soon forget.

Meydra stepped down onto the ground and bowed her head. Bryn placed a kiss on Meydra's neck and slid off to stand in the grass. She hugged herself and twirled, smiling widely. She turned back to Meydra and without realizing she was crying, felt the tears run down her cheeks. She wiped them away with the back of her hand.

"I will never forget this, Meydra. Thank you, thank you." Bryn embraced the dragon and felt their hearts beat as one and their breaths move as one. In the deeper recesses of her mind, a small light came on. She knew this feeling, but for the moment could not place it. Bryn released her hold on Meydra and stepped back. "I will go look for Thalynder."

Bryn went back into the keep and, after finding that Thalynder was not in her quarters, she walked toward the king's inner rooms. Nearing the private library, she heard Thalynder's voice coming from inside. Bryn stood at the open door and listened.

"Brymender has assured me that Bryn is quite capable of navigating through the countryside without using the road," King Thamen was saying. "I will not have you travel the roads. You would become easy targets."

"But Father, we will need to go into town and sleep at night," Thalynder said. Bryn heard the pleading tone in Thalynder's voice and winced.

"Yes, and you will do so cloaked by the cover of darkness. Thalynder, on this I must insist. You cannot enter town in daylight. There are too many eyes and too many of my enemies' spies," the king said, slamming his fist on the small map table they were standing against. "You test my patience!"

Bryn knocked lightly on the door and stepped where she could be seen. "Sire, if I may join you."

"Please, Bryn. Perhaps you can see the reasoning," he said, gesturing for Bryn to enter.

Bryn stepped inside and bowed to the king. She curtsied to Thalynder and stepped up to the table, glancing down at the open map. Smiling at Thalynder she said, "It is the same with my father, Sire. He does not wish for me to be seen until we are deep within the forest. At which point, he has granted me permission to seek out the local inns and homes of my kinsmen." Bryn pointed to a small river on the map. "Here is the path I plan to travel to Staenis." Bryn traced her finger along the river's winding path, stopping at an open plain. "Here we will need to make haste. Meydra will carry the princess over the open area while I, the guardsman, and the cook ride swiftly to reach the edge of this forest by nightfall." Bryn went on with the route, one devised by her, Thalynder, and Meydra while they were at the pool, but which Thalynder had obviously not shared with the king. Bryn frowned, wondering why Thalynder had failed to mention the plan to her father. She continued, "From there we take again to the woods and the small woodland hamlets. We will be at Staenis before the next full moon."

"That is a good plan," King Thamen said. "Your kin are in these woods?"

"Yes," Bryn replied. "Many Druids still live deep in the woods. We will stay with them, and some may even accompany us to the Stones. Pilgrimages are celebrated among the clanns. There is one thing though, Your Highness."

"And what is that, Bryn?" the king asked as he walked over to sit on a tall chair by the window. He glanced outside and down to the courtyard.

"It may be best to leave the cook behind," Bryn said.

"Why is that?" Thamen and Thalynder asked at the same time.

Bryn looked at Thalynder first before looking at the king.

"Sire, unless the cook can wield a sword, or use a bow, or ride like the wind, he will slow us down." Bryn hesitated before going on, not knowing now if Thalynder had even discussed with her father his plans for her marriage.

"Who will cook for us?" Thalynder asked.

"I will," Bryn said.

"Then you will need an extra guardsman," the king said.

"Father, would two men with two women be the best solution?"

"Sire, if you insist on a second guardsman we will accept, but would not four need more supplies and take more time to complete the journey?" Bryn sighed inwardly. "A delay in our journey would cause a delay in the marriage ceremony."

The king smiled. He stood up and approached Bryn. He placed a kiss on her forehead and one upon his daughter's cheek.

"I had expected Thalynder to be opposed to marriage, but here I find both of you so amiable about the whole affair," the king said.

Ah, Bryn thought, that is probably what delayed Thalynder. They had been long in discussing a groom. She smiled at Thalynder.

"Father, Bryn is right," Thalynder said. "Needless delays. Bryn and I can cook, and I know you will not send a guardsman who cannot boil water and loose an arrow at the same time."

The king laughed and took Thalynder's hand. "Come, girls. I am hungry after all this talk."

The king led Thalynder out of the library, while Bryn followed behind them. Once in the main hall, the king released his daughter and walked down the long corridor toward the dining room. Thalynder and Bryn were silent until he was well out of sight.

"Oh, Bryn," Thalynder said. "Why did you promise to keep me out of town? How will I ever meet my true love?"

"I did not promise the king anything," Bryn replied. "I merely showed him the road my father intended me to take. Nothing more. And since when did you learn to cook?"

Thalynder's mouth opened, but nothing came out. She smiled widely. "Bryn of the Skerrabrae, you may be better at pulling the wool over my father's eyes than I am."

"Now, where do you suppose I learned this trick?" Bryn said.

The two women spent the rest of the evening going over the proposed route and choosing what to wear on their journey. They settled on two dresses each—one in case a true love requested a dance and one for going into town for supplies or information. Bryn suggested tunics and hose for long days on horseback. One pair of boots, and one pair of slippers, again in case a dance was offered. Bryn would have liked to go barefoot when wearing a dress, but the slippers would serve. The thought of thigh-high boots caused her to frown. She practically lived in her short deerskin ankle boots with no heel. That were perfectly suited to her busy life in the keep.

"I would not need high boots if we're walking and not planning to take to the back of a horse," Bryn said between bites of warm bread. "Besides, taking a horse means grazing.

Grazing means meadows. As much as we think our fathers are being unnecessarily cautious, we should avoid the open fields whenever possible."

"You may be capable of walking all day among the trees," Thalynder said. "However, I am not accustomed to doing so. If you recall, I am more inclined to riding on the back of a dragon than riding on the back of a horse, much less walking."

Bryn sighed. To be on the back of a dragon, she thought, what a lovely thing indeed.

"Oh, let us not think of you having to walk," she chuckled. "If only we did not need to take supplies and a guardsman, we could both ride upon Meydra's back." Bryn pictured herself and Thalynder upon Meydra, with her sitting in front and Thalynder's arms wrapped around her waist. She closed her eyes and inhaled deeply.

"Not possible," Thalynder said as she pulled apart a roasted chicken. "There is not enough room."

Bryn looked at Thalynder and wrinkled her nose. "What do you mean, not enough room?" She wanted to say that two would fit nicely on Meydra's neck but she did not want to tell Thalynder yet about her own riding experience.

"No room," Thalynder repeated. "Where I sit leaves no room for others."

"Oh, Thalynder. I'm sure Meydra could accommodate three or four riders if they all sat close together."

"Perhaps. I suppose it would be up to Meydra."

Bryn knew Meydra would have no problem with both women on her back, but decided to keep quiet for the time being. A lot could happen to a horse and a guardsman.

Having supped and talked over their meal, Thalynder and Bryn walked out to say goodnight to Meydra. The sun had set and the waning moon had yet to rise. Thalynder carried a small lighted torch to see the ground in front of her. Bryn closed her eyes and let the earth beneath her feet guide where she would step. It was one of the first things she learned when she was taught to walk in the forest. *Let the forest floor guide you*, her mother had reminded her. It was one of the many things Bryn hoped to teach Thalynder while on their journey.

Meydra was sitting in the tall grass, her head alert as if listening for some distant wingbeat. She was so intent on listening that Bryn was surprised when she did not notice Thalynder's approach, despite the smoke from the little torch.

Bryn stopped at the linden tree arch and did not move. Off in the distance—though she did not hear so much as she felt— was the keening of an ill-favored wind. Something in the dark was crying, something distant and unrecognizable, perceived only through Bryn's deep connection with the earth. The sound caused Bryn to shudder in the warm evening air as if she had been plunged into a dark and icy well. She held her breath and waited.

"What is it?" Thalynder asked quietly. "Meydra, what do you hear?"

Bryn couldn't move. Her heart was so sad that she felt as if she would faint away if she moved. Her breath caught in her throat. She watched, from what seemed like many leagues' distance, as Meydra blinked and turned to look at Thalynder. Bryn saw Meydra give Thalynder a weak smile and turn slowly to look back at the spot where she was standing. Meydra inhaled and exhaled softly in her direction. In her mind Bryn heard, *Breathe, Bryn.* She felt Meydra's breath touch her face and she inhaled sharply. Finding she could move again, Bryn gently shook her head and rubbed her arms as if she were cold. Thalynder was looking at Meydra, but Meydra was looking past her to Bryn. The light in Bryn's mind, kindled by the ride on Meydra's back, glowed a little brighter, and Bryn caught a fleeting glimpse of something still unrecognizable: a face from her childhood. Bryn stared into Meydra's eyes and saw concern. Concern for me? Bryn wondered.

Meydra abruptly turned her gaze to Thalynder.

"It was a dragon cry," Meydra said. "There is another dragon somewhere in the kingdom."

"Another dragon," Thalynder said. "How, where, I mean, how do you know? Do you know where it is? I was told that you were the only dragon in the realm. *I'm* the only noble with a dragon."

"Yes, Princess, you are the only noble in the realm with a dragon, and no," Meydra replied, "I could not hear where the dragon is. I only heard an overwhelming sadness."

That was what that was, Bryn thought. Sadness. She walked over to join Thalynder and Meydra. "It felt like death," Bryn said to Meydra as she approached the two. She touched Meydra's cheek. "Such depth in that cry. Such sorrow."

"You heard that?" Thalynder said. "I didn't hear a thing. What could a dragon be sad about?"

"Perhaps it was because I was standing still," Bryn said and felt heat rise in her cheeks. "You were still walking and holding the crackling torch." She turned away from Thalynder. There were too many unanswered questions. She wondered why she was able to hear the dragon's cry. Why she could feel the pain in the cry and Thalynder could not. Unanswered questions that were beginning to weigh upon her mind.

Thalynder looked at Bryn. "You are a wonder, Bryn of the Brae. After seventeen years, you now begin to show me the little secrets you have kept from me for far too long. Druid secrets."

"We all have secrets, my princess."

Thalynder laughed and the dark spell was broken. She began to tell Meydra about the meeting with her father and was about to begin the part where Bryn came in to the library when Bryn stopped her.

Bryn rested her hand gently on Thalynder's shoulder. "I am sorry, Thalynder, but it's getting late, and unless you want to sleep with Meydra tonight, we should get inside before they bolt the locks of the inner keep."

"Sleep with Meydra?" Thalynder said as if the idea was something she had never considered. "What a great idea! Yes, let us stay out all night and sleep here with Meydra. She will keep us safe, and we can huddle together to keep warm, though I doubt we will need to do that as warm as the air is tonight."

"I am much safer than any locked inner keep, Princess," Meydra said. "It would be my honor to keep you two women tucked against my body, safe and warm."

"It's settled." Thalynder looked at Bryn and grinned. "Do you toss much when you sleep?"

"No, Lynder. I toss not at all."

"Good, you will sleep behind me. Now may I finish the story?" Thalynder sat down on the grass.

Bryn laughed. "Yes, and you may embellish and elaborate to your heart's content. I will sit quietly and listen as well." Bryn removed her outer tunic and placed it on the ground next to Meydra's chest. Snuggling down and getting comfortable, she pulled Thalynder's feet toward her and began to remove her slippers. As Thalynder resumed her story, Bryn slowly massaged her feet. Thalynder's voice grew softer and eventually she began to yawn. Finally she stopped and looked up at Meydra. With a rather large yawn, she kissed Meydra's scales and pulled her feet from Bryn's lap.

"I am tired now," she said. "I believe I will sleep. Will you lie behind me, Bryn?"

"Yes, Lynder," Bryn said. "Lay here on my tunic." Thalynder lay down on the garment and, reaching behind her, pulled Bryn's arm over her waist. Bryn moved down behind Thalynder and pulled her closer to her chest, her breasts resting against Thalynder's back. Bryn glanced up at Meydra and they smiled at each other. Bryn kissed Thalynder's hair, then settled herself onto the grass. The air was pleasantly warm and the night sounds hushed and comforting. Soon they were all asleep.

❧

The sun was beginning to rise and the day promised to be clear and warm. Meydra awoke long before the sun cleared the horizon and lay still while her two charges slept peacefully against her chest. She had dreamt of the other dragon, its sad and painful lament echoing deep inside her heart for most of the night. Bryn held Thalynder and during the night their legs and arms had became entwined.

Meydra smiled at the two and thought about the journey that lay before them. She knew Bryn wanted desperately to see the Stones at Staenis. She knew Thalynder wanted to find someone other than the suitors her father might present. The problem did not lie with the true love or potential suitors. It lay with the Stones. In Staenis, Bryn would learn the truth about who she was and her part in her Druid heritage. Meydra was not sure she was ready to tell that story to Bryn.

No, she decided. Doing that would change many things and she liked things the way they were. "I will not tell them," she said aloud.

"Tell us what?" Bryn asked quietly.

"That the sun rises and you will be missed in the keep."

Bryn hugged Thalynder closer to her. "I like it right here."

"So do I," Thalynder replied with a little morning yawn. She turned in Bryn's arms to look into her eyes. After a brief hesitation and a little inhale of breath, Thalynder kissed Bryn's mouth.

Bryn pulled Thalynder tight against her and slipped her hand behind Thalynder's neck.

Thalynder broke the kiss but did not move. She looked at Bryn and smiled. "You are blushing, Bryn."

"Why did you kiss me?"

"Because you looked so soft and beautiful in the dim light. And I've never kissed a woman before."

Bryn moved away from her. She did not like Thalynder's casual attitude. "Have you kissed a man?" Bryn asked.

"Yes, many times." Thalynder laughed. "The male attendants my father had chose to be my playmates when I was younger were anything but chaste." Thalynder reached out to touch Bryn's face. "Have you not kissed a man, Bryn?"

"Only once. It was part of my instruction."

"Oh yes, I forgot: you of the clanns have other areas of instruction." Thalynder's voice was thick. "Have you kissed a woman?"

"Yes," Bryn said but did not elaborate.

"Someday you should instruct me." Thalynder quickly kissed Bryn again, and this time she pushed her hand against Bryn's breast.

"Stop," Bryn said. "This is not a game."

"But it can be," Thalynder said and looked up at Meydra. She smiled and patted Meydra's chest. "We've got Meydra here to shield us from prying eyes." Meydra responded by slapping her tail against the ground.

Bryn shuddered at Meydra's gesture. "You don't understand," Bryn said, more to Meydra than to Thalynder.

"Oh Bryn, quit being so stuffy." Thalynder stood up.

Bryn glanced up at Meydra and saw that she was watching Thalynder.

Bryn rose to stand next to Thalynder. She was winded from the excitement of having Thalynder in her arms, but still perceptive enough to realize that Thalynder was playing. Thalynder's inquisitive nature—her persistent quest for adventure—were her only feelings for Bryn at that moment. Bryn sighed. Something she dreamt of doing had happened, and it had all been a game.

Bryn quickly pulled her tunic off the ground, shook it out and pulled it over her head and down over her hips. She felt flushed and knew it was not a blush that colored her cheeks. Bryn felt foolish.

Thalynder stood at Meydra's tail, looking out over the grassy meadow that lay between garden and keep. She looked back at Bryn. "Come on, Bryn, I'm hungry and we have to prepare for our journey."

Bryn kissed Meydra's cheek and heard the little moan of pleasure as it rose deep inside Meydra's throat. Bryn trotted after Thalynder and glanced back as she walked under the linden arch to watch Meydra lift effortlessly into the air—the only sound came from the wind as it moved beneath her wings.

CHAPTER FIVE

The dining hall was crowded with waiting ladies, guardsmen and attendants. Bryn and Thalynder walked over to the long table laid with a selection of food and drink and began to choose their breakfast fare. Thalynder began to pile food on a plate, and Bryn chuckled at the quantity she was amassing.

"What are you laughing at?" Thalynder asked and placed another slice of melon on her plate.

"You," Bryn replied. "You have enough there to feed you, me and all your other waiting ladies. Are you hungry, Princess?"

"Starving," Thalynder replied. "I think it was the restful sleep and that rousing kiss."

"Shh, Thalynder," Bryn said. She looked around at the others at the table. All were busy placing food on their plates, eating and chattering loudly to one another. She felt relieved that no one was paying attention to them. Bryn collected a small bunch of grapes, tore a piece of bread from a still-warm loaf and placed them on a plate. She grabbed an empty cup and held it out to the servant to be filled with mead.

When Bryn turned back to Thalynder, she saw that the princess had already taken her place next to the king's chair at his table and that Sir Arryn had seated himself next to her. Bryn found a place at the other end of the table and picked at her grapes. She watched Thalynder and the knight converse. Bryn sat with the rest of the attendants, thus reminded of her place in the court.

Thalynder smiled at Sir Arryn and Bryn felt a pang of jealousy. She beat it back and concentrated on her morning meal. She did not notice the young man standing in front of her until he spoke. It was Pilan, a kitchen servant.

"Excuse me, mistress," the young man said.

"Yes?"

"Her Highness has asked that you join her and Sir Arryn at the king's table."

Swallowing hard, Bryn stood up, picked up her plate and cup, and made her way to Princess Thalynder and Sir Arryn. Bryn knew of this knight's calm demeanor and his unequaled skills with a sword. He was a captain in the King's Royal Guard, and over the years had become quite fond of the princess. Bryn saw him at every function and event that she and Thalynder frequented. He was always coming over to speak with them or request a dance. He treated Bryn as an equal, and she always appreciated his kindness toward her. If he were a prince, he would be high on the king's list of possible grooms for the princess. Being in the guard precluded the chance to be on that list, but it did not keep him from wanting to be near Thalynder, or so Bryn believed.

"You requested my presence, Your Highness," Bryn said, her head bowed in deference to the title.

"Yes, Bryn," Thalynder replied with an easy smile. "Come sit and discuss the journey with Sir Arryn. Father has appointed him as our fellow traveler."

Bryn felt an inner sigh rise to her lips. She set her plate and cup down on the table and walked around to the other side. She started to take the chair next to Sir Arryn, putting him between the two women.

"No," Thalynder said. "Here, sit in my chair." Thalynder stood and moved to stand at the king's chair. Sir Arryn rose when the princess did and stood waiting for the two women to seat themselves before sitting again. Thalynder patted the chair next to her and grinned at Bryn. "Sit here and tell Sir Arryn the plans for staying to the paths in the forest." Thalynder shot a smile at Sir Arryn, then sat down in the king's large chair.

Bryn sat in Thalynder's seat and glanced at Sir Arryn. His face was calm, but there was a hint of a smile on his lips. He thinks us fools, Bryn thought.

"I have discussed the route with both my father and the king," Bryn began. She kept her words precise in hope of being taken seriously. "The road is not safe for the princess, and I am well schooled in the paths of the forest. I can lead us through on horseback and manage to keep us well hidden among the trees."

Sir Arryn looked from Bryn to the princess and back to Bryn. He retrieved a folded piece of leather from inside his tunic. He opened the leather to reveal a map of the realm and the surrounding countryside. It was a map of fine detail and Bryn sighed audibly at the craftsmanship.

"That is a map of great value," she said.

"It was my father's. A gift from old King Thafyn," Sir Arryn said and ran his hands lovingly over the leather. "It was a reward for loyalty, and passed from father to son."

Bryn tentatively stretched her hand to touch the map. When Sir Arryn did not object, she ran her hands over the leather and the markings placed upon the supple deerskin. She ran her fingers lightly over the edges and smiled a knowing smile.

"This map was given to King Thafyn by Brymeldan, Arch Druid," she said, her voice quiet. "It was designed by Brymeldan's mother, my great-grandmother Andelyn, and crafted by the elves of the Umbriel Forest. I have seen drawings of this map before." She looked up at Sir Arryn and saw him in a new light. He was a captain and all that it implied, and he would not risk losing that by playing with the affections of a princess. The realization that he might also be a Druid caused her to think of him differently. She felt she owed him an apology for having thought less of him. She ventured a question.

"You know I wish to see the Stones at Staenis. Have you been to Staenis?"

"I have not, but my ancestors made the pilgrimage. I am in service to the king," Sir Arryn replied. "As are you."

"Do you leave a family behind?"

"Why do you ask that?" Thalynder asked.

"Because, Your Highness," Bryn said and turned to glare at Thalynder, "this journey may take us away from kith and kin for many weeks, possibly months. It would be best to know what thoughts would occupy Sir Arryn's mind." She moved her foot under the table to tap against the princess's leg. She turned her attention back to Sir Arryn.

"I leave only my mother behind," Sir Arryn replied and smiled at the two women. "My clann is in the west, and she and I are the only ones living in this realm."

"And your mother will not miss you?" Thalynder asked.

"She will. But a long journey will be good for me and my horse." He laughed a quiet, playful laugh and Bryn relaxed.

Pointing at the map, Bryn said, "This is the route I propose. It will take us through the smaller villages where my own kinsmen dwell." Bryn continued to show Sir Arryn the route, as she had the king. She did not know whether she and Thalynder would be able to stray from the route now that the captain, who was to accompany them, possessed such a map. It will be hard to lose such a man as this, she thought. The ruse of going to Staenis may cause them to have to go there after all. To flit about the countryside at the whim of the princess was going to take some beguiling of this redoubtable knight.

Sir Arryn folded the map and replaced it inside his tunic.

"How do you plan to resupply while on the journey?" he asked.

"My kinsmen will aid us. They will welcome us as family."

"And where will you sleep?"

"When among my kin, in their homes. When in the wild, with Meydra, and under the trees if necessary."

"The king does not want the princess to be recognized. How will you accommodate that request?"

"You have many questions, Sir Arryn," Thalynder said.

"My first concern is always the safety of the princess," Bryn said. "But to answer your question, I do not intend to call her *Princess*."

Sir Arryn leaned close to Bryn. "I believe we understand each other." He stood and moved a step back from the table. "We will discuss provisions, but I will need only one horse. I will carry all I need on my mount." He bowed before both women and when he rose he addressed Bryn. "I am glad to see we will have your sure hand and sharp mind, Bryn of the Brae. Between us, the princess will be safe." He retrieved his sword from the table. "I will inform the king that we have met and that I am satisfied by the route you propose. By your leave, Your Highness." Sir Arryn bowed low before Thalynder. He turned and looked at Bryn. "Lady Bryn."

Once outside in the courtyard, away from the eyes of the inner keep, Bryn grabbed Thalynder's hand. She led Thalynder out of the walled courtyard to the grassland and a small grove of trees where she stopped in the shade of an old and stately oak tree. She went over the talk with Sir Arryn in her mind and several things bothered her. Confused by a mixture of anger and jealousy *and* pleasure at having Sir Arryn be the one to accompany them, Bryn frowned. Feeling Thalynder's hand in hers helped relax her furrowed brow. She pulled Thalynder close and spoke quietly, "Why do you suppose your father chose him?"

Thalynder leaned her shoulder against the tree and looked at Bryn. "Several reasons, I imagine." She reached out and pulled an acorn off the tree with her free hand.

"Several things? Could you elaborate?" Bryn watched Thalynder study the acorn and saw the little pout to her lips that indicated she was deep in thought. When distracted, Thalynder looked like a child confused by the big world around her.

"He is young, as you reminded me," Thalynder began. "He has neither wife nor child. He is a skilled rider and, as we both know, skilled with a sword."

"True," Bryn agreed. He was all of those.

"And," Thalynder paused. She leaned close to Bryn's face. "I think he likes you."

Bryn's face reddened, though not from Thalynder's words but from the nearness of her. She hesitated only a moment, then kissed Thalynder's mouth.

"I have no time for men," Bryn said, her voice thick with renewed passion. She ran her free hand over Thalynder's neck, touching lightly the cowrie shell necklace. Bryn gently kissed Thalynder's throat. Then another kiss on her chin and another on her mouth. She felt Thalynder's free hand touch her breast with the point of the little acorn, causing her nipples to harden, and she sighed against Thalynder's velvety lips. Bryn kissed those lips with desire and urgency, and was rewarded by a gentle squeeze of Lynder's hand on her breast. She felt Thalynder relaxing under the kiss and parted Thalynder's lips with her tongue. After a moment Thalynder relaxed against her. Here, Bryn thought, take a little instruction, Princess.

Bryn moved her tongue softly against Thalynder's, and Thalynder responded by pushing her own tongue further into Bryn's mouth. Bryn moved her hand to the back of Thalynder's neck and took the kiss deeper.

The lush dance of two tongues eager for the touch of the other, asking for more and pushing hard against each other to take all the other would give. Bryn felt Thalynder move both hands on her tunic and over her breasts. She moaned deeply in Thalynder's mouth. With one hand on Thalynder's neck, the other moved to touch the brocade tunic at Thalynder's breast. Bryn moved her hand in a circular motion over the brocade, feeling the shiver of Thalynder's body against hers. She moved to pin Thalynder against the tree, and positioned her leg so that she could raise her knee and rub against Thalynder's mound. Thalynder shuddered and abruptly stopped the kiss and pushed Bryn back.

"No," she said breathlessly. "A little at a time, Bryn. I am only now getting used to kissing you."

Bryn, as breathless as the princess, released Thalynder from her position against the tree. She touched Thalynder's cheek. "What am I going to do if you marry?"

"You will not leave my side, for one thing. You are still my attendant and even in marriage I will have need for your company. Besides, that is too far into the future to discuss. Come, let us go tell Meydra we have met the other member of our little traveling company." She started for the dragon garden and did not stop to wait for Bryn.

Bryn stared at Thalynder's back. Adjusting her tunic, she followed Thalynder to the garden. She knew she had crossed a line there at the tree. She had shown a glimpse of her true self, and she was not certain if Thalynder understood what had happened. Bryn felt confused by the event and frightened at the thought of losing Thalynder if she went too far. She ran her hands over her cheeks before quickening her step to catch up before Thalynder reached the linden arch.

Meydra had seen the two women come out from the walls of the keep and into the meadow. She saw them stop at the tree and waited to see if they were coming out to visit her. It was not long before she saw Thalynder come out from behind the tree and head toward the garden. Meydra looked past Thalynder to see if Bryn was coming along behind her, and she saw Bryn step out from under the tree and stare for a moment at Thalynder's back. Meydra's heartbeat quickened at the sight of Bryn. But soon a pang of sadness rose within her as she watched Bryn stare at Thalynder. She had known for several years that Bryn was in love with Thalynder. There was nothing she could do, no wise counsel, no kind words, nothing Meydra could say to help Bryn with the heartache she would feel when Thalynder married. Meydra knew Bryn would have to fight for Thalynder's love. She would have to fight convention and time-sown tradition. It would be a battle against all the princess had been taught and come to expect.

Bryn reached the arch in time to walk into the garden with Thalynder. The two women approached Meydra, and Thalynder sat down hastily on the bench. She had neglected to touch the dragon, as was her customary greeting. She drew her knees into her chest and sat in silence. Bryn touched Meydra's cheek and moved to stand next to the bench where her Lynder sat in quiet contemplation. Bryn took a breath and turned to face Meydra.

"Sir Arryn will accompany us on the journey," Bryn said.

"He is a skilled captain," Meydra replied. "He will be an asset."

"I don't want an asset," Thalynder said, her words muffled by her arms and knees. She raised her head and looked at Meydra. "I want to find true love. How can I do that if one of my father's own guard is following my every move?"

Meydra's tail twitched. She looked down at Thalynder. "Would you believe me if I said you will find love before you return home?"

Bryn looked at Meydra and remembered her words from the other day: Thalynder's true love was already close by. Could it be Sir Arryn?

Thalynder shook her head and said, "I suppose next you will tell me I do not even need to take the journey." Her tone was terse and it caused Meydra to snort.

Bryn stifled a laugh. She looked out at the grassy field to regain her composure.

"I will tell you that your true love will be found before you return home," Meydra said quietly. "I will also tell you that you should take the journey and find out for yourself whether you should have left home in the first place. I am charged with helping you find love, not persuading you to accept it. That is entirely up to you, Your Highness."

Thalynder reached down and picked at the grass at her feet. She looked up at Bryn and Meydra. "Enough riddles," she said. She stood up and smoothed her tunic down over her hips. "I will inform my father that we plan to leave in two days. We will make the journey, you Meydra, Bryn, Sir Arryn and I. Mark my words, I *will* find true love."

"Yes," Meydra said. The sadness in her voice did not bother Thalynder, but it hit Bryn squarely in the chest. Bryn looked at Meydra and frowned. She placed her hand on Meydra's chest and willed the dragon's heart to beat slower. As her heart slowed, Meydra's shoulders relaxed.

Meydra sighed as she looked at Bryn. Meydra hesitated, then quickly turned to look at Thalynder.

"I will be gone tonight," the dragon said. "I want to scout some of the forest before you set out."

"You have my permission to leave," Thalynder said and walked over to put her hand on Meydra's forehead, a perfunctory gesture not lost on Bryn. "Come, Bryn, we have work to do in the keep." Thalynder started for the arch and without looking back, left the dragon garden.

Bryn watched Thalynder leave and felt uneasy. She patted Meydra's cheek and smiled at her. "My chief concern is the section where we leave the forest and have to cross the expanse of open land near the wall. It will be necessary to know where an enemy could hide."

"I will be cautious," Meydra said.

"I know you will." Bryn kissed Meydra's cheek and started for the keep. She hesitated at the arch.

"Don't worry about Thalynder. She is a bit overwrought today," Bryn called back. "I will miss you tonight."

Meydra smiled at Bryn, then stood up on her four legs and lifted into the air. She continued to look at Bryn as she rose into the cloudless afternoon sky. Bryn watched her climb and turn to the west.

Sir Arryn walked the grounds that surrounded the keep with one of his fellow guardsman. They circled back and stopped at the horse paddock.

"You are pensive, Arryn. What worries you? Surely you are not sulking over the task of accompanying two beautiful women on a jaunt to the north?"

"Stop wagging your tongue, Dryst," Arryn said. "You speak of Her Highness Thalynder and her attendant Bryn is no less a lady herself."

"I meant no disrespect to either woman," Dryst said. "It's just not like you to be so quiet over an assignment. I could only guess."

"You are right. I mistook your words because I am distracted."

"Clearly. Do you want to talk about it?"

"Not now, but thank you. Stay here at your post. I'll continue to walk the keep." Arryn left Dryst at the paddock and went out by way of the back garden wall. He walked out toward the dragon garden and stopped at the open field by the linden arch. Arryn glanced into the garden but did not see Meydra. He stepped out into the open field and, placing his right hand on his heart, he held his left hand out, palm facing the sky.

"I am your servant," he whispered. "I am your guardian. I am he that breathes the same air, feels the same wind, embraces the same earth. I am your servant." He pulled a small object out from under his captain's cloak and held it in his hand. He ran his fingers over the object, caressing it like a precious gem. He kissed it, then placed it back under his cloak. Arryn turned to leave the field and saw Meydra step out from the shadows of the garden. He stared at the dragon for a long moment.

"I do not know if I am ready for this journey," he said in a whisper. Arryn did not expect a comment in return and was startled when his heart replied. *It is time you walked your own path, Arryn of the Epidii, Clann of the West.*

⬧

Bryn and Thalynder spent the rest of the evening going over the items they would take on the journey. Bryn knew that the long days of riding would eventually take a toll on the saddle ponies, and the lighter they traveled the better.

Bryn chose one pair of boots, a tunic and a pair of hose to be worn while riding or walking in the forest. The tunic was a dark leaf green. Embroidered into the cloth by the skilled hands of her mother was the Tree of Life symbol adopted by her clann.

The tunic would render her nearly unseen as she passed among the trees. She paired it with brown hose and dark brown boots. Bryn rolled one extra tunic, a dark blue one that resembled the night sky, into a blanket and set it down next to her bow and quiver. She laid a small bag of essential items—a comb and some dried herbs and flowers—next to her treasured sword and her shield.

Bryn's sword, a true expression of the early world of her ancestors, had been designed by her parents and wrought by the elves. On the handle was the clann symbol for the sun: rays extending out from the center orb. The entire sword gleamed brilliant in even the dimmest light. Engraved on the blade were the words *leug camhanaich* ~ "precious jewel of the dawn" on one side and *till gu talamh* ~ "return to earth" on the other.

The shield, a resplendent example of Druid and elf collaboration, had been fashioned for her arm three years ago as a gift for the seventeenth anniversary of her birth. Bryn did not grow much after that time and the shield remained a good fit. Emblazoned upon the shield was the Tree of Life as it stood in a field of concentric circles joined so there was no beginning and no end. The shield rim was fashioned with silver and could be used to reflect the sun into an enemy's eyes. With the shield and the sword and her many years of training, Bryn was as formidable a swordsman as any of the knights of the Royal Guard. Paired with her knowledge of alchemy and herbs, Bryn's sword and shield set her apart from her peers. Nevertheless, Bryn kept her knowledge to herself. Not even Thalynder knew of all that Bryn held hidden inside.

Bryn left her little room and made her way to the courtyard and the outer wall of the main keep. She gave a nod to the guard at the gate as he opened the small door that allowed her to exit and walk through town. The evening meal hour was approaching and the town was busy with merchants closing upshop for the day. Bryn stopped at a small ironware stall next to the village smith. She stepped up to the table and glanced at the items laid out for sale or trade. She turned several knives over, looking at both sides carefully.

"Is there a particular blade you wish to see, my lady?" the man at the stall asked as Bryn hefted a small knife in her hand.

"This will do," she said. She placed a small coin on the table.

"That coin will buy a second knife as well, perhaps one a little larger to complement the smaller?" the man said as he picked up the coin. He started for another knife.

"No thank you," Bryn replied. "However, if you have a small cup that can be used in travel, I will take that and you may keep the small change."

The man looked under the table and found a small cup, one that might be used by a child. He showed it to Bryn. "Is this what you had in mind?"

"Yes." Bryn thanked the man, took her purchases and left the stall. As she continued through town, she began to think of the journey she was about to embark upon with Thalynder. The dangers, both foreseen and unknown, were real, and the need for stealth was paramount. Bryn felt better with the little knife in her hand and looked it over as she walked. She ran her thumb over the maker's imprint, having seen the mark when she first saw the knife. She smiled as her thumb gently rubbed the carved letters. The imprint, still clear after all these years, was in the rúnir used by her clann.

The light burned brightly from inside the small happy home before Bryn. The house was surrounded by raised flower and vegetable beds tended by her parents. Small, iron loops caught the wind and the rain and lent a calming chime to the warmth that came from within. Bryn loved the little house. She tapped lightly on the door and pushed it open. Her father was helping her mother with some little task at the table and they both looked up and smiled as Bryn stepped into the room.

"Daughter, as always you are right on time," Bryn's mother, Arlendyl, said. "I have dried the first of this season's berries and they are ready for you to take on your journey."

"Good evening, Mother, Father," Bryn said. She kissed both parents on the cheek. She placed the little cup and the knife on the table. "Thank you, Mother. The berries are much appreciated." She sat down next to her mother. "I have come to borrow the book."

Brymender picked up the knife and hefted it in his hand. He glanced at the maker's mark and smiled. He looked over the cup, turning it in his hands. "Why so small a cup?" he asked.

"I wanted something small to crush the herbs and berries in," Bryn replied. "I have a small bowl, but this will serve other uses as well."

"Sound idea," her mother said. She placed the dried berries into a small cloth sack and tied it closed with a strip of cloth. "These are the hips from last year's roses." She placed the sack next to the knife and cup.

"I may have need of much before this journey is over," Bryn said. She touched her mother's hand. "I saw Andelyn's map today. Sir Arryn has it in his possession."

"It is in good hands. Young Arryn comes from good stock," Arlendyl said. "I am glad he has been chosen to accompany you and Thalynder to Staenis. He may wish to make this his pilgrimage as well."

Bryn felt a slight remorse at having lied to her parents. She hesitated and looked at her mother.

"There is something I must mention," she said. "I have neglected to tell you the true reason behind the request for the journey."

Bryn's father shook his head slightly and smiled at his daughter. "We knew there was another reason. Will you tell us now?"

Bryn ran her hand over the well-scrubbed table. "Princess Thalynder does not wish to marry someone her father chooses for her. She wishes to find her own true love."

Arlendyl looked from Bryn to Brymender.

"That map of Arryn's does not include Staenis or Skerrabrae," Arlendyl said. "Brymender, would you hand me the bundle from inside the box?" Brymender rose from the table and walked to a small wooden box at the back of the room. He removed a small item from the box, walked back to the table and handed the item to his wife. He remained standing and watched the exchange between mother and daughter.

"A royal's obligation is always a concern to them when they are young," Arlendyl said to Bryn. "Love will find her when it is ready, not before. The princess was brought up to be a ruler. That will not change. For now, be concerned with the journey. Here, look at the book." Her mother opened the book Brymender had handed her to a page in the front.

"I have added a passage that will help you identify some of the writings on the Stones, as well as a map of the land around Staenis and out to Skerrabrae," she said. "The book is my gift to you, Daughter."

"Mother," Bryn said as she looked over the much-cherished book. "This belongs to an elder. I only wish to borrow it."

"When you return from this journey, we will discuss your returning it," her father said.

Arlendyl lay her hand over her husband's and looked at their daughter. She smiled and said, "If the book is yours, you will not be quite so upset if something happens to it."

Bryn looked at her mother and understood. Anything could happen along the journey, and to worry about returning the book should be the least of her concerns. "I am most pleased with the gift." She looked at her parents and thanked the stars for their kindness and understanding. "I was afraid you would not understand Thalynder's own reason for the journey." She stood up and embraced her father. After a warm embrace, she stepped over and kissed her mother's cheek.

"Her reasons are her own. Perhaps we should ask if you truly intend on a pilgrimage to the Stones."

"I did not at first," Bryn confessed. "But I do now. Will I see you tomorrow night at the departing feast?"

"Nothing will stop us," her father said.

Brymender walked with Bryn to the door and stood outside with her a moment in the cool evening air. He took a small object from his pocket and fingered it before speaking. He sighed.

"Bryn, there are revelations waiting for you and Arryn at Staenis," he said quietly. "Meydra will be able to assist you in understanding what you see and read. Do not hesitate to ask questions of her. She is beyond reproach; loyal and honest."

"She is," Bryn agreed. "However, I am not her Companion as you well know. I can, however, instruct Thalynder to ask those questions."

Brymender laid his hand on Bryn's arm and looked into her eyes. "No, Bryn. Do not instruct Thalynder to ask those questions that will come to your mind. Ask them yourself." He held her gaze for a long moment. "Meydra will answer you." Brymender released his daughter and gave her a warm smile. "Go on now. Your mother and I will see you again at the feast."

Bryn wanted to ask her father many questions, but his dismissal was firm. She kissed his cheek and left the circle of comfort that emanated from the house. She carried the book, cup, knife, and sack in her hands, holding them all close to her breast. Her father had not commented on the maker's mark on the knife but Bryn knew he recognized it. The mark belonged to her eldest brother—long since dead at the hands of raiders from the east. It was a good omen to be starting a journey with her brother in her hands.

Bryn felt something tapping her thigh as she walked toward the keep. She stopped and felt in the pocket of her tunic, pulling out the small stone. It was the one her father carried with him everywhere. On the face was a deeply carved rune with one half of the rune missing, the stone having been split or splintered long ago. Its polished surface was the result of constant rubbing by human hands. She sighed and felt the sting of unshed tears as she looked back toward the contentment that was her parents' home.

CHAPTER SIX

The sun rose behind a veil of clouds and cast a pale gray hue over the keep, promising its inhabitants a much cooler day. The inner sanctum was still quiet in the early morning hour, but the servants' and attendants' quarters were already producing a steady hum.

Bryn had already seen the pack ponies laden with bags, despite her urging to keep the load to a minimum. She didn't wait for Thalynder to come down from her room. She left the sleeping quarters to go downstairs and find Sir Arryn.

The halls were filled with light conversations as attendants and servants scurried like mice to and from the Grand Hall. Bryn passed one hall that led to the servants' quarters and heard voices arguing. She heard the word "ponies" mentioned and, glancing down the hall, saw two young men engaged in a debate, bags full of who knew what at their feet. She paused and listened.

"Fetch another pony," one of the groomsmen said to the other. "We can redistribute the loads and lessen the weight on each pony."

"I can't believe all the things they are taking," the other replied. "It is as if the princess means to stay away longer than just a few weeks."

That comment caught Bryn by surprise. Talk like this is not good, she thought. She stepped into the hall and cleared her throat.

"What is in those bags?" she asked and pointed at the groomsman's feet.

"Lady Bryn," the young man said and bowed his head quickly. "Dried provisions for your journey."

"And what is in the bags that are already causing the ponies distress?"

"Food, medicine, cooking pots, bowls, cloth to cover the ground."

Bryn grunted. She had heard enough and looked the young man in the eye. "You will do nothing with these bags, and you will not lay store on any other ponies until you hear back from either Sir Arryn or myself. Is that understood?"

"Yes, Lady Bryn."

Bryn left the two men and walked back toward the dining room. I have to make this right, she thought, and the place to start is with Sir Arryn. "Let us hope he does not need persuading," she said to the cat in the hall.

In the corner of the dining room, standing and speaking with an attendant, was Sir Arryn. Bryn locked her gaze on his face and after a brief moment, he looked her way. She nodded at him and waited. Sir Arryn quickly walked over to her.

"Good morning, Lady Bryn," he said and bowed his head.

"Good morning, Sir Arryn," she replied and gave a quick curtsy. She lowered her voice: "I am in need of your counsel. Could you join me at the pony paddock?"

"I can accompany you now," Sir Arryn replied, matching Bryn's hushed tone.

Bryn turned and left the dining hall, hastening toward the doors that led out back to the horse stalls and pony paddocks. She felt Sir Arryn at her elbow and turned to look at him. "So long as we are to be traveling companions, it would be suitable for you to call me Bryn. You may drop the title."

"I would like that, Bryn. You may call me Arryn."

Bryn shot him a hard glance and did not like the familiarity in his voice. She frowned. "I will only do so once we have left the keep tomorrow morning." She quickened her step to put some distance between her and the knight.

"Why?" Arryn asked as he increased his step to match Bryn stride for stride.

"Because you are held in higher esteem than I. I am a waiting lady, you are a knight. We are not of the same social status. You may condescend to call me by my name, but for me to do so in the presence of others connotes familiarity," she said quickly.

Arryn touched her arm. "Lady Bryn, you are a Druid. And not only a Druid, but the daughter of a Druid elder. In my world, that is a higher place than that of a waiting lady. If you wish me to call you Bryn, it is I who am flattered by your condescension."

The hall that led to the back door was dark, and Bryn did not like the way the walls made her feel—as if they were closing in on her. She reached the exit before Sir Arryn and pushed open the heavy wooden door. As she stepped out and into the gray mist, she sighed audibly.

Mistaking her sigh for a comment on the weather, Sir Arryn said, "It will clear."

"Yes," Bryn said. *It will clear, when you and I come to an understanding*, she thought. Bryn slowed her walk and allowed Sir Arryn to walk beside her again. "I am concerned about the provisions we are bringing with us."

"I was told to leave the planning of provisions to you."

She laughed. "Who, then, do you think has been requesting all of this?" she said as they approached the pony paddock. Tethered to the fence were three ponies. Each was laden with several leather bags on each side. "I gave no word stating we would be taking so many ponies, let alone this much in the way of provisions. Surely, this is not all at the request of the princess?"

Sir Arryn chuckled. He lifted the flap of one of the leather bags and looked inside. "This one contains what appears to be a finely woven tunic, by the cut of the cloth." He pulled out a rolled piece of fabric and showed it to Bryn. He placed it back into the bag and lifted the flap of the next satchel. "Ah, here we have bathing items." He pulled out a brush of soft bristles.

Bryn laughed. "That girl will be the death of me," she said and quickly paled at her informal familiarity in referencing Thalynder before the knight. "Excuse me, Sir Arryn, I meant no disrespect to the princess."

Sir Arryn placed his hand on the pony's back and looked at Bryn. "You and the princess have been inseparable since you were young girls. I would expect that by now you have become quite used to having her cause you no end of grief. I take no offense at the casual way you refer to our princess, your friend."

"Thank you," Bryn said, relaxing. "I need to speak with her again regarding what we will be taking on this trip. I presume that she will insist on some things, and that may require one pony. My things I will carry on my own mount."

"As will I," Arryn replied. "Between us, I am sure we can convince Her Highness that one pony will suffice."

Bryn patted the pony's nose and smiled at Arryn. Perhaps he will not be as hard to deal with as I first suspected, she thought. "I will find the princess and ask her to reconsider."

Arryn resumed his knightly demeanor and touched his fist to his chest and bowed his head. "I do not envy you your task." He raised his head and looked at Bryn.

Bryn gave him a quick smile and left him and the ponies to make her way back to the inner keep to find Thalynder.

Thalynder was sitting on her bed, still dressed in her loose-fitting bed gown, and looking over trinkets she had amassed over the years. Bryn giggled first, then tried to frown at the idea of Thalynder even considering taking jewelry on the journey. She picked up a small brooch from the floor.

"You aren't planning to take these, are you?" Bryn asked, tossing the brooch onto the bed. She sat down next to Thalynder.

"I must take something that will catch the eye of my true love," Thalynder replied.

"Lynder, you are already taking too much." Bryn reached over to touch Thalynder's neck and the cowrie shell necklace lying there. "The servants are beginning to talk about how much you are taking."

"Do you think I care what the servants think?" Thalynder asked as she picked up another bauble and looked it over.

"No, I don't think you do, but you should. If you pack fancy clothes, jewels, many shoes and foodstuffs that is better left behind, you will cause your servants to talk. If they talk, the attendants talk. If the attendants talk, your father will hear. This is supposed to look like a journey to Skerrabrae and Staenis, not a hunt for your true love."

Thalynder frowned and looked down at the items she held. "I guess I was more concerned with how I would appear to someone who might love me instead of considering the consequences of my actions. I've overpacked, haven't I?"

Bryn laughed. As much as she wanted to remain stern with Thalynder, she couldn't. She wrapped her arms around Thalynder and squeezed. "Yes, you have, naughty girl." She kissed Thalynder on the cheek.

Thalynder laid the trinkets down and turned in Bryn's arms. Wrapping her arms around Bryn's waist, she pulled her close and kissed her on the mouth.

Bryn hesitated only a moment before returning the kiss. Pressing her lips to Thalynder's, parting them to allow tongues to dance. Bryn sighed as she felt Thalynder's hands move over her back. She gasped only slightly when Thalynder again touched her breast as she had the previous day. She wished she was still dressed in her own loose bed gown, and not her tunic, so that she could feel Thalynder's touch all the more keenly. She moved her right hand to Thalynder's shoulder, and when she felt no resistance, moved her hand to Lynder's breast. The princess pressed her breast forward to fill Bryn's hand. Bryn held Thalynder's breast through the loose, gauzy material of the gown and rubbed her thumb over Thalynder's nipple. Thalynder moaned in Bryn's mouth and Bryn felt her own pulse quicken. She wanted to lay Thalynder on the bed, to kiss her mouth, her neck, her breasts. She did not know how far Thalynder was going to let this go, and she was afraid to go too far.

Bryn broke the kiss and, still holding Thalynder's breast, said, "You tempt me."

Thalynder smiled warmly at Bryn. "You make it easy," she said and moved her body against Bryn's hand. "I like being in your arms."

"Lynder, I want more but am afraid I will offend you." Bryn squeezed Thalynder's breast, causing her to jump a little.

"What more do you want, my Bryn?"

"I want to fill you with delight." Bryn continued to stare into Thalynder's green eyes, watching for signs of distress. Seeing none, she continued, "I want to kiss your skin from head to foot. I want to kiss your nipples. I want…"

Thalynder's body pulsed under Bryn's hands. She began to speak but was interrupted by a knock on the door. Bryn quickly pulled the gown up over Thalynder's shoulders as the door came open.

"Good, I find you together. I have need to speak with both of you," the king said.

King Thamen waited outside the door while Bryn helped Thalynder dress. The severe look the king had given the girls diminished all trace of desire, and Bryn was quiet while she handed Thalynder her dress and tunic. Thalynder had chosen a simpler dress for the day and did not need Bryn's assistance with the laces. Bryn found Thalynder's matching slippers and handed them to her. She looked at the princess's face and noted she was concerned—and well she should be, Bryn thought. The king rarely came to this part of the keep unless it was of great importance.

"Do you suppose he means to stop us from going?" Thalynder whispered as she took the slippers from Bryn. She sat down on the bed and pulled them on over the dark blue hose.

Bryn watched with fascination as Thalynder poised her foot to accept the slipper. The dainty and delicate way Thalynder moved her foot had Bryn mesmerized.

"I'm ready," Thalynder said to Bryn. "Please tell my father."

Bryn opened the door to let His Majesty enter the room. She did not speak but waited until he was inside. She closed the door behind him and stood still.

"Come, girls," King Thamen said. "Sit here with me." He sat at the little table by the window in one of two chairs. Thalynder sat in the other.

Bryn walked to the table and stood between her king and her princess.

"You are packed for a long journey, Thalynder," he said.

Bryn shot a quick glance at Thalynder and saw the flush at her cheeks.

"I am beginning to suspect you have other plans." The king reached across the little table and took his daughter's hand in his. "Will you tell me the truth now and save me having to stop your journey?"

Thalynder swallowed and glanced at Bryn. Bryn took a little breath and cleared her throat.

"It is my fault, Majesty," Bryn said, bowing her head. "I had planned the journey to get us to Staenis and back within six weeks. I then realized to avoid the open we would add another three weeks to the journey." She raised her head. "I knew you would wish us to hasten our return, so I thought perhaps with the extra supplies and ponies, we could avoid the forest villages altogether and thereby not be detained by my kin. I should have made my change in plans clear to you before having the extra things packed."

"Yes, you should have, Bryn," the king replied. "Had you discussed this with me first, you would have found that I would rather you take the forest path and stay with your kin and not have you rush needlessly. In haste you would be vulnerable."

Bryn inwardly sighed. "It is a mistake I will avoid in the future, Your Highness." She curtsied low before him and waited.

King Thamen touched the top of Bryn's head. "I can see you have the best interest of the princess and her father in your heart. Let us make sure it reaches your head before you make any more decisions without consulting me. Now, I have other news."

Bryn rose and stood a little closer to Thalynder. He will mention a suitor next, she thought. She laid her hand on the back of Thalynder's chair and rested it against Thalynder's back. She wanted the contact so Thalynder was conscious of her presence; it always served to keep Thalynder calm.

"King Heli of Caer Troia is sending his son, Lludd, to see me while you are away," the king said with a large grin. "Britannia is growing and an alliance between my realm and that of King Heli would be greatly strengthened should you consider becoming Lludd's wife."

Bryn could feel Thalynder's back tense and moved her hand over a small section of Thalynder's shoulder. Bryn desperately needed Thalynder to be calm and allow her father to say this one thing.

"Caer Troia's realm is south of the River Thames," Thalynder said. "How could an alliance help us? We are leagues and leagues away from Caer Troia. Would our realm not benefit more from an alliance with, say, someone closer?"

"Dearest daughter," King Thamen said as he stroked her hand. "I know that you would be far from home, but the alliance is needed to keep the middle realms protected from invasion. You would be far, yes, but we could build you a keep in between and I could come and visit."

Bryn knew there were many reasons why Thalynder did not want to move to the south, and distance was only one of them. She rubbed Thalynder's shoulder.

Thalynder looked at her father. She took a little breath and said, "I will await word from you on the meeting. I appreciate your seeing him first, but please, Father, if possible, make no promises without my consent. Remember our bargain."

"I will remember our bargain," the king said and stood up. "By the time you return, I will have a fair number of possible husbands awaiting your approval."

Bryn grimaced and turned her head to cough, hoping Thalynder would keep a civil tongue. Much to her surprise, she did.

"Thank you, Father," Thalynder said and stood up. "You will make my choice that much easier if you have weeded through the chaff while I am away."

King Thamen kissed his daughter on the forehead, smiled quickly at Bryn, then left the room. He left the door open and when he had left the hall and started down the stairs, Thalynder turned to look at Bryn. "I bet you thought I was going to get angry with him," she said and took a step closer to Bryn. "You were right. I have overpacked."

◈

Soft music filled the warm air inside the Grand Hall. The room was lit with hundreds of candles and sparkled with flickering light. The hall, large and spacious, could be icy cold in the winter and blisteringly hot in the summer. It was humid this night and the lords and ladies who had come to the feast, dressed in their finest regalia, looked more than a little uncomfortable. The Royal Guard captains—easily recognized by the silver brooches at their left shoulders and the matching swords at their sides—were dressed in uniforms of the realm with heavy cloaks held in place with the brooches. The room was a steam bath and everyone looked ready to wilt—everyone, that is, except for Bryn of the Brae, her father and mother, and two of the other Druid elders of the Brae Clann.

Bryn had anticipated the heat of the night and the close proximity of many bodies and had chosen to wear a floor-length deep blue dress of a light and airy gauze material. A lighter blue thigh-length tunic, embroidered with the Tree of Life in fine silver thread, and matching silver ribbons at her wrists, completed her attire. Her hair was pulled into a braid that hung down her back, interlaced with more of the silver ribbon. Bryn's parents and the elders wore gowns and tunics of the same light gauze, in colors of dark brown and green. They all wore the silver-embroidered tunics, and the silver Trees of Life glinted in the candlelight.

Thalynder had taken Bryn's advice on wearing her hair in a braid, but she had not dressed as casually as Bryn. She had opted to wear her best dress of royal purple with long sleeves cuffed in rabbit fur. The fur also adorned the neck opening of the dress, as well as the hem. She wore an embroidered tunic the same color as the dress, with her family crest embroidered in gold thread on her bodice. She was truly beautiful with her blond hair braided and flowing down her back over the rich purple and gold fabric.

Bryn spent most of the evening with her parents and the Druid elders. Her parents appeared more anxious than she had seen them in many years.

"Why do you suggest I go to Staenis first, Elder?" Bryn asked when her father paused. "I have mapped out a route to Skerrabrae first with a visit to Staenis later. It would be the most direct route."

"True," the elder replied. "However, it would be better for Bryn, daughter of Arlendyl and Brymender, to see the Stones of Staenis first. There you will learn many things that will make the journey to Skerrabrae all the more important. To journey to Skerrabrae first would pose many questions in your mind. To journey first to Staenis, those questions will have answers."

Bryn began to regret devising this ruse. What had started out as a way to get Thalynder out of the keep and allow her to look for her true love was becoming a quest of epic proportions. Add to this the insistence of a clann elder that Bryn actively seek the Stones where she was to supposed to find answers to questions she had yet to pose. Inside, she wanted to scream. Outside, she could see the logic in the older man's reasoning and nodded her head. She touched the Tree of Life symbol on the elder's tunic and pressed softly. She looked into his face, where she saw many things: a quiet resolve shown as a peaceful continence, depth of knowledge from years of study shown in the creases around his eyes. In his gaze she saw something newer, something younger than his years would normally portray. She saw anticipation and expectation. Expectation for what? she wondered.

"I will go to Staenis first and find the answers," she said to the older man. "I will go to Skerrabrae to ask the questions."

The elder leaned over and placed a trembling kiss on Bryn's forehead. His hands shook as he patted Brymender's shoulder. He turned to Bryn's mother, Arlendyl, and said, "Worry not. Bryn will return and all will be put right." With that the elder left the room.

Bryn heard the words the elder had said to her mother and frowned. *What was wrong that had to be put right? What have I gotten myself, and Thalynder, into?*

Thalynder overheard the small speech the elder had given to Bryn, and she too wondered what was ahead. She knew she was in line to rule a kingdom. That gave her certain rights and privileges among the realm, but she couldn't help thinking that Bryn would be more affected by what they discovered on their journey. The Druid elders, with their secret ways and secret teachings, always left Thalynder feeling inferior. She didn't like the way they made her feel. When we are away from the keep and the elders, she thought, then I will have more control.

CHAPTER SEVEN

Bryn dressed quickly in her brown hose, green knee-length riding tunic and green hip-length overtunic embroidered with the Tree of Life. She decided to add a darker green bodice to her outfit and slipped it on over the embroidered tunic. She laced up the front, covering her clann's symbol. As she braided her hair, Bryn looked about her room. At least you will be waiting for my return, she thought. She pulled on her riding boots and picked up her sword and scabbard, fastening them around her waist. She positioned her quiver at her right shoulder blade, slung the bow over her left shoulder, and grabbed the bag and bedroll that lay on the floor. She blew out the candle and left her room, closing the door softly behind her.

Bryn entered the stalls quietly and found her own mount, a dark brown Galloway mare with long mane and tail, and light feathering at her pastern. A sturdy horse from the Northern Isles that could be ridden all day without tiring. The mare and Bryn had a good rapport, and when Bryn entered the barn, the mare whinnied softly.

"Yes, little sister, I am here," Bryn cooed as she opened the door to the stall. She placed fresh grass in the horse's feed bucket and rubbed her hand over the mare's forehead. "We will be leaving soon, Pymmar. You will have no oats along the way, but there will be plenty else to eat, and I promise you are going to love the clear water of the northern lands." Bryn hung her bedroll, her bow and quiver and her bag on the hook outside Pymmar's stall. After giving the mare one more rub on the forehead and a kiss on the jowl, Bryn closed the stall door and went to find Meydra.

Meydra had arrived back at the garden long before the festivities began that evening, and she now lay resting in the tall grass. As night fell, she listened as the revelers left the inner keep and returned to their own houses. She expected either Thalynder or Bryn to join her once the keep was quiet, and so bid sleep depart until she had her visit. She smelled Bryn's scent long before she heard or saw her. Bryn's step was always light and left no mark behind her. She was rarely heard, and if she wanted, Bryn could remain unseen. Meydra smiled knowing Bryn was coming alone. She sniffed the air and could tell the rain in the east was ebbing, which would mean a warmer day tomorrow. She shifted her head slightly to watch for Bryn's approach.

"Meydra," Bryn said as she approached the linden arch. The trees swayed as she passed.

"I am here, Bryn," Meydra replied softly.

"It will be warmer tomorrow when we set out on our journey," Bryn said and ran her hand over the scales on Meydra's neck. "The air feels lighter."

"It has stopped raining in the east," Meydra replied. She nodded at the way she and Bryn were reading the same things. "When do you wish to leave?"

"I spoke with Sir Arryn at the feast and he agreed we should leave before the keep wakes," Bryn said and sat down with her back against Meydra's thigh. Meydra shifted behind Bryn to curl her tail around her leg and rest it in front of Bryn, creating a little circle of protection. Bryn sighed. "The king would rather we wait for him to rise and see us off."

"Thamen is always one for the dramatic," Meydra said. "I am glad you were able to talk him out of the parade."

"Yes, my one compensation," Bryn replied. "When he first told me of his plan of an armed escort through the realm with banners and drummers, I scowled. He saw my face and laughed. Thankfully, Sir Arryn and I were able to convince His Highness of the need for secrecy even in the realm. This morning, while you were away, I managed to convince Thalynder that she need not take three pack ponies *and* her mount."

"Three pack ponies? My, we would have had a long and slow march through the forest." Meydra adjusted her heat to keep Bryn from becoming too warm, as the night air was still humid and heavy. The last little sliver of moon had not yet cleared the trees and the breeze had died down. "How many ponies are you taking now?"

"None," Bryn said and leaned her head back and closed her eyes. "We are carrying our small bags and bedrolls on our own mounts. No pack ponies, of that I am much relieved. Tell me, did you find any trouble spots along the wall?"

"I did. When we near the open expanse, I will accept Thalynder and take to the air." Meydra hesitated.

Bryn sat back up and looked at Meydra's face. "What is it? You hesitated."

"You and Sir Arryn will be in the open, Bryn. I know you are skilled, but you will be exposed. I do not like the idea."

"It is the risk we have to take, but at least Thalynder will be protected," Bryn said. "There is one other thing." Bryn removed her boots and tossed them over Meydra's tail and into the grass.

Meydra shifted and sensed a change in Bryn. She brought her tail closer to her body, tightening the circle around Bryn. "A change in plans," Meydra said.

"Yes, Elder Regmar has suggested—no, that's not the right word. He has *told* me to go to Staenis first and to Skerrabrae only after seeing the Stones."

Meydra nodded. "He wants you to see the writing on the Stones." She adjusted her heart to beat slowly, calmly. She raised her body temperature slightly and began to breathe deeply.

"He said I would find answers at the Stones. Answers to the questions I would ask at Skerrabrae," Bryn said and lay down in the grass, protected by the dragon's body and tail.

"Yes, you will," Meydra said and closed the gap between the end of her tail and her body, providing Bryn with the perfect place to sleep a dreamless sleep. She heard Bryn's breathing deepen and she knew Bryn was asleep.

"You will ask questions, and you will have the answers. What matters most, little sister, is what you do with the answers." Meydra lifted her head and inhaled deeply. She sensed nothing amiss in the air. She stretched her ears and listened to sounds off in the distance. The soft call of an owl to its mate was all she heard. All was still in the realm. She lay her head down on her thigh and closed her eyes. Tomorrow they would begin a journey that would result in only one thing of certainty—and that was change.

Bryn stretched and rubbed Meydra's chest. The sun was not up but the sky was growing lighter in the east. Meydra smiled at Bryn, and Bryn kissed the dragon's cheek. She straightened her tunic and bodice, found her boots and put them on. She stood in front of Meydra and leaned her forehead to touch the creature's forehead. It was an intimate touch, one of complete trust for a dragon that was not hers. Bryn knew it was dangerous. Some dragons became protective of their Companions and would let no other touch them in such an intimate manner. Bryn sensed Meydra was no threat. Never once in all the years she had been with Thalynder had Meydra ever showed anything but kindness toward Bryn. She wanted to let Meydra know she trusted her. She needed Meydra to know. As Bryn approached the dragon, she knew Meydra understood what she wanted to do. Meydra bowed her head and as Bryn neared, she moved to meet Bryn halfway. Bryn smiled and without fully realizing what she was doing, she brought her two hands up to place them on either side of the dragon's head. She held the position and in a whisper, said, "*Mo anam.*" My soul.

Meydra remained with her head bowed until Bryn was out of the garden and had passed through the linden arch. She had heard that term, *mo anam*, used by Bryn's great-grandmother, Andelyn, and her grandfather, Brymeldan, her former Companions. Meydra could only guess that Bryn had, without knowing, tapped into a childhood memory. Meydra sighed and felt the tear fall down her cheek. The tear solidified as it hit the earth, turning into a glittering drop of clear stone. Meydra used her talon and dug a little trench, pushing the stone into the rut and covering it with earth. The diamond would remain buried until needed.

Thalynder was still in her bed gown when Bryn came into her room, and when she saw Bryn, she ran straight into Bryn's arms. She kissed Bryn quickly, then took her hand and led her to the bed. "Where have you been?" Thalynder asked.

"I went to check on the horses," Bryn said. "Why aren't you dressed? We should be on the road soon, or we will spend the first night in the thick of the forest where it will be difficult for Meydra to provide protection."

"Don't be angry, Bryn. I was waiting for you. I thought that before we go, you could finish what you started yesterday." Thalynder rubbed her body against Bryn in a provocative manner—her breasts pushed against Bryn's arm.

Bryn sighed. "I would like that very much, Lynder, but I am serious. If we do not leave within the hour, we will sleep in a thicket and Meydra would be unable to come into the forest to provide protection. I only fear for your safety." Bryn kissed Thalynder's mouth, which was screwed up into a pout.

"Oh, Bryn, you are perplexing and sometimes quite annoying."

"I will continue to be so until we are well away from the keep and away from Sir Arryn's view," Bryn said. "Come, let us get you dressed. Your morning meal is being prepared and we still need to find Sir Arryn."

Bryn watched as Thalynder removed the bed gown and stood in the early light, naked and unadorned. She handed Thalynder her dark green hose and watched as she slipped them over her long legs. The hose were held in place with matching ribbons. Her riding attire was next: the undergarment, an ankle-length dress of a durable linen the color of wheat, the outer garment, a hip-length tunic the color of rich earth with her family crest embroidered in gold. Over these she placed a wheat-colored bodice, hiding the crest. She looked like a young sapling with her hair crowning the ensemble like gold leaves hanging off slender limbs. Bryn smiled at Thalynder.

"You did that all by yourself, Princess," she mocked.

"None of your lip, Bryn of the Brae." Thalynder gave Bryn a big smile. "I need my sword and my bow. Have you seen them?"

"They are with the horses. Now, let us eat. I am suddenly quite hungry," Bryn said and touched Thalynder's arm when she came toward her. "You look beautiful, Lynder."

"As do you, Bryn. You are flushed and quite pretty this morning. You must be careful though, or Sir Arryn is likely to sweep you away and leave Meydra and me to finish the quest alone," Thalynder teased.

"That will never happen," Bryn said and let Thalynder lead her to the dining room.

The women ate their meal while Bryn explained the first leg of the day's journey. It would take them past the grouse-hunting grounds and through the small villages that ringed the inner realm. Bryn had finished her meal and started to stand when an attendant placed three cups and a small jug of mead in front of her. "I did not ask for mead," Bryn said to the attendant.

"No, my lady," the attendant replied. "Sir Arryn asked that I bring it, and bade me tell you he will join you shortly."

"Very well," Thalynder said before Bryn could respond. "Where is Sir Arryn now?"

"He is having the horses brought to the inner courtyard," the attendant replied. Then he bowed his head and backed away from the two women.

"We *are* leaving soon," Thalynder said with a note of surprise. "Will I have time to bid my father farewell?"

"You will," Bryn said and glanced toward the entry to the dining room. Sir Arryn was approaching their table. His stride was brisk, and Bryn could see he was as anxious as she to start the journey. Sir Arryn knew the inner realm, knew where the forest would be thickest, and would realize the need to seek shelter that Meydra could defend. Bryn poured a small amount of mead in each cup and stood as the knight approached the table. She offered him a cup.

Sir Arryn nodded at Bryn and accepted the cup. He held it up for a toast. "To a safe journey," he said.

"Safe journey," the two women echoed. They took a long drink of the mead, after which Bryn set her cup down and looked at Thalynder.

"Go now and find your father. Tell him we are in the courtyard and await any last instruction he may have for us."

Thalynder left the table and quickly walked across the room. When she was out of sight, Sir Arryn looked at Bryn.

"The king and your father are in the dragon garden with Meydra. I did not tell the princess, as I knew that the king and your father wished a moment alone."

Bryn frowned, trying to determine why the king and her father might want to speak with Meydra. If it was regarding the journey, they should be talking to her or Sir Arryn. The fact that they were not left a note of bitterness on Bryn's tongue. She moved from behind the table and stood next to Arryn. "We should go to the horses and make ready to leave." It was then that she noticed Arryn was not dressed as a captain but was wearing traveling attire much like her own. A green knee-length tunic over dark brown hose and knee-high boots. His thigh-length jerkin was a much-worn and weathered leather the color of a fawn's coat. His scabbard was not ornate, and the hilt of his sword showed that he carried not his sword of the realm with its richly ornate hilt, but one with a hilt engraved with rúnir like her own. How did he come by that? Bryn wondered. The ensemble created a softer look for the always stern-looking knight. She smiled inwardly. The illusion the three would cast would indeed serve them should they meet with a threat in the forest. She was pleased.

Bryn and Arryn waited with the horses for Thalynder, who had not yet returned from looking for her father. Bryn walked to the back of the courtyard and looked toward the dragon garden to see if Thalynder had gone out to Meydra. As she approached the edge of the low wall and looked toward the garden, she saw her father, the king, and the dragon in the open field at the edge. She could not hear what they were saying, but she could see that Meydra's head was bowed in deference to the men. She watched her father touch Meydra's forehead. To the casual observer that would have been remarkable in itself; to Bryn it was only unexpected. She knew Meydra had been her grandfather's Companion and that her father had been present when Meydra chose her new Companion. She hadn't considered that her father might be close to the dragon. So many things of late perplexed Bryn. Things she saw and things she felt. "Perhaps the journey will open some doors," she whispered. Bryn left the wall and went back to where Arryn waited with the horses. Thalynder had joined him, and the two stood in silence as the grooms held the animals. A step was placed for Thalynder to mount her horse. As Bryn approached the horses, the king and her father came through the pavilion and into the courtyard to join them.

"Ah, here they are," King Thamen exclaimed. "It is time for you to depart." He kissed Bryn lightly on each cheek. He patted Sir Arryn's shoulder quickly and turned to his daughter. "You will see much on your journey, my daughter. Take it all in. Relish these coming days of what remains of your youth. Upon your return we will have much to discuss."

Bryn heard sadness in the king's words. She watched as the king embraced his daughter tenderly. Her own father came to her and pulled her aside. He stood close and spoke scarcely above a whisper. "You will remember all I have taught you. Of that I am certain. Remember what I said the other night—ask Meydra if you have questions. She will not fail you. There is one other thing."

"Yes?"

"Arryn is also a Druid. You can depend on his strength."

"I had suspected as much. Thank you, Father," Bryn replied. "Where is Mother?"

"She is waiting at the house, and she has a gift for you. Be sure to stop for a moment."

"I will," Bryn said and embraced her father, pulling him close and tight. "Is there anything I can bring back for you from Staenis or Skerrabrae?"

Brymender hesitated only a moment. "Return to your people, Bryn of the Brae."

"It will be done," she replied.

The three mounted their horses, Thalynder with the help of a groom and a step—though she did not need either—as propriety would have it no other way.

Sir Arryn offered Bryn a leg up onto her mount's back, and though she did not need that, she allowed him to be the gallant knight. It made her father smile and caused Thalynder to chuckle. Sir Arryn mounted his own horse, and the three began to ride out of the courtyard toward the main gate of the inner keep. The need for an extra pony was no longer necessary with Bryn's instruction, thus the travelers would be able to travel light and unencumbered. Bryn led the way, followed by Thalynder, with Sir Arryn at the rear. There were places along the way where they could travel three abreast, but the exit to the inner keep was not one of them.

A shower of rose petals greeted them as they approached the wall at the gate, and a flurry of trumpets announced the departure of the princess. Bryn thought the pomp a bit much, but clearly Thalynder enjoyed it, as she waved and smiled at all those who turned out for the early-morning event. Bryn passed through the gate and slowed her horse until Thalynder and Sir Arryn were outside. Bryn checked her horse and waited for Meydra to step toward them. Meydra had been waiting outside the gate in the tall grass to the left of the road. When Bryn's horse stepped through, Meydra had bowed her head for a moment at Bryn, then straightened and waited for the others to come out.

Bryn acknowledged Meydra with a warm smile and a nod of her head. In her mind she spoke to Meydra. *There is much I want to know.* To her surprise, her thoughts were answered by what she believed was her own voice. *You will be shown much.* She shook her head slightly and smiled. Thalynder rode up beside Bryn, and Sir Arryn placed himself on the other side of the princess. Meydra stepped onto the road and bowed her head before Thalynder. Thalynder reached out and lightly touched Meydra's forehead with her hand.

"We will stop momentarily at my mother's house before we take to the path that leads behind the village and out toward the grouse-hunting grounds," Bryn said. "Our first stop will be the hamlet of Tetton. There we will have a midday meal." Bryn looked at Meydra. "You will be able to see us clearly until we reach Tetton. Once we leave the confines of the hamlet, we will be unseen from the air but for a brief glimpse now and again."

"I will be able to hear you, and I also know your scent," Meydra replied. Bryn sensed a little humor to her words.

"You will also be in contact with your Companion," Sir Arryn said. He had kept his tongue since mounting his horse.

"That is as it should be," Meydra replied and added, "I will always know the whereabouts of my Companion, provided she is alive." Bryn heard the warning to Sir Arryn and listened as he returned the arrow and said, "We both have a job to do."

"Come," Bryn said, before the two began to debate their respective duties. "Let us make for my mother's house and set these horses to the path."

Bryn saw her parents' house and felt a tug on her heart. Something deep inside told her she would return a different woman, and somehow that made her wish to be a child again— at play with her mother. Arlendyl stood at the foot of the garden with a small bundle in her hand. Bryn approached ahead of the others and checked her horse before reaching her mother. She slid off the mount easily, embraced Arlendyl, and accepted the bundle. She opened it and for a moment the sun caught the item and glinted brightly. Bryn wrapped the item back in the cloth. They talked for a brief moment and then Arlendyl bowed her head to the princess. "Safe journey, Your Highness."

"I am in good hands, Lady Arlendyl," Thalynder replied. "Your Bryn and Sir Arryn will have me home in good order."

Arlendyl nodded at the princess and turned to speak to Sir Arryn.

"There is much about you we do not know, but you come from good stock," Arlendyl said. "Keep them safe." Arryn nodded at her and touched his fist to his chest. Arlendyl turned back to her daughter. They embraced one last time. Bryn returned to her horse, where Sir Arryn waited. Bryn placed the small bundle in her other sack, grabbed the horse's mane, and accepted Sir Arryn's assistance up into the saddle. She took the reins and urged the horse away from her childhood home, onto the path that would see the end of all childlike things.

CHAPTER EIGHT

For three days they traveled the small roads that ran between the hamlets of the Realm that Touches Two Seas. The days had been uneventful, even pleasant, with easy talk between the travelers, good company in the hamlets and restful nights in the homes of Bryn's clann members. The third night, though, stirred some unusual feelings in Bryn, as her clann that lay in the outer reaches of the realm began to treat her differently than those closer to the keep. They seemed more in awe of her than they were of the princess. Meydra, who was now able to fly closer to her group and even walk beside them on occasion, was also being given a far more reverent greeting than those she received from the inhabitants of the inner forest. Thalynder had mentioned it to Bryn that morning, and Arryn had put it down as simple awe of a dragon. Meydra was the only dragon he knew of in the realm. Bryn suspected that something else drove the clann to act as they did toward Meydra, but she said nothing to the others. During the days when conversation lulled, Bryn spent her time pulling all the facts she could from the recesses of her mind, and she was beginning to form a picture. She hoped that the closer they got to the region of Caledonia, the clearer the explanation for the silent veneration would become. The forest was beginning to thin, and they were near open land with heather moors stretched across the horizon before them.

Bryn checked her horse before walking out into the meadow. "Thalynder, would you ask Meydra to join us?" Thalynder called softly to Meydra and in a moment they heard the dragon's wings as she came to stand before them.

"Your Highness."

"We will be in the open for several hours," Bryn said before Thalynder could speak. "Have you seen anything that would delay our progress?" In her mind she asked, *What is it I am sensing?* She did not believe Meydra could hear her, but she thought perhaps the dragon would sense her discomfort.

"There is a small group of hunters camped on the forest edge on the other side of this moorland, and they are not of your realm," Meydra said, looking directly at Bryn. Meydra gave her a small, barely perceptible nod.

"Can you tell me their colors?" Arryn asked, his captain persona coming quickly to the forefront.

"They are wearing blue with a gold eagle on the outside of each boot," Meydra said. "They are from Danelagh."

"We will need to be careful, but only because they are hunting," Arryn said. "I do not believe they would do us harm. The King of Danelagh has long been a friend of King Thamen."

Bryn considered the options. "May I see your map, Arryn? If they are regular hunters of these woods, they may have had word that the princess is traveling. We will either need to consider having Meydra take her across and wait for us, or we need to find another way around them."

Arryn moved his horse closer to Bryn and handed her the map. Bryn pointed out the original spot she'd planned to make their camp—the first night they would sleep on the ground in the open—and pointed to the spot where the men were camped. She shook her head. "I think Meydra should take Thalynder here," she said and pointed to a new spot on the map. "We can make our way out there, you and I, avoiding the men, and when we clear the moorland, we could gallop the horses to reach Meydra before nightfall."

"It is a good plan," Arryn said and smiled at Bryn. He got off his horse and made ready to help Thalynder off hers.

"Meydra," Bryn said. "Do you know the Peak Stone and the pool west of it?"

"Yes, Bryn," Meydra replied and her tail twitched. "It is a favorite of dragons."

Bryn grinned. "Yes, I understand it was once a place for dragons to meet. I need you to take Thalynder to the small pool and wait for us there."

"If that is my Companion's wish," Meydra said.

"It is," Thalynder said.

"Good. We will have a meal here first, after which I need you to take Thalynder directly to the pool." Bryn turned to Thalynder. "Take whatever you want in the way of bathing things. The pool is secluded and you can bathe while we bring the horses."

"Oh, I'd love a bath, and it has been far too long since I rode on Meydra's back," Thalynder said and moved her horse so that she could dismount.

"I need you to do one more thing," Bryn said. She got down off her horse before Arryn could come to help her. "I need you to ride her shoulders and not her back."

"Why would I do that?" Thalynder asked.

Arryn looked first at Meydra. He turned back to Bryn and immediately understood. "Because if Meydra has to maneuver quickly, you will be able to hold on with your legs and not just your arms, Princess."

"Now why didn't I think of that?" Thalynder said and accepted Arryn's arm as she slid off her horse.

Meydra gave Bryn a sideways glance and moved her tail to touch Bryn's back as a thank-you. Bryn responded with a little giggle and set about preparing a meal.

The meal was eaten quickly and all foodstuffs were returned to the horses. Thalynder retrieved a small bag from her horse,

gave Bryn a quick kiss on the cheek, and walked over to where
Meydra was standing in the heather. She waited for Meydra to
lower her head.

Bryn watched the dragon bow low and saw Thalynder climb
onto Meydra's back, sliding forward to rest her legs on either
side of Meydra's neck. She waved at Thalynder and smiled at
Meydra. Her heart soared as she watched Meydra lift up into
the air.

Bryn and Arryn quickly mounted and headed across the
moorland. They did not take the seldom-used but quite visible
path. Instead they turned west and headed over open country.
They kept their pace even and relaxed until they had crossed the
open moorland and were again near the forest. They stayed to
the thinner edge of the wood where the heather was less dense
and increased their speed to a gallop. The wind caught Bryn's
hair and tugged at the sides of her braid, causing little wisps of
her dark tresses to come loose and flow freely behind her as she
rode. She clung to Pymmar and let the wind caress her face as it
had when she soared with Meydra.

The route she was taking narrowed and became thick with
crowberry underbrush, so she turned her horse toward the trees
and slowed to walk through the bramble until the thickets and
thorns were left behind. Approaching the woods, Arryn was
again next to her. He cleared his throat as if to speak and Bryn
turned to look at him. His face was flushed from the gallop, and
his hair was windblown. She reached up to tuck her own errant
locks behind her ears.

"That was exhilarating," Arryn said after a couple of
moments. "I haven't had that good a run in months."

"Nor I," Bryn replied. "It is seldom that Thalynder is on a
horse and even more unusual for us to run them when we're
together. That was exciting."

"You and the princess are close," Arryn said. He kept his
horse close to Bryn's, the two touching now and then.

"As you know, I came to court at a very young age to be an
attendant to the princess. Many days and nights since I have
spent with her, so yes, you could say we are quite close," Bryn
said. Over that past few days Thalynder had done most of the

talking, and hearing Arryn speak was a pleasant respite. She encouraged him. "Thalynder is excited about this journey, as you can tell by her nonstop chatter."

Arryn chuckled. "You handle her well, Bryn. She clearly believes she is in control, but I know better."

Bryn laughed and turned to look at Arryn. "Do not let on, or we may both rue the day."

It was Arryn's turn to laugh. "That is so true," he said, as his breath returned and he found his words. "Do you truly believe she will find true love on this quest?"

Bryn returned her gaze to the path before her—a well-used game trail—and was silent for a long moment. She swallowed before continuing. "I was not sure how the knowledge that we had lied to the king about our real reason for the journey would appear to you. Thalynder had not even told me that she intended to share the true reason of the quest with you. I was a bit shocked yesterday when her tongue loosened enough for her to disclose the secret. She does not want the crown, as she has said. She prays nightly that her father will sire another heir long before she is wed to some prince for whom she has no love."

Bryn saw that the path was leading into a denser section of forest and wove her way back out to the edge of the trees and the thicket that grew outside. There was a narrow path, wide enough for only one horse at a time, and that ended the conversation for the moment. Bryn needed to explain things to Arryn before they reached the princess. With Arryn and Thalynder's mounts walking behind her, she checked her horse and slid off. She waited until Arryn did the same, then left her horse to munch on berries that grew in the thorny thicket and walked under the trees. Leaning against the smooth silver bark of a young tree, Bryn watched as her horse nibbled away at the berries. Arryn removed the water bag from his horse, and as he drew near, Bryn spoke again.

"What started out as a harmless way for Thalynder to put a little distance between her and her commitments to the crown has now become something entirely different."

"So to disguise the real reason, you came up with the plan to go to Staenis," Arryn said. He removed the stopper from the water bag and handed the bag to Bryn.

Bryn took a long pull from the bag and handed it back to Arryn. She wiped her mouth with the hem of her sleeve and watched Arryn take a drink, the apple at his throat bobbing as he swallowed. He lowered the bag and offered it to Bryn a second time. She shook her head no and waited as he replaced the stopper and set the bag on the ground. He leaned back against a tree facing Bryn. "Do you not intend to visit the Stones?"

"I must now," Bryn replied. "My father has sent word ahead of me."

"That may explain why as we travel further out of the realm, the members of your clann are regarding you and the dragon somewhat reverently."

"You have noticed it too? Good, I thought it was my imagination playing tricks." Bryn sighed with relief.

"I have noticed it, and if I may say, I believe they are in awe of you." Arryn stood up away from the tree. "As am I."

Oh no, Bryn thought, and a moment of panic gripped her. It must have been evident on her face, as Arryn stepped back and leaned against the tree. He blushed slightly and that made Bryn even more panic-stricken. But as she watched him struggle, she began to understand. It was the way she felt around Thalynder, in awe of her, and in love with her. Oh, poor man, she thought, I must set this right. She took a deep breath, looked Arryn in the eyes, and said, "Arryn, I am in love with Thalynder. There is no turning back for my heart. I know it will be unrequited, but I cannot turn it aside. On the day that she marries, my heart will be frozen."

"That leaves hope for me," Arryn said and again took a step toward Bryn. "If you can live with unrequited love for Thalynder, I can do the same. I will live with the love I hold for you kept deep inside me. I too cannot stop my heart from choosing this path." He took another step toward her. "I have loved you since I was a youth and you were a skinny little girl. I watched you turn from a girl to a woman, long before your age of consent. Tutoring you, watching you, hearing you speak—these privileges I accepted, all the while waiting for you to come of age and notice me."

Bryn held her ground and did not flinch as he neared her. She raised her chin slightly and raised her hands so that he could come no closer. "Arryn, I admire your courage as a soldier. I admire your competency as a swordsman and hunter. I admire those things you can do as a man that I cannot. I admire all that you are and believe that we can be the best of friends. Nevertheless, I could not make love with you, a man. It is not in my nature. I love all the same things about a woman that you do," she said and felt him press against her palms as she held him back. "Please, Arryn. Allow us to be loyal and comfortable friends."

Arryn leaned in toward Bryn's face. He looked into her eyes and after a moment's hesitation, he took her hand and stepped back. "I can see the truth to your words, Bryn of the Brae. I will defend and protect you with my sword and my oath of fealty. I will be your friend, Bryn, but know this too: I will love you until my death." He placed a kiss on her palm before releasing her hand.

⧉

The sun dipped below the range of hills that surrounded the Peak Stone by the time Bryn and Arryn found the hollow where Meydra had hidden Thalynder. Meydra was sitting with her tail wound around her body to shield Thalynder, who lay sleeping on the ground. Bryn slid off her horse and spoke softly, "Has she been asleep long?"

"No, she has only now begun to dream," Meydra replied. "She has bathed, and I believe she was getting bored."

Arryn chuckled behind Bryn, which caused her to chuckle. "Thalynder is the only one I know who can become bored by fresh air and clear water," she said. "I would like to bathe and then I will start a meal. We can let her sleep until I return."

"You cannot go alone," Meydra said. "There are two other dragons by the pool. I will need to go with you."

"Other dragons?" Arryn asked.

"Yes, they have come from the west and take rest here at the pool," Meydra replied.

Bryn took a small bag off her horse and set it on the ground near a small circle of rocks. "I will prepare the meal first. When it is ready, I will wake Her Highness. While she eats, you and I will go to the pool."

"I too would like the benefit of washing some of the journey off my body," Arryn said. "If there are other dragons, perhaps it would be best if we all went to the pool together, since we cannot both go with Meydra and leave the princess here. Besides, I have never seen more than one dragon at a time: the princess's Companion."

Bryn thought a moment. "Agree: food first, bath second," she said. "We will all go to the pool with Meydra as our guide and ambassador."

"Did someone say food?" Thalynder asked. She rose to sit against Meydra and yawned. She was exceedingly skilled at yawning.

Bryn looked out over the landscape and took notice of the changes. They were approaching a deep valley where heather moorland gave way to glen and tall grass. The shelter of the forest had given way to rock outcroppings and so Bryn had Meydra flying lazy circles above the travelers. Her keen eyes could spot much in the open and for several nights the travelers dined on grouse and rabbit. The herbs Bryn had brought along served to season the game, and each meal was a little feast.

"I wonder why the other dragons back at the pool were riderless," Thalynder said as they packed again for another day's ride.

"Perhaps, they were only momentarily riderless, Princess," Arryn said. He handed Thalynder the next small bag to load on her horse.

Bryn was silent for the moment, remembering the words she'd heard at the pool. *There will be another, if only for a short time. Do not despair, Caraid, change is nigh.* Bryn didn't understand the words or why she had heard them in her head. The two dragons at the pool had greeted Meydra with great concern and Bryn could see that Meydra was still agitated two days later.

"What do you think, Bryn?" Thalynder asked. "Surely, you must have something to say. You've been pensive for two days now.

Bryn shook her head. "I too believe the dragons were only momentarily riderless. There was something in the way they deferred to you, Thalynder, that makes me believe they are also Companions. We may meet up with them again."

The company approached the northernmost highlands, having passed over the high moor mountain range. The highest peak was known by the Brae Clann as the Brow of the North Wind. The group was descending into a long wide valley known as the Great Glenn. It was believed that in this region, dragons from all over this part of the world came to mate and nest, the Twaylings being the rarest and most revered. Several lochs—the larger lakes—were found in this valley, and one in particular, Loch Nis, was important to Meydra's breed. It was to Meydra what Skerrabrae was to Bryn: the land of her ancestors.

Meydra dropped down to the grassy meadow and waited for the three horses to approach her. Bryn had asked the dragon to scout for a suitable place to rest for the night and Meydra had found a small group of large boulders that could be easily defended, with a small stream for water located nearby. She raised her head to listen as the horses stopped beside her. Her nose twitched as it caught a distant but familiar scent.

Bryn sensed something in the air, and as she slowed her horse she thought she heard a far-distant cry. The same sad lament she had heard the night at the dragon garden. She felt the anxiety coming from Meydra like heat from a flame, and saw the continuous flick of her tail. She pulled up beside the dragon and started to reach out and touch her, when Meydra breathed a heavy sigh. Thalynder came next and did not notice the agitation in Meydra's tail. She reined in next to Bryn and touched Meydra's shoulder.

"Have you located a place for the night?" Thalynder asked and gave Meydra's shoulder a little pat.

"I have, Princess," Meydra replied. "A small outcropping with a water source that will serve lies to the east of the small rise." Her tail slapped the ground.

"You are agitated," Bryn said. "Is there danger?"

"No danger," Meydra replied. "I will meet you at the outcropping."

"Wait," Thalynder shouted as Meydra began to lift up into the sky. Meydra came back down and stood in front of Thalynder.

"Princess," she said and bowed her head.

"It is not like you to fly off without my leave to do so."

"Yes, Princess."

"Tell me what concerns you," Thalynder said and her tone softened. "If we are not in danger, are you?"

"No, Princess. Not in danger."

Arryn cleared his throat and looked at Thalynder. "Princess, if we are in no danger, we should head for the outcropping. There is not much daylight left."

Bryn hoped that Arryn's concern would distract Thalynder from her interrogation of Meydra. Bryn understood that Meydra had a *need* to leave, a compulsion to find the source of the deep sadness. Arryn had sensed something in her manner, as had Bryn. Thalynder was the only one unaware of Meydra's heightened unrest.

Meydra waited, her body tense and rigid.

"I wish to know what takes my dragon away in such a hurry," Thalynder said tersely to Arryn. "She may leave once I know what is in her mind."

"Princess," Meydra said, her head still bowed. "I have heard the call of another dragon, and there is urgency in the cry." It was as close to an explanation as she could express in words. From the depths of her soul, she had heard the plea in the cry. Words could not describe why she had to leave. She looked into her heart and, grasping at the only thing she could, she held the vision of Bryn's brother in her mind.

Bryn grabbed Thalynder's hand. "Let her go now. Trust me, Thalynder. Meydra must go now!"

Thalynder looked at Bryn, then to Meydra. "Go!" She turned back to Bryn and pulled her hand closer so that Bryn was pulled nearly off her horse.

Meydra lifted immediately and her swift rise stirred the air around the horses. Thalynder was still holding Bryn's hand when the dragon disappeared over the rise. She stared at Bryn for a moment, her demeanor stiff and regal.

Bryn knew she would bear the brunt of Thalynder's wrath, but she had to get Thalynder to release Meydra. The deep sadness coming from the other dragon's heart had conveyed a single image to Bryn: death. Death for the other dragon. How could Bryn explain that to Thalynder, knowing Thalynder was not feeling it herself? How could she tell Thalynder that she could understand Meydra's thoughts when clearly Thalynder could not? As Bryn waited for Thalynder's admonition, tears welled in her eyes. Tears for the death that was imminent. She hung her head and as the feeling increased she began to shake. She pulled her hand away from Thalynder's grip and gathered her horse's reins.

"Bryn!" Thalynder demanded her attention. "I will have an explanation as to why my dragon needed to leave and why you encouraged it."

Bryn swallowed hard, fighting back her own frustration. "And I will give that explanation, Your Highness, once we reach the safety of the outcropping." She urged Pymmar forward. Tears stung her eyes as she ran headlong into the wind. Bryn did not look back. If Arryn was half the man she expected, he would have already urged Thalynder to follow.

They rode hard and as they crested the rise, Bryn did not stop. She saw the outcropping in the distance and continued to push her horse onward. If anything, she thought, this will tire Thalynder and she will be less angry. As a precaution, she gripped her sword by the hilt and drew it from the scabbard, bringing it to the ready. Meydra had not yet returned and Bryn was taking no chances that the outcropping was still safe. If it appeared as a safe, defensible place to Meydra, it could appear so to others. Bryn leaned over and spoke into her horse's ear. "*Greas ort, am caileag.*" Hurry, little sister.

Pymmar whinnied and, without a tap or a whip, bolted forward, gaining speed. Bryn stayed low against the horse's neck, disguising her form should anyone be watching. She held her sword across her chest. She did not slow her speed as she approached the outcropping, instead she sailed past the rocks, turning her horse in a long sweeping turn. On the other side she saw nothing of concern, so she rode up to the rocks.

In the distance, Bryn saw Arryn and Thalynder coming toward the site with Arryn in front, sword drawn. Thalynder held her horse back behind Arryn, and Bryn was glad to see the princess thinking straight again. She waved her sword toward Arryn and dismounted. Being occupied with Thalynder's anger and the exhilaration of the ride, Bryn had not noticed the deathlike stillness to the air around her. Here, waiting for the others to reach the rocks, she felt the hush to the air, the quiet of the grass and the land around her. It was as if the glenn were holding its breath waiting for something, and in an instant, Bryn understood. As she stood there with her horse, a mournful wail began to fill the air. It was deep and heartbreaking. Pymmar began to move her head up and down slowly as if acknowledging the cry. Bryn felt her chest growing heavy and her heart filled with sadness. She dropped her sword and sank to her knees, waiting for the inevitable.

In the distance, a gathering of dragons began a requiem for a fallen king. Their voices carried over the glenn like a gale in winter and touched all that could hear the song. Bonded Companions that resided in the high and low lands, the coasts and the forests, stood still in reverent respect for the fallen. Meydra knew Bryn would hear and understand. She sought

Bryn with her heart and, finding her still and quiet, Meydra called to her: *Ar n-athair-ne marbh.*

Bryn felt Meydra's call before she heard the dragon's song. "Our father is dead," she repeated. Bryn could hear the sorrow all around her. The sky, the grass, the hills, the earth itself was mourning the loss. She did not know why the world lamented so for the dying dragon, but she felt it as she sat on the ground and waited. The desolation of the song covered her in a dark thick wool, taking the breath from her and shutting out the light. At the moment the dragon's heart stopped, Bryn lost consciousness.

"She's fainted," Arryn said as he came off his horse.

Thalynder got off her mount and bent down to touch Bryn's face.

Arryn watched in amazement as the grass folded up and over Bryn's arms and legs, cradling her in its soft, cool touch. He shook his head at the sight.

"You have not been around her much," Thalynder said and took Bryn's hand in hers. "I have seen this twice before. Once when she was thrown from a horse and was unconscious. The trees bent low and shaded her—it was frightening. The other time was when we slept outside for the first time. We were twelve, and Bryn made me lie down on a cloth and stare at the stars. She was on the ground without a cloth and the grass folded itself over her bare legs. That night she told me the story of the dragon stars."

"She is a very special Druid," Arryn replied. "No wonder her clann clings to her every word."

"You have noticed that too." Thalynder stood up and grabbed the water bag from Arryn's horse. "I believe up here in the north she is more revered than I or my father."

"They have their own ways," Arryn said, wanting to ease Thalynder's concerns. "Your father's realm thins as we move north, and you and I will become less and less important to the people up here."

"You too are a Druid or Bryn was a poor teacher. You wear clann symbols on your wrist and your scabbard."

"I am nothing like Bryn. I have long been away from my clann and did not grow up with an elder as a tutor."

"You hear the call, I can tell." She poured some water in her hand before returning the water bag to Arryn. She rubbed her hands together and placed one on Bryn's throat, the other on Bryn's forehead. "If I am to find *true love*, Sir Arryn, it benefits me to be less than a princess, do you not agree?"

Arryn smiled. He placed the water bag on the ground beside him, reached under Bryn's neck, and gently lifted her to a sitting position. He could see the color returning to her cheeks and knew she would soon wake. Thalynder leaned in and kissed Bryn's mouth.

Bryn awoke to see Thalynder's face near hers. She leaned toward the princess and eagerly kissed her. Thalynder laughed and looked at Arryn.

"That is how she acted when she fell off the horse too," she said.

Bryn frowned at Thalynder's words. She swallowed first, then took a cleansing breath. Smiling at Arryn, she said, "Thank you, I believe I can stand now." She looked around and saw the light leaving the evening sky. Night was falling and a dragon was dead. The deed was done, and the night sky would have a new star to watch over the earth. It was an end and a beginning. That thought cheered Bryn somewhat, but where was Meydra?

Arryn stood up and pulled Bryn up with him. Thalynder hugged Bryn tightly. She kissed her cheek and said, "You take my anger too deep to heart, Bryn. You know full well that my anger fades when I see your clear blue eyes." She kissed Bryn's other cheek, and for good measure, kissed her mouth again. Arryn watched the two women kiss and saw the way they felt about each other. Bryn was immediately drawn into the kiss, leaning her body closer to the princess. Thalynder, on the other hand, took longer to react, but eventually she did. Arryn could see the flush to her pale skin and watched the vein at her temple pulse. In his heart, he knew he witnessed one thing of certainty: love given. He wondered when Thalynder would realize where she would find her true love.

Arryn shifted on his feet. Time was fleeing and he wanted them deep within the rocks before the last light of day slipped under the coming veil of stars. It will be a moonless night, he thought.

Bryn said to Thalynder: "Your anger added to the conflict already building between our needing Meydra here with us, and her need to be with the other dragon, is what set my mind to fail. I have borne your anger on many occasions, my princess, and always you ask forgiveness for the outburst. I worry only that the time will come when your anger strikes my heart and kills me dead."

Thalynder stroked Bryn's cheek. "My anger was lost when we found you still as death," she said. "What other dragon?"

"I believe you asked for an explanation," Arryn reminded Thalynder. "If it pleases the princess, I would ask that we wait until Meydra has returned. In the meantime, let us move into the rocks and make a fire. The night will be moonless and cold."

The outcropping was well-suited to hide them and keep them safe for the night. Arryn prepared a fire for a hot meal, all the while watching Bryn and Thalynder interact. He kept his gaze fixed on Thalynder, gauging her reactions to Bryn's orders. During the time they had been out in the country and not in the care of hamlet or burg, Bryn had assumed a heavier hand with Thalynder. Arryn understood Bryn's control; they were nearing where the raiders from the east were known to keep winter encampments. The raiders did not stay into summer, as the winds made the summer seas treacherous. The cold winter days were best for sailing the open sea between their homeland and the lands they raided. The cold kept the fog at bay, thus the fog of the warmer months had become friend and ally to the clanns of the north. Still, the need for stealth was foremost in his mind.

As the night grew darker and the stars began to dot the sky, Meydra returned to the little group. She stood on top of the rocks and looked down at Thalynder. "Princess," she said with her head bowed, and waited.

"There is sadness in your voice," Thalynder said. "Come closer and explain what has happened." The clearing was wide enough for Meydra to step down into. She knelt before the fire and placed herself so that she could see through the opening to the clearing, beyond the rocks out to the north and to where Loch Nis lay nestled in the Great Glenn. Her back acted as a shield to the only other opening in the rocks. Meydra settled in and her tail lay out around the little clearing, filling the small space. She did not look at Bryn, but kept her gaze on Thalynder.

Arryn stoked the fire with additional dried peat and sat down to listen to Meydra's explanation. He was as curious as Thalynder, but noticed that Bryn had become silent. She was sitting near the fire with her knees drawn to her chest, hugging them tightly. Arryn could see her whole body responding to Meydra's own sadness. More and more about the little Druid began to make itself known to Arryn. He remembered Bryn saying *the other dragon* as if she had already known what had happened.

Thalynder touched Meydra's forehead with her hand and quietly said, "Tell us."

CHAPTER NINE

Meydra took a deep breath. She looked quickly at Bryn and Arryn before turning to gaze at Thalynder.

"When dragons first came to the island that is now the home of Druids, Picts, Britons and Romans, there was only a small group of humankind. The dragons found themselves drawn to humans and to a certain group of men and women in particular: The offspring of the mating of elf and man. The dragons were drawn to the half elven."

Thalynder started to speak when Arryn laid his hand on her arm. "Wait," he said. Meydra nodded and then continued.

"The first dragon to come to Alban was Menchor, named so by the men who first encountered him. Several dragon breeds from countries far afield came to inhabit many parts of the island, and after a time new breeds evolved. One was the Twayling, my breed, direct descendants of Menchor and his mate, Melod. The Twaylings, along with the Nomic Reapers—native to the western string of small islands now inhabited by the Epidii Clann—remained with the people that would eventually become the Druids. It was Menchor who helped the peoples of this island understand the ways of the earth, sea, and sky. It was Menchor's children who chose to continue that education and the Druids became servants and guardians of the earth alongside the dragon. When Menchor reached an age where his strength waned, he asked his daughter to take over the care and education of the Druids. Thus the dynasty of the Menchor dragons began.

"How many Menchor dragons have been on Alban?" Arryn asked.

"Dragons live long lives, but direct descendants have been on Alban for over two millennia."

"Over two thousand years? How is that possible? What happened to their Companions?" Thalynder asked.

Meydra looked at Thalynder. "I will try to explain."

"A Menchor descendant would assume the mantel of High Dragon, settling any disputes that arose between the different dragon breeds, or disputes that arose between dragon and human. The title High Dragon was merely ceremonial, and either a male or female dragon could hold the position so long as they were descended from Menchor. Given that dragons can live for hundreds, even thousands, of years, there have only been four High Dragons since Menchor. Menchor was followed by his daughter, Melodi, then her son, Meldred, who had been ruler for eight hundred years, a short time for a dragon, but he was wounded by a raider while sheltering his human Companion.

"Dragons are forbidden to engage in the warfare of men, but they can shelter their Companions, forsaking their own life for the life of the human. Dragons can and do live to find new Companions, but if mortally wounded they die as any other creature that draws breath. For this High Dragon, his Companion perished in the conflict. It was not long after that the dragon's heart began to beat less frequently, eventually weakening him to the point that he knew he was dying."

"That was what you heard?" Arryn asked. "His last call?"

"Yes. But I heard the first call when we were still in your father's realm, Princess," Meydra explained. "It was a short time before we left on this journey."

Bryn closed her eyes. "It was the cry I heard at the linden arch," she whispered. "So long ago it now seems."

"That was the knell," Meydra said to Arryn. "The High Dragon's death was nigh."

"And when we came into the glenn?" Thalynder aske.

"I heard the calls of my kind and knew the High Dragon was near death," Meydra continued. "I had to leave quickly if I was to be there at the last hour. I apologize for not being able to take the time to explain."

"He is dead," Thalynder said and reached out to touch Meydra's cheek. "Was he close kin to you?"

"My brother," Meydra said and for the first time since returning, she looked at Bryn.

Bryn's face was buried in her arms and she was silently weeping. Meydra knew the vision she sent to Bryn would allow her to understand. The vision of her own brother and his death. Meydra knew it would catch Bryn off guard. It was meant to tell Bryn that Meydra had her own family to worry about, as well as her human Companion. Meydra could feel Bryn's need to rush to her side and comfort her, but it could not be permitted. *Not yet*, Meydra said silently to Bryn's heart. Bryn pulled her knees closer to her chest.

"I am sorry, Meydra," Thalynder said. "My anger at your abrupt leaving is forgotten. What becomes now of the High Dragon?"

"My brother, Meldred, has taken his place among the stars," Meydra said. "His daughter, Meylarn, is now High Dragon. She will be a good representative, as she is fair and just and known for her intelligence."

"I will breathe all the better knowing we have a good dragon with whom to arbitrate," Thalynder said, sounding like a well-schooled princess.

"Your father would have said that," Arryn said to Thalynder. "You will make a good ruler yourself someday."

"Bite your tongue, Sir Arryn." Thalynder shot a mean glare at him. "I do not intend to rule."

Before the sun was fully up, Bryn left the outcropping to stand in the open air of the heather moor that splayed across the glenn. She stood waiting for Meydra to return from her morning hunt because she wanted to speak with her before the others awoke. She saw Meydra's form high above and sent a greeting up to her. Meydra dropped swiftly and surely from the heights to land at Bryn's feet.

"Good morning, Bryn," Meydra said. "I am glad you finally slept."

"It was not easy," Bryn replied. "It was a great shock. I felt the death so keenly."

"You saw your brother?"

"Yes, he was dead, but I saw a dragon with him. Was that Meldred?"

"Yes," Meydra replied but did not elaborate.

"My parents never told me."

"They could not."

"The law of the realm," Bryn said quietly and shook her head.

"It had to be," Meydra said and sighed. She raised her chin. "Are you ready to set out?"

"I am. Our route takes us past Loch Nis. Do you need to return there?" Bryn asked. She could think of nothing else to do or say to ease Meydra's loss.

"It is not necessary." Meydra lowered her voice to a whisper. "The tears will wait."

"I do not understand."

"In time you will, Bryn. For now, the tears will wait."

"As you wish." Bryn took a step toward Meydra and touched her forehead to Meydra's brow. She brought her hands up to each side of Meydra's head and closed her eyes. "I feel your grief, *mo anam*."

Meydra sighed. She paced her heartbeat with Bryn's and they stood forehead to forehead, eyes closed. She knew Arryn was watching and was glad. The closer they got to Staenis, the more intense the pull to Bryn became for the dragon and the Druid knight. Meydra knew the worst was yet to come. She asked Bryn's heart to remain strong.

I feel strength coming from you, Bryn said in response. *I will take that and lend it to my heart for a while longer. Do not worry about me.*

Meydra smiled. Bryn was communicating with her from some deeper level and probably did not realize that what she said was not spoken aloud. Meydra could see the light in Bryn's mind grow brighter.

Bryn stepped back to look at Meydra. "There is much we have to discuss, dragon heart. You and I will have a long talk once we reach the Stones."

Bryn walked back to the clearing and found Thalynder finishing the lacings on her bodice. Arryn was not in sight, so Bryn approached Thalynder and placed her hands on her shoulders. She grinned. "Did you sleep well, my princess?" Bryn asked.

Thalynder stopped and wrapped her arms around Bryn's waist, giving her a little pull. "No, I did not sleep well. You were not at my back, and my dragon was not at your back. I missed your breath in my ear and your breasts against me to keep me warm. Not to mention a good-morning kiss."

"I can remedy that," Bryn said and moved her hands from the tops of Thalynder's shoulders to her back. She pressed her lips to Thalynder's mouth and felt the princess moving into her. Her body yielded, as did her mouth. Bryn moved her tongue to touch Thalynder's lips and Thalynder quickly sucked Bryn's tongue into her mouth. It was taking Lynder less and less time to fall easily into the kiss.

The kiss took on a desperate, needy quality, and Thalynder pushed Bryn against a rock. She drove her body against Bryn, cloth-covered breasts rubbing against each other. Bryn moaned and moved her hands inside the unlaced bodice, cupped Thalynder's breasts through her tunic, and squeezed softly. Thalynder's body responded and she parted her legs slightly.

She took one of Bryn's hands and held it against the cloth that covered her thighs. Bryn moved her hand up to rest against Thalynder's sex, waiting for Thalynder's next move. Thalynder continued to kiss Bryn, but her hands did not touch Bryn. Bryn wanted the touch to be mutual, so she released Thalynder's breast and sex, and brought her hands back to Thalynder's shoulders.

"Why are you stopping?" Thalynder breathed against Bryn's lips.

"Because I do not wish to do this alone," Bryn replied.

Thalynder backed up slightly from Bryn. She ran her fingers over Bryn's mouth and said, "I don't know how to start." She moved away from Bryn. "I will need you to teach me."

"Lynder, you are a woman. I can't believe that you are that naive," Bryn said. "You're playing with me."

Thalynder tried to look hurt but failed and wound up laughing.

Arryn cleared his throat and entered the clearing.

"The horses are ready," he said.

"A quick breakfast and we will be on our way," Bryn said. She was flushed from the kiss and tried to hide it by being lighthearted. "I have good news for you, my princess."

"Oh, and what is that?" Thalynder too was flushed.

"By nightfall we will be in the town of Skiel. You will have a warm bath, a large meal, and you may even meet some fine noblemen."

Thalynder hugged Bryn and kissed her soundly. "That is for making me happy, my little Bryn."

Arryn took out his map and placed it on the top of a flat rock. "Could you show me today's route?"

"Yes," Bryn replied. "There will be a slight detour, but the route is clear and Meydra has already scouted ahead."

Thalynder continued to lace her bodice while Bryn and Arryn discussed the map. She sat down to pull on her boots when Meydra came swooping down and landed on top of a rock.

"We are being followed," she said, not waiting to be addressed by Thalynder. "There is a group of raiders coming down from the creag."

Arryn scrambled to the top of the rock and looked south. A small dot was moving among the heather far to the south. He jumped back down and pointed to a location on the map. "They are still quite far out. We can defend from here, or we can ride hard to the loch," he said.

"Meydra, are there dragons at the loch?" Bryn asked.

"Yes."

"Will they aid us?"

They will aid you.

Bryn ignored the inner comment and looked back over her shoulder to Meydra.

"Yes," Meydra replied. "They will aid the company."

Bryn looked at Thalynder. "We make for the loch and the other dragons. We will need to ride hard." She folded the map and handed it to Arryn.

Arryn smiled at Bryn. "You want this battle."

Bryn touched Arryn's arm and gave him a quick wink.

Though the land across the glenn was open, the path that would take them to Loch Nis wound its way around smaller rivers and lochs. They were crossing north and back south— back and forth—for the entire trip. As they neared the west end of the loch, they found Meydra waiting with three dragons. Each dragon had a rider and Bryn wished she could be on Meydra's back, taking her defense of Thalynder straight to those that followed. Meydra walked toward the horses, leaving the other dragons to walk up behind her. She bowed her head to Thalynder.

"Princess," she said, "these Companions have traveled far to be here for the High Dragon and though they have their own kingdoms, they are willing to render aid now."

Thalynder walked her horse toward Meydra and reached out to touch her forehead with her hand. She dipped her head slightly to the other dragons and their Companions. "I am Thalynder, daughter of King Thamen of the Realm that Touches Two Seas. I am on a pilgrimage to the north with my traveling company, Sir Arryn of Epidii," she said and waited for Arryn to join her, "and Lady Bryn of the Brae."

Bryn brought her horse up to join the others and was at once greeted by the other dragons with a flood of inner thoughts. She held her hand to her heart in a gesture that said she understood and appreciated their thoughts. The newness of being able to hear the dragons all at once was foreign to Bryn and she wondered how the other Companions managed the onslaught.

"We heard you were headed north," a young man on the back of the lead dragon said to Bryn. "There are two here who hoped to cross your path before we left for our homelands."

"Where are your homes?" Thalynder asked.

"My home is in Northumbria," the young man replied, still looking at Bryn. "I am Lothan of the Iceni. Queen Betony is my liege."

"Greetings, Lothan of Iceni," Thalynder said.

"My home is far to the south," a dark-haired man said to Thalynder. He held her gaze and said, "I am Malcolm, Prince of Wessex."

Bryn shot a glance at the prince. She felt a pang of jealousy knowing that this man would attract Thalynder.

"Greetings, Prince Malcolm of Wessex. You have indeed come a long distance," Thalynder said and gave the prince a little nod.

"My original home, like yours, Bryn of the Brae, is in the far north on the island of Roan," the last of the three spoke. "Since the raiders destroyed our home, my clann has been living in the Western Isles on the Isle of Sky. I am Kenna of Clann Bridei." She leaned over and spoke to her dragon, who bowed her head and allowed Kenna to step off her neck. Kenna walked over to Thalynder and offered a little bow of her head. Kenna then nodded at Arryn and said, "Well met, cousin Epidii." She walked over to Bryn and touched the hem of her tunic with her forehead. "I wish you good fortune on your pilgrimage, my sister. My people ever look to the north in hopes the Jewel will be found."

Bryn reached down and touched Kenna's head. Her hair, the same sunlight gold as Thalynder's, was soft under her hand.

Kenna looked up at Bryn, and the blush on her cheeks caught Bryn by surprise. Her eyes were a soft brown and her lips were full. Bryn leaned over and touched Kenna's cheek. "As do my people, sister. We will again be united, do not let that leave your thoughts."

Kenna took Bryn's hand and kissed her palm. She walked back to her dragon and stood waiting. It was clear to Bryn that Kenna was not the least interested in Thalynder's title. She gave little perceptible deference to Thalynder.

Bryn looked at Thalynder, who nodded, and Bryn looked at the new Companions. "We are in need of your strong arms," she said. "The princess's dragon has informed us that we are being followed by a group of raiders. A small band headed for the coast would be my guess, but should they discover they have found not only a princess but now a prince as well, we may be in for a fight." Bryn moved Pymmar forward a step.

"I suggest we dismount and allow the dragons to take positions in the air. We can confront the raiders and make an effort to learn where they are headed and why. We know that your dragons cannot interfere with the fight, but they can remove you if you are in danger. Prince Malcolm, you may wish to change out of your royal robes."

Bryn was off her horse before any of the men could come to her aid. She waited while Arryn assisted Thalynder before she approached him. The other Companions gathered around Bryn and Arryn. Prince Malcolm had removed his outer tunic and left it in a sack on his dragon's back.

"I would suggest we make a fire. We could draw them in with the smoke," Arryn said. "Lothan of the Iceni, have you a sword?"

"Lothan, please call me Lothan," the young man said. "No, I have no weapons. I am still being schooled in the art of warfare."

Sir Arryn smiled. "Lothan will be our lookout. We will also leave the horses to your care." He patted Lothan on the back and then drew a small blade from his belt. "Take this and keep it in your belt. If the fighting gets close, you can always stab with it."

The young man beamed at Sir Arryn, and Bryn nodded. "Kenna, I see you have a sword and a bow. Which do you prefer?" Arryn asked.

"I am a skilled archer," Kenna replied. "I will position myself on high."

Bryn gave her a quick smile. It was exactly what she would have asked her to do. Bryn focused her attention on the prince. "Your Highness, I would rather see you secreted away in the forest, but I am not your keeper. What would you prefer?"

"I will stand on the ground with my sword at the side of the princess," Malcolm said.

Oh no, Bryn thought. She had not considered what to do with Thalynder. She frowned. "Princess, you know I would prefer that you stay well out of sight. I would suggest that you take up your bow and stand in the trees where you cannot be seen."

Thalynder smiled widely. "I think I'd like that little game." She removed her belt and scabbard and strung her bow. Then she watched as Bryn began to remove her own belt. "What are you planning to do?"

"I am the bait," Bryn said. "I will be the first they see when they reach the fire."

"I am not sure I like that idea," Thalynder replied.

"I know I don't," Arryn said.

"We will not risk the princess," Bryn said to Arryn. "You know I am skilled with a sword, and I speak their tongue."

"That she does," Thalynder said. "Her schooling far surpasses my own."

Bryn bowed low before Thalynder and when she rose she gave the princess a beautiful sunrise smile. "Thank you, Your Highness. Now let us see what the bait brings in."

※

Arryn intentionally made the fire with green and wet wood so it would smoke, in hope that the raiders would spot the plume and be lured to the clearing. The group remained quiet and waited for word from the dragons. The advantage was the number of bonded Companions, or so Bryn thought. She ventured a question. "Prince Malcolm, do you have a special word you use to call your dragon?"

"I simply state her name and she appears."

"How does she communicate with you? Will she be able to tell you when the raiders approach?"

"She never speaks to my thoughts, if that is what you ask. I call and she comes. It is never the other way around," the prince said and frowned at Bryn.

Hmmm, Bryn thought. "And you, Lothan, do you hear your dragon's call?"

"No, Lady Bryn, but as I said, I am new to the whole dragon idea," Lothan said. He was up in a tree, sitting on a large branch and facing south. "Do dragons eventually answer our thoughts?"

Thalynder cleared her throat and said, "After a time you will be able to understand your dragons' movements and even their mannerisms. I have been Companion to my dragon since I was three years old and I have yet to hear her voice in my head. I think that notion was thought up by an elder to urge us to work closely with our dragons."

Bryn stared at Thalynder. The callous way she dismissed Meydra grated on every fiber of her being. *If Thalynder does not hear Meydra, then what am I hearing?* Bryn thought. Though her mind had opened and some light was shed, there were still dark corners with secrets yet to be revealed. For one, why could not the other bonded Companions hear their dragons?

"Kenna, you remain quiet," Bryn said. Kenna had taken a post among some rocks where she could remain hidden and use her bow.

Kenna did not answer immediately and in the short pause, Bryn heard Meydra say: *She does, but not as you do.*

"As the princess has said, over time you get to know your dragon's mannerisms, even their characteristics," Kenna said. "I have yet to meet anyone who hears and understands the call of their dragon."

Bryn decided that was the right answer, and that it might be true. Kenna may have never met a truly bonded Companion as described in the Druid lore, and it now appeared they were indeed rare. Whatever she was hearing, Bryn decided now was not the time to discuss the subject.

Meydra called a warning, signaling the raiders' approach. Bryn stood and drew her sword, Kenna followed Bryn's move and drew an arrow from her quiver as Lothan called out from the tree. Bryn looked at Thalynder and the princess stepped back into the trees. They understood each other. The raiders were upon them.

Bryn stood near the fire, her dark hair loose about her shoulders and her bodice unlaced to expose the Tree of Life symbol on her tunic. Thalynder was out of sight in the trees, her bow at the ready. Kenna hid behind the rocks above the clearing, and Lothan withdrew high into the tree. Arryn positioned himself back against the rocks and out of view, and Malcolm stood in the trees with Thalynder. They waited. The sound of horses echoed among the rocks, and the mounts of Bryn and her company, tethered to the trees, moved anxiously against each other. Bryn backed up to where her sword leaned against a stone, shielding it with her body.

The men entered the little clearing with swords drawn. Bryn stood her ground, making no motion toward either the men or her sword. She watched the first man take in his surroundings before he moved closer to the fire. Two others came in behind him. The men moved closer to Bryn and did not see Arryn move out and behind their three horses, blocking their escape.

Bryn focused her attention on the second man. His clothing was finer, and when he came into the clearing he looked right at her and did not bother to look around. His demeanor was that of someone who controlled others. He made eye contact with her. Risking that he was the leader of the small party, Bryn addressed him. "*Velkommen, Herrer. Hvor er du ført?*"

The second man smiled at her and with his knees nudged his horse forward. He dismounted and walked toward Bryn. He ran his eyes up and down her body, stopping at the unlaced bodice. He started to reach out and touch her, but Bryn took a step back.

"*Jeg taler din tunge*, little maid," he said. "You speak my tongue, and I speak yours. This will be a pleasant conversation. How is it that you come by this symbol?" He pointed to the Tree of Life on Bryn's tunic.

"It is my mother's clann," she replied and gripped the hilt of her sword tight. Behind her in the trees, Thalynder readied her bow, pulling the arrow back to shoot it when Bryn gave the next signal. The two women had practiced this move many times with Arryn and the other guards. When Bryn gripped the hilt, Thalynder notched an arrow; when Bryn opened her hand to adjust her grip, Thalynder would loose the arrow. Timed correctly, Bryn would be able to react to the man standing in front of her, while Thalynder took out the man on the foremost horse.

The man before her remained calm. He looked again at the embroidery and said, "Your mother is a Druid." He spat out the word *Druid* as if it burned his tongue.

"She is."

"She lives?"

"She does." Bryn kept her eyes on the man's face, gauging his reactions.

"We have your kind in my country."

"*Dette er sant*," Bryn said.

"Of course, I only speak the truth. We have a shared history, little maid."

"Do you have Druids in your village now?"

"No, the Druids left my village," the man replied and frowned. "You are trying to find out where I live."

"I am. Perhaps we are kin."

"I doubt that," the man chuckled.

Bryn shifted her foot to stand more erect. She looked at his clothing. "How do you explain the fact that I speak your language?" He was dressed like a noble. His boots bore an emblem on the calf but she could not tell what it was. She guessed he was a noble who would be granted the lands he sacked for his liege. It would explain why he was still in her country this late in the year.

"You are a clever Druid, little maid. Too clever for your own good, but since you will not live to tell anyone, I will indulge you. I will answer three questions before I take you for my pleasure. When I am finished with you, my men will eat your heart."

"*Meget snill av deg*," Bryn said.

"It *is* kind of me. Now ask your questions. I grow hungry," the man said, licking his lips.

Bryn shuddered inwardly. She could imagine what he wanted. "You are heading to the coast to return to your homeland. Where is your homeland?" Bryn asked.

"My home is in Götaland. Do you know it?"

"Yes, and your king is Heardred. How many of you are still in my country?"

"I am the last, for now. I will take my small party home and return with my longboat full of men when the weather turns colder." He took a step closer to Bryn. His fingers played with the laces of her tunic.

Bryn swallowed but remained still. She raised her chin slightly, a signal to Arryn, whom she saw take position behind the last man. Glaring at the warrior in front of her, she leaned forward against his hand where it touched her laces, pressing her body against him to both tease him and give her leverage. She spoke in a calm, soothing voice. "*Er du forberedt?*"

"Am I prepared? Prepared for what?" he asked and ran his hand over her breast.

Meydra dropped lower to where she could be immediately on the ground if called. She descended and held her position above the tallest of the rocks, but still out of view of the marauders. She watched as Bryn adjusted her stance.

Bryn opened her hand behind her and grabbed the hilt of her sword, swinging it around and catching the man off guard as Thalynder's arrow pierced the shoulder of the first horseman.

"To join your ancestors!" Bryn ran the sword edge across the man's neck as he turned to look at the front man on the horse. As the noble fell back and was pinned against his own horse, Bryn thrust her sword between the laces of his thick leather jerkin. He could not free himself from his horse, and Bryn pushed through the leather and into his flesh.

Thalynder hit the first man with her arrow, and he fell off his horse with a cry. Prince Malcolm was upon him as he hit the ground. Sir Arryn had the third raider down off his mount and was driving him with his sword toward the rocks. He did not see another man charge in from behind him toward Bryn, his sword drawn. Bryn pulled her sword from the noble and swung around in time to take a sword blow to her left arm, feeling the blade meet flesh. She faltered from the force of the blow and fell to her knees, raising her sword to defend against a second strike, only to have the man go down at her feet, an arrow buried deep in his throat.

Kenna waited for the last warrior to come in. She had seen him move between the rocks and had moved to follow his every step. He had been momentarily hidden behind the horses and thus able to swing his sword at Bryn, but only once. As he moved to strike Bryn a second time, Kenna's arrow had found its mark.

"No!" Thalynder cried as Bryn fell to her knees.

Meydra dropped out of the sky and was at Bryn's side before anyone else could reach her. The dragon's defensive posture kept all but Thalynder at bay. She bowed her head to smell the wound on Bryn's arm. "It is not poisoned," she said as the princess rushed out of the trees to where Bryn knelt. Thalynder quickly dropped to her knees, pulling Bryn to her.

Bryn released her sword and let Thalynder hold her. The pain in her arm threatened to blind her to what was happening around her. Her sight narrowed and she could see Arryn dragging a body toward the center of the clearing. Lothan was gathering the horses, and Malcolm was moving the body of the first man toward Arryn. Bryn looked for Kenna but did not see her. The brave sister from the west had saved her life and she needed to acknowledge that, but where was Kenna?

Kenna had walked behind the rocks looking for the fourth man's mount. She found the horse and a young man holding the reins. He carried no sword, so Kenna slung her bow over her shoulder and drew a small sword from her belt. She snuck up behind the youth and had her blade at his throat before he knew she was there.

"Are there others?" she asked.

"No," the young man replied, startled by the blade at his throat.

"You are not from the land over the sea," Kenna said, hearing the boy's speech. She moved the blade from his throat and turned him around. "You are a Pict!"

Kenna led the youth and the horse back to the clearing where she saw Bryn sitting on a rock, her bodice removed and the sleeve of her underdress cut away from her arm. Kenna handed the reins to Lothan and took the youth to Bryn.

"We have rescued a Pict," Kenna said and moved the boy to stand in front of Bryn. She noted that the others had received minor scratches during the skirmish. Arryn had taken a gash to the cheek and Thalynder had scratched herself coming out of the trees. Bryn's arm, on the other hand, was bloody, and Kenna winced. She released her grip on the boy. "He was tending a horse."

Bryn looked first at Kenna and smiled. She looked the boy over. "Why are you here?"

"This one wanted something to warm his bed." The boy kicked at the dead noble who lay on the ground. "I was the only one that survived the raid on my village."

"I am sorry for the loss of your village." Bryn inhaled sharply as Thalynder began to clean her wound. "We will not leave you alone. We are heading north, and you are welcome to join us." She turned to look at her arm and scowled. "Thalynder, please retrieve the small leather pouch from my horse. This wound needs some attention. Kenna, I need hot water. Arryn, could you assist me?" Thalynder rose and went to the horses, and Kenna went to the fire. Bryn waited until the women were gone to address the boy. "You are not from the coast. From where did they take you?"

"We need to know what villages have been raided," Arryn explained.

"My village was in the high north near Beinn Hob. The men came ashore in Gallaibh near the Inbhir Theòrsa."

"What is your name, Pict?" Malcolm asked.

Bryn shot Malcolm a heated glance. She didn't like the way he spat out the word *Pict*. It reminded her of the way the Norseman had said *Druid*. She looked back at the young man.

"I am Bryn of the Clann Brae. The woman who brought you to me is Kenna of the Clann Bridei. This man is Arryn of the Clann Epidii," she said, holding the boy's gaze. "What is your name, lad?"

"Who is the mean one?" the boy asked, pointing to Malcolm.

"He is Malcolm, Prince of Wessex," Bryn replied. "Do you know where Wessex is?"

"No, mistress," the boy replied. "But I do know of the clanns you mentioned. Are you looking for the Jewel?"

"That is not our quest." Thalynder returned with the sack and opened it to find several smaller pouches, each a different color. Bryn turned to Thalynder. "Make a tea from a few leaves that are in the darkest green of the pouches. Pour the tea into the wound." Thalynder walked to the fire, and Bryn continued with the boy.

"That was Thalynder, Princess of the Realm that Touches Two Seas."

"If you are not seeking the Jewel, why the company and the dragons?" the boy asked.

"Some of us are here to bid farewell to a friend. Others are on a pilgrimage to the Stones of Staenis."

"Still a worthy quest," the boy said. "My name is Rylan. I am of the Clann Donii and I have kin in the north. If I could ride with you until we reach the village of Skiel, I would be able to offer you food and shelter."

Bryn smiled at the boy. "Skiel is where we planned to go. Come sit down, Rylan of the Clann Donii, and rest for a moment. We will be leaving soon. Are you hungry?"

CHAPTER TEN

"I think we should hack them to bits and leave them for the wolves," Prince Malcolm said.

Thalynder had washed and dressed Bryn's wound, and the company was finishing a small meal before starting out for Skiel.

"The fire is hot, why not just burn them on a pyre?" Thalynder said.

"Yes," Lothan said. "A pyre is how we handle the dead in Betony's realm. Surely, the Picts do the same."

Rylan did not comment, but sat eating a second chunk of bread, dipping it into mead.

"No," Arryn said. "We need something more severe. Something others who follow will think twice about."

"I agree with Arryn," Bryn said. "We've gone through their bedrolls and pockets. We know the man was not just a noble but a jarl. An earl or even a prince. He will be missed. We need to send a message to his countrymen." She shifted to rest her bandaged arm in her lap.

"We've learned two important things from the jarl. One, the raiders do not linger during the summer months, which had long been suspected and is now confirmed, and two, they are arrogantly confident. They rode into a possible trap boldly and without hesitation. They were sure they would meet no resistance. That gives me hope."

"Bold, confident raiders gives you hope?" Kenna said.

"Yes," Bryn smiled and raised her chin a little. "They suspect nothing, no resistance, no defiance. We have the best opportunity here to change their perception. To give them pause before they strike again."

Arryn nodded. "Something sorely needed."

Thalynder patted Bryn's hand. "What would you have us do?"

"Call your dragons. We will ask them to take the bodies and leave them on the shore. I want whatever boat the raiders have waiting to be burned and left where it will be seen," Bryn said to Prince Malcolm and Thalynder. "Prince, your dragon is a FireBreather. I would ask that you direct him to set the boat ablaze. Princess, it would be helpful if the bodies were a bit torn up." Bryn winked at Thalynder, knowing the princess would understand. Meydra was quite skilled at tearing limbs from animals.

"I am not sure I like you taking charge," Prince Malcolm replied. "I am not used to taking orders. I too am a captain of the Wessex Royal Guard and not just a lazy noble."

Arryn rose and stood beside Bryn and Thalynder. He looked at Prince Malcolm.

"Your Highness, I suggest that you leave now and return to your home in Wessex. Lady Bryn is in command of this company and we will do as she suggests. You may watch, or you may leave, or you may contribute, but you will not comment. It is entirely up to you."

Prince Malcolm took a step toward Arryn, his hand on the hilt of his sword. Thalynder stepped up and placed her hand on the prince's arm. "Stay your sword, Prince," she said. "Sir Arryn and the Lady Bryn were charged by my father to protect me. They only do what they think best. Do you not agree that it is about time we send the raiders a message?" She smiled up at the prince, and Bryn was sure she saw Thalynder bat her eyelashes at him.

Prince Malcolm released his sword and backed away from Arryn. Thalynder kept her hand on the prince's arm and guided him back to the fire. "Call your dragon, Malcolm," she said.

Meydra and the prince's dragon dropped in from the sky. Meydra landed in front of Thalynder, and the prince's dragon perched himself atop the rocks. The clearing was not wide enough for a dragon of his size. Thalynder touched Meydra's forehead and instructed her to take further instruction from Bryn. Meydra bowed and faced Bryn. She took a step toward her and bowed her head. *It is a good idea, Bryn,* Meydra said with her heart.

Bryn shook her head slightly at the inner comment. She found the conversation with herself confusing. Am I truly hearing voices? she wondered. I hear things no one else does. She closed her eyes. *I want a message sent. I mean to bring this to the attention of the elders,* Bryn replied with her own thoughts. She opened her eyes and looked at Meydra.

"Meydra, I ask that you take these men and drop them near their boat at the mouth of the Inbhir Nis. I would ask that you not treat them kindly. When you have done this, I ask that you return to find us traveling north."

Meydra bowed low and said, "As you wish, Lady Bryn."

Prince Malcolm moved to stand next to Bryn and he addressed his dragon. "Coeur de Fer, you will obey the Lady Bryn."

IronHeart, Bryn repeated in her mind, using his name as it was said in her tongue.

I am at your command, Bryn felt the reply.

"Coeur de Fer," Bryn said to the dragon. "Set the boat on fire at the stern so that it may burn slowly and be left for all who approach to see."

IronHeart bowed his head in acknowledgement.

"There is one more request," Bryn said and turned to look at Kenna and Lothan. "I need one other dragon to help carry the raiders, the other should stay near."

Kenna's dragon appeared before Lothan could speak. Bryn suspected that Kenna had already spoken with her Companion and prepared her. The small but beautiful Angelwing, with bright yellow spots that disappeared in the sunlight, giving her wings a lacy look, was sometimes mistaken for several large birds when viewed from far below. She landed delicately on a rock and waited.

Kenna placed her hand over her heart and said, "Caraid, go with the others. Take these men and drop them so that their limbs may break as brittle twigs."

Bryn heard the reply in her head: *At your command, Lady Bryn.* Caraid bowed her head.

Meydra grabbed one man in each foreclaw, her talons digging deep into the flesh, and lifted up and into the air. Caraid dropped in and picked up the remaining two men, lifting quickly behind Meydra. IronHeart followed the two smaller dragons, and they disappeared beyond the trees.

"Thank you," Bryn said to the company. "We will leave a message that will not soon be forgotten."

The village of Skiel was one of the last strongholds in the region. Surrounded by high walls of stone, the fortified village had yet to fall prey to the raiding hoards. The company approached Skiel and Bryn could smell the scent of roasted goat. Her stomach grumbled. She glanced at Thalynder and gave her a warm smile.

"You will dine on roast of goat and boar tonight, Princess," Bryn said. She absently rubbed her left arm where the wound had been bound tightly. It was beginning to ache again.

"And a bath," Thalynder said. "You promised a bath."

Prince Malcolm moved closer to Thalynder and said, "You shall have whatever your heart desires, Princess."

Mounted on a horse that had been stolen from the Picts, Prince Malcolm had ridden next to Thalynder for most of the day. Bryn could hear them laughing and talking, and though she was jealous and wanted to interrupt them, she did not do so. She kept her emotions in check. There was much on her mind, and the ride to Skiel gave her time to reflect on the things that had happened. Arryn was at Bryn's side, behind them were the prince and princess, followed by Lothan and Kenna.

❖

When the dragons had returned from their errand and Bryn was assured that her plan had been carried out, Prince Malcolm announced he was joining the company. Lothan and Kenna asked and were granted permission to join.

"You are welcome to join us so that the horses may be turned over to the Picts," Bryn said. "Once that is done, you are again on your own. I cannot be responsible for the fates of other dragon Companions."

❖

The company neared the gate, and Rylan, who was riding point, stopped. "I will approach the gate, my lady, and ask for my kinsmen."

Bryn nodded and checked her horse. Arryn rode up and stopped next to Bryn.

"They have archers on the ramparts," he said.

"Yes, I see them too," Bryn replied. "I hope we look friendly enough."

"On stolen horses with Pict harnesses?" Arryn asked, and sighed. "Let us hope our little Pictish fellow can convince them we are friends."

"I love his markings," Bryn said absently. "They remind me of the rúnir of the clanns. I rather think I'd like to be painted."

"And spoil that beautiful skin?"

Bryn bit her lip to stop the blush from reaching her cheeks but reddened before she could stop herself. Thalynder approached her.

"I am sure the scar will only add to her beauty," Thalynder said to Arryn. "I don't think she will be spoiled at all."

Arryn grinned at Bryn and bowed his head toward Thalynder. "So true, Your Highness, Bryn's beauty will not be diminished by the reminder of her deed."

Rylan came back to the party and nodded at Bryn. "My lady," he said. "You and your company are welcome. There is an elder inside who has been waiting for you to arrive. I will lead us through the gate."

Arryn grabbed Bryn's uninjured arm as she started forward. He looked up at the archers and waited until they lowered their bows and stepped back from the ramparts. He gave Bryn's arm a gentle squeeze. "Allow me to follow Rylan. I suggest next in line should be Lothan, followed by Kenna, the princess, the prince and you to come up behind us," he said, his voice low. "If you are expected, we can all go in ahead of you, thus staying their hand for a little while."

"Do you expect trouble?"

"No, but I want them to pay more attention to where you are and not be focused on the princess."

"Good idea," Bryn said and smiled at Arryn. "I am afraid my stomach was overriding my need for caution." Bryn turned to Thalynder. "You will go behind Lothan and Kenna. Prince Malcolm, you will follow the princess, and I will bring up the rear."

"My lady," Kenna said as she came forward and stopped her horse in front of Bryn. "I do not like your back unprotected. I will ride behind you."

Bryn glanced at Arryn and he nodded his approval. Bryn smiled at Kenna. "You will be at my back. Come, let us not keep our hosts waiting any longer. Rylan, lead us in."

The gate was opened to allow the riders and horses to pass. Bryn watched the ramparts and the archers did not return. Coaxing her mount forward, she felt her arm react to the grip on the reins. She grimaced at the sharp pain. She tried to hide the pain from the rest of the company, but the wound was raw. A small trail of blood had worked its way down her arm and dripped off her hand. Pymmar carried a dark red stain where the blood had pooled on her mane.

"My lady," Kenna said from behind Bryn. "Your arm bleeds."

Bryn looked at her hand and frowned. She moved her hand to hide it in under her bodice, raising her hand to keep the blood from dripping; she didn't want a panic as she entered the village. She gripped the top of her tunic under her bodice and hoped the gesture would not be taken as hostile.

She passed through the gate and was immediately approached by two men. "The boy has told us you are injured, Bryn of the Brae. We ask that you follow us so that your wound may be tended," the smaller of the two men said. They were dressed in similar tunics and their jerkins each had a small bird embroidered in the shoulder. Bryn recognized the clann.

"You are of the Sìldeag Clann?" she asked.

"Yes, milady," the smaller man replied.

"Is Elder Anethar here as well?" she asked.

"Yes, and it is the elder who asks that you follow now," the smaller man said. He took the horse's bit in his hand. "Will you come?"

Bryn glanced at the rest of the company. "When I know my company is inside and given food, I will go with you."

Arryn got off his horse and went to Bryn. "Go with them, Lady Bryn. I will see to the others."

Bryn looked at Thalynder and saw her nod. "Very well, I will join you shortly. Do not eat all of that fine-smelling roasted meat."

The others laughed and got down off their horses, grabbing their bags and nodding back at Bryn. Several young boys came and took the horses away, and the company was led to the center of town. Bryn remained on her horse and allowed the two men to lead her away. Following at a discreet distance behind her on foot, and unbeknownst to Bryn, was Kenna.

The men led Bryn's horse to a small house where a bright and welcoming light came from the windows. It reminded Bryn of her parents' house and she knew she was being taken to the home of a Druid. Still gripping the top of her tunic, she attempted to slip off her horse one-handed. She would have fallen had not Kenna quickly caught her.

"I have you, Lady Bryn."

"You have been my protector all day," Bryn replied and settled herself against Kenna's arm. "I am not quite sure how I will repay you, not only for saving my life at Loch Nis but for saving my dignity now as well." She lowered her voice. "I am in great pain, and I do not believe my feet will carry me far."

Kenna wrapped her arm around Bryn's waist and spoke into her ear. "Lean hard against me. I will see to it that my legs carry us both." Bryn leaned against Kenna. She led Bryn around the horse to where the two men waited. Upon noticing that Bryn was leaning into Kenna, the smaller man came to Bryn's other side to render assistance, but when he touched her arm, she gasped and turned her face into Kenna's neck.

"Do not touch her," Kenna pleaded. "Her left arm bears the injury."

The smaller man backed away and let the two women move toward the house. The other man opened the door and held it. Inside, the light and warmth flooded Bryn's senses with familiarity. The scents and even the sounds reminded her of her parents' house. She still had her face buried in Kenna's neck and could not see the place clearly, but in her mind's eye she could see the inside of the room: a box in the corner for the clann book, a table in the center for friends and family, and a mantel at the fireplace with small treasures of the earth, sea and sky. At home, her mother's mantelpiece had a pinecone, a seashell and a small rock with a hollow in the center that held rainwater, which was often replenished with each rain. Bryn felt something at the back of her knees and realized someone was providing a bench for her to sit on. Kenna sat beside her, still holding her upright. Bryn looked around the room. Standing beside the bench and looking rather concerned was a woman who closely resembled Bryn's mother.

"Elder Anethar," Bryn said. "I am happy to see you."

Older sister of Bryn's mother, an elder of the Síldeag Clann by marriage, Anethar leaned over and kissed Bryn's brow. She placed one hand over Bryn's heart and one on her forehead. "You are fevered," she said. "Let me tend to that arm first. There will be time to embrace and talk about your visit later."

Bryn looked at Kenna and smiled. "Your assistance is no longer needed. Thank you for being in the right place at the right time." Bryn kissed Kenna's cheek. "You may join the others."

"If it is not a bother to you or Mistress Elder, I would like to remain," Kenna addressed Bryn and nodded at Anethar.

"That is entirely up to the Lady Bryn," Anethar replied. "As for me, Kenna of the Clann Bridei, you are always welcome in this house."

Kenna bowed her head to the elder and looked at Bryn.

"I would like you to stay," Bryn replied.

Kenna released her hold on Bryn and moved to watch from the other side of the table. The skilled hands of the elder began to peel away the dressing on Bryn's upper arm. She motioned for the men to leave the house and then removed Bryn's bodice.

"I want you out of that tunic, Daughter," Anethar said. "Kenna, please go to the chest that sits beside the bed and bring me the tunic the color of dried peat."

Kenna went to the little sleeping alcove and brought back the tunic as instructed.

"I will have this bodice washed, Bryn. Your mother's handiwork should be saved; it will have a little blood stained into it, but for good cause. Now I will cut away the remaining tunic," Anethar took a knife from the belt at her waist.

"Mother, it is the second tunic that has been cut open at the sleeve."

"We will see if we can save one," Anethar replied. "Kenna, unlace her overtunic and remove it gently."

Kenna moved to stand before Bryn and began to unlace the bloody laces. She moved the tunic over the good arm first, then gingerly moved it off the injured arm.

"My lady," Kenna said. "I do not believe we can salvage the inner tunic. It is quite stained."

Bryn glanced down at it. "I have an extra one on my horse. Could you retrieve it for me?"

"No need," Anethar said. "There is another tunic in the chest by the bed. Please fetch it, Kenna, it is the color of wet peat." She turned back to Bryn. "I will save this tunic for you. The embroidery alone is worth keeping in the family."

Kenna did as she was asked and placed the fresh tunic with the other on the table.

"Now take this knife and lower both tunics to Bryn's waist," Anethar said to Kenna. "We will wash your arm, Bryn, before we change your clothes."

Bryn leaned back against the table. Her face paled and Kenna grabbed her. "Elder, Bryn is very pale!"

Anethar removed a small piece of cloth from her tunic pocket and held it to Bryn's nose. Immediately Bryn's color returned and her eyes opened. "Better?" Anethar asked.

"Yes, thank you," Bryn replied.

"We must tend to that arm."

"I had Princess Thalynder apply the Ladies Mantel to the wound and it was painless for several hours."

"She applied a good dressing," Anethar said. "I will apply one that will provide you with some relief, but I can do nothing for the scar. Too much time has elapsed."

Bryn chuckled, "The scar will serve me."

"That is truer than you realize, Bryn of the Brae," Anethar mused.

The company waited in the tavern in the middle of the village. Arryn watched Prince Malcolm introduce himself and heard him prepare to introduce the rest of the company when Thalynder took his arm. She interrupted the prince and addressed the little crowd that had gathered. "I am Lynder, a traveler from the Realm that Touches Two Seas," she said before Malcolm could speak. "I have come with Bryn of the Brae."

Arryn gave a quick smile to Thalynder. She was still being careful, and that pleased him. Many years of many lessons had stuck with the princess. He stepped toward her and said, "I am Arryn of the Epidii, and I too travel with the Lady Bryn."

Rylan came up to the group and lowered his head slightly to Arryn. "If you or the lady would care to bathe, there is a tub provided in the sleeping chambers."

Thalynder released Malcolm's arm and smiled at Rylan. "That is the best thing I have heard in days."

Bryn sat with her arms, shoulders, and breasts exposed while Kenna washed her arms and Anethar looked over her wound. The gash was deep but not as deep as first expected. Yet the bleeding had not slowed. Bryn knew what needed to be done and sensed that Anethar knew it too.

"You will need to stop the bleeding," Bryn said.

"Yes," Anethar replied.

Bryn grabbed for Anethar's hand. "Beloved mother, do not worry. I am strong and the pain will subside. You must close the bleeder."

"How is this possible?" Kenna asked.

Anethar looked at Kenna. "Has your mother taught you nothing?"

"My mother keeps to herself," Kenna replied. "I do not ask these questions of her."

Anethar shook her head. "There is much you have missed."

Bryn touched Kenna's hand. "The Druids are by far the most knowledgable when it comes to the body. We are taught how the body works, the veins, the pumping heart, the bleeders, the breathers," she said. "A vein has been nicked and the bleeding will not stop until the tear is closed. The best way is by fire. Anethar will apply fire to the inside of the wound to stop the bleeding. It will be painful and I may be overcome. You must hold me still and do not let me fall." Bryn turned to straddle the bench. "Come sit behind me and take me in your arms."

Kenna moved to sit behind Bryn. She saw the flush of fever on Bryn's skin and moved closer to wrap her arms around Bryn's waist.

"Higher," Anethar said. "Move your arms up under her arms and pull her close."

Kenna moved her arms up under Bryn's armpits, covering her breasts. She pulled Bryn close.

Bryn laid her head back on Kenna's shoulder and said, "I am ready, Mother." She closed her eyes and waited.

Anethar removed a short metal poker from the fire. She spread the wound slightly. Bryn flinched and Anethar waited for Bryn to adjust to her touch. Once Bryn was again calm, Anethar touched the tip of the red-hot metal to the inside of the wound. Bryn gasped, her body tensed and she fainted. Kenna kept Bryn upright and kissed her hair, tears fell silently down her cheek.

"She will sleep for now," Anethar said. "Hold her while I dress the wound."

Outside, high above the village sitting on a creag, four dragons bowed their heads as Bryn was overcome with pain. Meydra could not stand the scream she heard come from Bryn's mind, and lifted high into the night sky. When she was high enough that her own cry would not be heard by human ears, she let out a sorrowful wail. She flew higher and higher to separate herself from the pain.

Kenna opened the door and Bryn walked into the tavern. The other companions had bathed and eaten and they stood as Bryn approached. Her left arm was wrapped in a strong gauze-like material and smelled of heather and moss. Bryn was dressed in clean clothes and her hair had been rebraided. Thalynder shot a glance at Kenna.

"You look much better," Thalynder said, kissing Bryn's mouth. "How do you feel?"

"Hungry," Bryn replied.

Thalynder led Bryn to the table, arm in arm, and sat down beside her, leaving no space for Kenna.

Bryn sat down and the rest followed suit. Kenna remained standing. Bryn saw that the others wore clean clothes and looked rested. She turned to Rylan and said, "Rylan, could you please see that Kenna is provided with a bath and some clean clothes?"

"Yes, milady," Rylan said and left to speak with a man carrying a platter of cups.

"You will bathe first and afterward you will join me for a meal," Bryn said to Kenna. "I will await your return."

Kenna smiled at Bryn and walked away to join Rylan.

"I am sorry I was not with you when the elder tended to your arm," Thalynder said and pulled Bryn closer to her. "You have bathed?"

"Elder Anethar and Kenna bathed me," Bryn replied. She heard a curious hint of jealousy in Thalynder's voice and grinned at the thought of the princess being jealous. She moved her right arm around Thalynder's waist and kissed her cheek. "Anethar is my mother's sister," Bryn explained, but she did not elaborate on Kenna's participation.

"We should be leaving," Thalynder said. "Will tomorrow be too soon?"

Arryn overheard Thalynder and moved to sit closer to the two women. "It will not be soon enough for my tastes," he said. "Still, I think we need to rest a day or two. Bryn, you need to recover some strength in that arm or you will be useless to me should we again meet with raiders."

"True," Thalynder said. "I wonder how long the other dragon Companions will remain in the village? Surely, they and their dragons will want to return to their own homes."

Bryn looked around the tavern and saw Prince Malcolm engaged in conversation with the tavern keeper. Probably arranging for lodging, she thought. Kenna was in the sleeping chambers at the back of the tavern, taking a well-deserved bath, while Rylan and Lothan were speaking with a group of young men their own age. Bryn saw the young men glance back at her and the little group. Surely by now the knowledge of who they were and what they done at the loch, including Rylan's rescue, must have been discussed. The tavern was filled with many village folk and though they kept to themselves, Bryn could tell they were discussing the arrival of the company, which included not one but four dragon Companions. As the evening darkened and candles were lit, the room took on a cheery glow and Bryn began to relax. The herbs Anethar had applied to the wound numbed the pain and she was feeling quite calm. Too calm for her liking, as she began to feel numbed to the people around her.

Arryn leaned past Thalynder and looked at Bryn's face. He could see she was wrestling with some inner thought. "What troubles you, Bryn?" he asked.

Thalynder looked at Bryn and tightened her hold on Bryn's hand. "Are you in pain?"

Bryn looked at them both and smiled warmly. "No, I am not in pain. On the contrary, I feel quite relaxed, and that has me thinking my mother's sister has given me something to aid my sleep. I want to eat a meal, but I think I may be asleep long before Kenna finishes her bath and food is set before me."

Thalynder frowned. "Do not wait for the Bridei. Eat a little something now so that you may retire."

Bryn shook her head slightly. "Thalynder, dear Thalynder, do you not remember it was she who saved my life? I am showing her kindness for a debt I can surely never repay," Bryn kissed Thalynder's cheek. "Please, be kind to her."

"I will be kind and courteous," Thalynder replied. "She did save your life, and I too am forever in her debt, but I do not have to like her much."

"Ha!" Arryn said. "You sound a bit jealous, Thalynder. Surely you do not think anyone could take your place?"

Bryn shot a glance at Arryn and immediately he reddened. He had openly said what was in Bryn's heart. She held her breath waiting for Thalynder to react.

Thalynder placed her hand under Bryn's chin and turned her face so they could look into each other's eyes. There were unshed tears in Bryn's deep blue eyes. Thalynder kissed Bryn's mouth and softly said, "No, I don't believe anyone will take my place in your heart, and for that I am a little sad."

The herbs Anethar had used to reduce the pain traveled through Bryn's blood and soothed her anxiety. They worked well enough for Bryn to hear Thalynder's words and feel no shame or guilt, knowing Thalynder understood that she held Bryn's heart in her hands. Bryn smiled at Thalynder. She turned and laid her head on Thalynder's shoulder. Sleep had found her.

Anethar watched the interaction between the two women from the far side of the tavern. She wanted to be at Bryn's side when the time came for her to sleep, but did not want to tell Bryn that the herbs would cause her to sleep for at least twelve hours. Anethar knew that Bryn would be worried about her companions. Bryn had come close to losing her life with the amount of blood she had lost. Had she bled to death, the loss to the princess would be small compared to the loss the clanns would suffer, but Anethar was in no position to divulge anything about Bryn to anyone outside the clanns. She walked over to Thalynder as Arryn lifted and held Bryn in his arms.

"She will be fine," Anethar said to Thalynder. "If you will follow me, I will show you where she may sleep. I must tend to her wound again soon, and she will sleep deeply for at least twelve hours."

"Your medicine is strong," Arryn said. "My guess is that you did not tell the Lady Bryn how long she would be asleep."

Anethar grinned. "I did not. I am sure you know by now the stubborn streak that is Bryn of the Brae." Anethar took Thalynder's hand in hers. "Do not trouble your heart. She was in danger, but that danger has passed. She needs the rest. Once she wakes she will be hungry and her strength will gradually return. Come, I will show you where she may sleep."

"Will there be room for me to sleep with her?" Thalynder asked as Anethar led her out of the tavern.

"Tonight that would not be wise," Anethar replied. "I will watch her and tend to her arm. There is still much to do."

"I thought you said she was out of danger," Arryn said from behind the two women. He held Bryn close to his chest and felt her heartbeat steady and strong against his hands. She was dressed in a lightweight sleeveless tunic, and Arryn thought he had never seen her look more lovely, bandaged arm and all. Her hair was braided with silver thread that matched the thread along the hem of the tunic. She smelled of lavender and wild honeysuckle, and Arryn couldn't help but take deep breaths of the comforting scent.

"She is out of danger of bleeding to death, which she came quite close to doing," Anethar scolded. "She is not, however, out of danger when it comes to infection. The wound must be washed and dressed every hour for the first night. Bryn will sleep through these, thankfully, as they can be quite painful. Thalynder, would you bring me the pouch you used to make the dressing for the wound?"

"Yes. It is in one of Pymmar's saddlebags," Thalynder said.

"Bryn's mount is tethered outside my house. After we have Bryn inside, I would like for you to retrieve the pouch for me."

"Certainly, Lady Anethar."

Arryn remained quiet as he carried Bryn to Anethar's house. Inside, Anethar released Thalynder's hand and moved aside a wool curtain to reveal a small bed and single chair. Arryn placed Bryn down on the bed and stood back. He walked to the table in the middle of the room and looked at the surface.

The table had been scrubbed clean recently, and Arryn guessed this was where Bryn's blood had been washed from the surface. He sat on the bench and waited. Thalynder spoke with Anethar but he could not hear their words. Thalynder started to leave the house and Arryn jumped up to stop her.

"You should not go alone," he said.

"I only go to Bryn's mount to retrieve a pouch of herbs," Thalynder said. "I will not be long."

Thalynder found several pouches. She tried to remember which one contained the herbs, but her mind was preoccupied with Bryn. She grabbed the entire sack and took it inside. There she began to remove the pouches from the satchel, placing them side by side on the table. One of the bundles was not a pouch but something wrapped in a cloth. Without thinking, Thalynder began to open the cloth. Inside was a delicate headpiece with three circles on the front. She tilted her head and looked at the piece. "What is this?"

Anethar looked back at Thalynder from the alcove and saw the headpiece in Thalynder's hand. She walked over and gently took the piece from Thalynder.

"That, Princess, is a Druid headpiece. It is worn on special occasions. I will venture a guess and say that Bryn's mother, Arlendyl, sent this along with Bryn."

"It looks a little like a crown."

"Yes, I suppose it does." Anethar wrapped the headpiece back in the cloth and placed it in the sack. She picked up the dark green pouch. "This is the one I need. The rest can go back into the sack."

Thalynder sat down in the little chair next to the bed and ran her hand over Bryn's face. Arryn nodded at Anethar as she stood at the table.

"If you would like to teach us how you want it done, we can stay and help change the dressing," he said. "It is the least we can do to thank you for tending to our friend."

"As I told Thalynder, the washing of the wound must be done carefully. I will attend to that myself," she took a little breath and lowered her voice. "It would have been best if one of the dragons had brought Bryn to me. She has lost much blood and it will take her body many days to fully recover."

Arryn shook his head, "As you said, Bryn of the Brae is a stubborn woman. She insisted on bringing the stolen horses to the Picts and to do so with the full company meant riding them. She would have it no other way. She never once let on that she was in great pain."

Anethar nodded. "She has always been of a mind to think of others. I will tend her wound and you can be sure she will heal. However, if you wish, you can watch her between the times I apply a fresh dressing." Anethar turned to the mantel and took down a book. She sat down opposite Arryn and placed the book between them on the table. Opening it, she thumbed through the pages until she came to one that contained several concentric circles and the Tree of Life. "Bryn's fever must not be allowed to spike between dressings. I will rest easier if I know someone is watching her while I ready the herbs. If you would like to stay and help, you can sleep now. I will wake you when Thalynder tires." She ran her hands over the Tree of Life. "Do you recognize this symbol?"

"Bryn wears it on her shield and her finer clothing," Arryn replied. "It is the symbol of her clann."

"It is more than a symbol of *her* clann," Anethar said and leaned closer to Arryn. She glanced once at Thalynder before continuing. "It is the symbol of *our* highest clann. Bryn is descended from the earliest leaders of the Druids. She is the daughter of a most important person."

Arryn had always considered Brymender to be a good and knowledgeable man but never knew he was important to anyone other than his immediate clann. "Is this knowledge a secret?"

"It is. Brymender has long since hidden the fact that he married a half-elven princess."

"An elf princess? Bryn's mother is the important one?" Arryn asked and shook his head. "How is this possible? Bryn should not be a waiting lady in the court. She should be a royal in her own right."

"You are still young, but I believe you are beginning to understand the ways of the world. Many things are possible but not all things are probable," Anethar said. "The hierarchy within our clanns is not complicated like that of the rulers and lords of this land. We have only one route of accession. Because of our spiritual beliefs, we have had to hide much of our ways. Many before us have been slaughtered because of those beliefs."

"Why are you telling me this?" Arryn asked.

"Because, Epidii clannsman, you must not only protect the Princess Thalynder from harm, but you must also protect Bryn. She does not know she needs protection and would strongly deny it, but now after the incident at the loch, she will need it more than ever. I do not want you to go forward without additional swords at your side. If you do not wish the other dragon Companions to accompany you, I will suggest others of the clann."

Anethar turned the book to show Arryn the page more clearly. On it was a scene of a baby held up before the Tree. Woven around the trunk of the tree was the tail of a dragon. Arryn followed the tail into the tree and saw the rest of the dragon's shape. "The high clann tied to the dragons," he mused. "Bryn's clann tied to the dragons. Bryn tied to…" Arryn looked at Anethar.

"Do not speak what is in your mind," Anethar said. "You, Arryn of the Epidii Clann of the West, must now realize the hardship the dragon Meydra has come to bear. Do not let on, but if you do not wish to carry this burden with you, you must ask to return to the Realm that Touches Two Seas. There are others here to take your place."

"Is Meydra tied to this also?" he asked.

"That too is not widely known. You *must* bear this secret, Epidii."

Arryn said nothing. He ran his hand over the illustration as if to take in all that it suggested; the Tree of Life—the eternal symbol of the clanns of not only his country, Alban, but of the lands and countries that lay across the North Sea and of all the ancient tribes—was tied to the dragons. The arrogance of the nobles had robbed the Druids of their birthright, and that effrontery stuck in Arryn's throat like bitter bile. He looked again at the picture and could see in his mind the little Bryn, held high to the Tree, her dragon close at hand. He looked toward the bed where that same little girl, now a waiting lady and Shieldmaiden to a princess—strong and ever loyal—lay in induced sleep to keep pain at bay. All this because a princess wanted to take a little journey to find true love. He stood up and closed the book. He gently pushed it back toward Anethar. "There is something I must do, but I will return to relieve the princess in short order. Do not tell anyone what you have told me tonight."

"Arryn of the Epidii Clann of the West, I only told you because I trust in your love for Bryn over that love which the princess professes," Anethar whispered. "The Lady Bryn deserves to be happy, but she has already chosen a path that will test that happiness. You, I believe, will remain by her side because you understand the many sides of love. The love of a captain for his queen."

Arryn bowed his head and touched his right fist to his heart. He left the little house and headed toward the livery.

In the sack tied on the back of his mount was a weathered and seldom-used leather jerkin. It had belonged to Arryn's great-grandfather and never had been worn by anyone since. Those men had given up the clanns for service to a king. Arryn had followed in his father's footsteps and had become a member of the king's Royal Guard. He had excelled and became a captain of the Inner Guard, the special chosen few to be at the hand of the king. Arryn had always wondered about the clanns and their heritage. He had kept his great-grandfather's things hidden from the rest of the guard out of guilt and shame for a past he had never understood. Now, the call of the clanns was ringing loud in his ears. His heart filled with something it hadn't felt before. Arryn struggled to put a word to the feeling as he removed his old guard jerkin and put on the one bearing the Fish symbol of the Epidii Clann of the West. One word came and held him in a tight embrace.

Belonging.

CHAPTER ELEVEN

Each time Anethar removed the bandages from Bryn's arm, Thalynder felt her stomach rise in her throat. The first time was the worst. Thalynder thought she was prepared to see the deep gash in Bryn's arm, having seen it when it was fresh and bleeding. But now, to see it with Bryn lying motionless, she could only imagine what Bryn must have felt when the blade ripped through her skin. Bryn's wound could have been avoided if they had fled before the raiders came upon them, she thought. Bryn's insistence on staying to glean information had been sound, but it was useless if they were not going to put the knowledge to work for them. What had they learned that they did not already know? Now, her Bryn lay silent, being washed and prodded time and again by the Druid elder, and Thalynder could not help but think it was all for naught.

My father would have done things differently, she thought. Could we have reasoned with them?

She slept fitfully after Arryn insisted he relieve her from watching over Bryn, and she lay now listening to Anethar prepare another dressing. She turned on the bedding laid out on the floor and looked into the room where Bryn lay sleeping and Arryn sat with his hand on her brow. She watched Arryn stroke Bryn's forehead as a parent strokes the head of a child—a soothing repetition of loving touches. She watched him and thought that something had changed in him since Bryn was injured. He was solemn, yes, but something more. Something she could not quite put her finger on, though she could trace it back to the conversation about the raiders before they had arrived. Arryn had sided with Bryn from the beginning, wanting to glean information from the raiders and to slay them before they could leave the country. Thalynder thought that foolish, as it was sure to ire the raider's own king, sending more men back to take out his wrath on another helpless village. She was schooled in warfare as Bryn had been, but she failed to see why it was important to anger the enemy.

Thalynder got up and stretched. She straightened her tunic and glanced out the window. The sun was rising and she'd had maybe four hours total sleep throughout the night, but she could not lie still any longer. She entered the little alcove and placed a hand on Arryn's shoulder. He appeared deep in thought and did not at first acknowledge her hand. Thalynder sat on the bed and placed her hand next to Arryn's on Bryn's forehead.

⛬

Arryn heard Thalynder moving about but was not going to stop his prayers to Harimella, the goddess of protection, to acknowledge the princess. He kept his hand on Bryn's forehead and finished his thoughts and pleas to speed Bryn's recovery. It had been a long time since he referred to himself as a clann member, let alone admit that he too was from an old and well-established Druid sect. The book Anethar had shared, and his own building belief that Bryn was something special, awoke a long-quiet song in his soul. Besides the jerkin he now wore, there was something else he had always carried but which had seldom seen the light of day: a simple disk of stone with a small hole at the top. It was etched with concentric circles representing his clann and polished to a brilliant sheen by many hands of the long since dead. A stone, removed from the hallowed ground at Staenis and carried by the eldest son of each succeeding generation, with the etching still visible but in need of a little work. Arryn threaded the disk on a strip of cloth torn from his bedding and fashioned it around his neck. When the chance arose, he would string the stone on a leather thong. He no longer considered himself Sir Arryn, captain of the king's Inner Guard of the Realm that Touches Two Seas in his heart or his mind. That man had been replaced with Arryn of the Epidii Clann of the West, son of the earth, sea and sky.

Arryn withdrew his hand from Bryn and looked at Thalynder. "You look pale," he said. "Did you not sleep?"

"I slept in fits," Thalynder replied. "I could not stop thinking that this wound could have been avoided."

Arryn nodded slightly. "It could have, but then not only would we have allowed the raiders to leave unchallenged, but Rylan would be a slave to those men. Even without knowing the Pict was involved, I don't believe any of us could have persuaded Bryn to let these men leave Alban."

"Why does she have to be so stubborn?" Thalynder said, touching Bryn's forehead.

"She lost brothers to the raiders," Arryn replied. "Have you forgotten why her clann is under the protection of your father's realm?"

"No, I have not forgotten. I am reminded everyday when I see Bryn. She would not be in my court if it had not been for the raids. I would have grown up without her."

It was the first honest admission of Thalynder's true feelings and Arryn smiled. He touched Thalynder's hand. "I knew you loved her more than you admit."

"I love her more than I can stand," Thalynder said. "I must marry a prince, I know that. This quest for me to find my true love is a lie. Oh, certainly I wanted to find my heart, but when Meydra told me that I would find it in the realm, my only thought was to postpone the inevitable and have Bryn all to myself for a few weeks."

"And now?" Arryn asked.

"Now I know she holds my heart with her own. It will be difficult to go our separate ways."

"Do you think you must?"

"I do. I am my father's daughter, and you know full well that I am expected to marry a man. It is the law of my realm."

"Keep your heart and mind open, Thalynder, daughter of Thamen. There may be another path you have yet to discover." He rose to let Thalynder sit in the chair. "I am going to the tavern to speak with the others. Those who wish to leave should do so today. Those who wish to accompany us to Arcaibh, I will advise that we will be spending another night here in Skiel. Have you spoken with Meydra since we arrived?"

"No," Thalynder replied. "I have not wanted to leave Bryn's side."

Anethar stepped into the alcove and touched Thalynder's shoulder. "You must tell the dragon that Bryn will recover. I will sit with her for a while. The two of you should stretch and go to the tavern to conduct your business. Return in one hour," she said and took Thalynder's place in the chair.

Thalynder grabbed Arryn's arm as they left the little house. She stopped him and turned her face to his, smiling sweetly. "See if you can't persuade Kenna to return to Skye."

Arryn chuckled. "You should not worry about the Bridei. She loves Bryn for the same reason I do. Because Bryn is Bryn and for no other reason."

⬥

Bryn felt the wind in her face and laughed with pleasure. "Higher!" she called. She held tightly with her legs and her mother sat behind her on the dragon's neck. "Faster!"

The dragon obliged the child and soared higher, careful to make the flight level. Lifting faster was not something she was wont to do even without the child riding her, but flying higher, *that* she could do. "You are a brave one," she said to the child.

"Mummy, what is brave?" Bryn asked her mother.

"Someone who is not afraid to try," Arlendyl replied.

"Oh, I am brave," Bryn squealed.

Suddenly the wind was gone and all was dark again. Bryn felt the cry deep in her heart; the wailing of many voices echoed in her head. *The High Dragon is gone, she said to herself. I have witnessed in my heart the death of a beloved. My heart aches*, she thought. *Will I ever feel joy again?* She could hear mumbling around her but she could not stir and acknowledge the distant voices. She waited. The cool touch on her head resumed and she found the wind again.

"Do you know what a *parting* is?" Brymender asked her.

"It is when someone leaves," the child Bryn replied.

"Are we sad at partings?" he asked and lifted the child in his arms.

"No, because we know we will meet again," Bryn said and wrapped her arms around her father's neck. "Who is parting?"

"Your dragon is parting. She is going to live with another little girl."

"Was I not brave enough?"

"You are a very brave girl, brave enough, my little Bryn," her father said and his words became soft. "You are a brave girl who is going to allow her special dragon to belong to someone else for a little while."

"Will it be long before I see my dragon again?"

"You will see her every day, my brave girl. One day, when you are grown and your path is clear before you, you will have your dragon back as your own."

"Won't the other little girl be sad?" Bryn asked and laid her head on her father's shoulder. "I never want anyone to feel as sad as I am at this parting."

Brymender could not answer his daughter. He hugged her tightly and after a moment he said, "No, Bryn, the little girl will understand."

"Let us say goodbye to Meydra. The other little girl must be waiting."

Bryn felt the tears fall from her eyes but could not reach up to wipe them from her face. She said goodbye in her heart, and the darkness deepened.

Bryn woke to the sounds of her stomach. She did not move, not knowing where she was. She slowly opened her eyes. Beside her, Thalynder sat in a chair, her chin on her chest and a blanket over her shoulders. Past Thalynder, she saw Arryn sitting at Anethar's table. He was holding a book and talking quietly with Anethar. He had shed his battered captain's jerkin for another. This one had stitching and embroidery that she could not distinguish from where she lay. There is something in his hair, or perhaps his hair is braided, she thought. Arryn and Anethar were raptly reviewing the contents of the book. Bryn looked back at Thalynder. How beautiful she is in sleep, Bryn mused. Beautiful and at peace.

"Lynder," she whispered.

Thalynder stirred but did not open her eyes. Bryn tried to touch Thalynder's knee that was resting against the bed, but her arm would not move. She felt a momentary sense of panic that her arm was dead. She looked down and discovered it had only been bandaged to her chest, thus preventing her from moving it. She sighed.

"Lynder," she said a little louder.

Thalynder opened her eyes and stared at Bryn. Coming fully awake, Thalynder squealed like a child and stood up, looking at Anethar and Arryn. "She is awake!"

"Yes, Thalynder, I am awake. No need to wake the rest of the world. Help me to sit up, please."

Thalynder placed her arm under Bryn and lifted as Bryn brought her legs over the side of the bed. Thalynder sat down next to Bryn and put her arm around her waist. "We will not be waking anyone, as they are already awake," Thalynder said. "It is after midday and you have slept a very, very long time, lazy girl." Thalynder kissed Bryn's cheek softly. "We have all been worried about you."

Bryn saw the tears in Thalynder's eyes. She reached up and ran the back of her free hand over Thalynder's cheek. "Do not cry, Lynder. I am healing."

"You are," Anethar said from the opening to the alcove. "Your arm has been washed and dressed several times over the past fifteen hours. Your body is healing itself now."

"I am in your debt," Bryn said. "How can I ever repay you?"

"Return to your people," Anethar said. "That is all I ask."

"You are not the first to ask. It must be one of the answers Elder said I would find at Staenis. Now, if I only knew the question." Bryn smiled at Anethar and leaned a little to see Arryn.

"I believe I see a changed man standing in that room," she said to him. "If I am not mistaken, that is the Fish Circle of the Epidii Clann of the West you have embroidered on your jerkin."

"It is," Arryn said and returned her smile. "I have carried it with me since my elder father died. It was his, as was the map I carry. I think the time has come for me to embrace my past."

"I am glad to hear that, Arryn. However, it is not only your past you should embrace but your future as well. Before we return the princess to her father, I believe you and I will find some interesting answers at the Stones."

Arryn nodded and touched his fist to his heart. "I am glad to hear your mind is clear."

"My mind is clear, but my stomach is empty," Bryn said as she turned back to Thalynder. "If I ask nicely, would you bring me something to eat?"

"I'll do something even better," Thalynder said and kissed Bryn's mouth. "I'll even spoon-feed you if you ask."

Bryn ate soft bread, coddled eggs, melon, early lingonberries and a broth made of steeped elder bark, wild fennel and meadowsweet. She did not need Thalynder's help to eat; nevertheless, she allowed the princess to wait on her. The meal filled her nicely, and the broth, which she suspected contained roseroot as well, gave her spirits a lift. She sat at the table and ate, while the others came and kept her company.

Of the four who traveled with them from Loch Nis to Skiel, only Prince Malcolm and Kenna would remain with the company. Lothan left to warn his queen in Northumbria of the raiders. It was Northumbria that would bare the brunt of a return attack.

Rylan left with his kinsmen and was heading for a small village located at the sea's edge north of Skiel. He too had taken his leave of Bryn and had bowed low, only raising his head when Bryn asked him to. He gave Bryn a small round stone as a parting gift. Engraved on the stone was the Pictish image that represented the Arca, a giant sea creature. This creature was also the Pict symbol for the name of the island that holds the Standing Stones and the village of Skerrabrae. To Bryn and Arryn it was Arcaibh; to Princess Thalynder and Prince Malcolm of Wessex it was known as Orkney.

Bryn placed the stone in the pocket of her tunic. She had been bathed again, this time by Thalynder and Anethar. She was wearing an undertunic the color of the sky on a bright spring morning and an overtunic of a deep cerulean blue. Both were sleeveless, which allowed her injured arm to be bound and reset in place against her chest. Her hair was loose on her back and her feet were bare. She was quite comfortable in the company of her companions and was glad to see that Kenna had decided to continue with them. Secretly, she wished the prince had returned home.

Thalynder had her hand on Bryn's back the entire time Bryn was eating. She curled Bryn's hair around and around her finger, absently caressing the curls. She sat close to Bryn on her injured side and had placed Bryn at the table such that no one could sit on her other side. Kenna was left to sit across from Thalynder because Arryn was directly across from Bryn. Thalynder kept watching Kenna for any little sign that she wanted more from Bryn, but after a while she became bored watching Kenna hang on every word that came out of Bryn's mouth. Prince Malcolm was on her left, and Thalynder, with her hand still on Bryn's back, turned to speak with the prince.

"Why have you decided to go north with us, Malcolm?"

"I have no pressing business in the south," he replied. "We are not fighting any battles at the moment, the grouse is not yet in season, I may be wed by next spring and I want a little adventure."

Bryn looked around Thalynder to the prince and said, "Did you say you will be married next spring?"

"Yes, my father is negotiating as we sit here enjoying your leisure."

"We know you are from Wessex," Arryn said. He was beginning to see where Bryn was headed with this. "What is your father's name?"

"He is known as King Heli in Wessex. Here in the north he is referred to as Beli Mawr," Malcolm replied.

Bryn looked at Thalynder, who stared at Malcolm with her mouth open. Bryn moved her knee to tap Thalynder's thigh, and Thalynder closed her mouth and swallowed. Bryn leaned over to look at Malcolm a little closer. "Your full name wouldn't happen to be Malcolm Lludd Llaw, would it?"

"My younger brother is Lludd," Malcolm replied. "Lucky sot is destined to marry some little princess from a small kingdom and rule a slice of Wessex between my father's kingdom and her father's realm. Never to have to worry much over anything of consequence, except perhaps siring children. I have to hold out for a foreigner. Most probably a Gaul or Cimbri to keep the peace and be destined to rule Wessex and whatever country from whence my wife hails."

Thalynder chuckled. Bryn started to laugh, and Arryn could not contain himself. The older brother of the prince that Thalynder's father wanted her to marry was here with them on this quest to find Thalynder's true love! The prince smiled and said, "Clearly the joke is on me. Would you mind letting me in on the ruse?"

"You would not believe us if we told you," Arryn said when he was able to speak again.

Bryn took a deep breath and looked at the frowning prince. "You are sitting next to the little princess that is destined to marry your younger brother. Though I dare say, they will not rule some little slice of Wessex, but the Realm that Touches Two Seas. By far, a much better prospect now, wouldn't you say?"

The prince turned red. He bowed his head to Thalynder. "I hope you will not hold my behavior as example of my brother. Lludd is the more refined of the two of us," he said.

Thalynder wiped tears of laughter from her face and placed her hand on Malcolm's arm. "No," she said. "I will not set judgment of your brother by your roguish nature. I do wish to know one thing. Which of you has larger feet?"

Bryn spit out the mead she had in her mouth and laughed, as did Kenna. Thalynder, who had tried to keep a straight face, smiled sweetly as Malcolm looked quizzically at her.

"I do," Malcolm replied. "Why do you ask?"

"Curiosity," Thalynder said.

Prince Malcolm looked at Arryn and they both shrugged.

⟐

Bryn walked with Anethar out to where Meydra sat under the canopy of a bright blue sky. Skiel was set in the open country, a situation that allowed them to see far around the village and take note of anything that approached. Meydra was lying down, her tail curled around her body and her head resting on her forearm. As Bryn approached Meydra, she felt their hearts begin to beat as one. Bryn greeted Meydra first with her mind and her heart. *Mo anam*, she said in silent greeting. *I am glad to see you.*

Meydra looked into Bryn's eyes and saw the light behind them. *I was worried.*

Bryn's hands moved to rest upon Meydra's chest. Meydra felt the syncopated rhythm as her heart kept time with Bryn's, and she closed her eyes. She helped Bryn look deep into the recesses of her memory and saw the light grow bright and clear. Meydra moved Bryn further into her memories to hear the peals of laughter of a small child, the sound of joy—pure, unadulterated and unsullied by grown-up ideas.

Meydra bowed her head to the Druid elder. "Greetings, Elder Anethar," she said to the older woman.

"Greetings, Meydra, it has been a long time," Anethar said and placed her palm on Meydra's forehead.

Bryn stepped up to Meydra and laid her own forehead against Meydra. "Thalynder is taking a bath," Bryn said. "We have come to speak with you about Staenis."

"Yes, Bryn. You already have questions," Meydra said.

"I do, but that is not why I have come now. Anethar wishes to address you, and I have come to ask you to speak with her. If you agree, I will leave you two and return to Thalynder."

"It is always good to speak with an elder," Meydra said. "You are welcome, Anethar."

"Thank you, Meydra. Bryn, I will return in less than an hour." Anethar dismissed Bryn with those words.

Bryn left Anethar and Meydra, glancing once over her shoulder at them. She saw Anethar sit down in front of Meydra and watched as the dragon circled her tail around Anethar's back. It was a friendly gesture and Bryn silently thanked Meydra.

❧

"Does she know?" Meydra asked.

"She only guesses," Anethar replied. "Little time is left before a decision must be made."

"Yes, Elder Anethar, very little time."

❧

Thalynder did not see a cloth to use to dry her skin. She thought about using her tunic, but it needed to be washed itself and the idea of the sooty residue from the tavern lingering on her skin made her frown. She would have to call for someone. That too made her frown, not knowing who was around in the back of the tavern where the bath and the bedchambers were located. She was about to raise her voice when she heard a knock at the door.

"Who is there?"

Bryn grinned from behind the door. She carried a thick soft cotton cloth draped over her arm. "The chambermaid, milady," she replied with a high squeak. "I have your drying sheet, milady."

"Oh, thank you. I was about to shout for someone. You may enter."

Bryn opened the door and looked at Thalynder with a smirk. "And if I had said I was the stable boy?"

Thalynder laughed and stood up in the large tub. She held out her arm and offered it to Bryn. "You may dry me."

"Hmmm," Bryn replied. "As my left arm is no longer wrapped to my chest, I could do that if that is what you truly wish."

"What else would you suggest? I can't stand here naked for too long and not get a chill," Thalynder stepped out of the tub to stand on her discarded tunics.

Bryn opened the clean dry cloth and held it for Thalynder to step into. She waited until Thalynder was closer and wrapped the princess in the sheet, leaving her neck and shoulders exposed. Bryn placed a kiss on Thalynder's left shoulder.

"More," Thalynder whispered.

Bryn kissed the same shoulder and moved to kiss the back of Thalynder's neck.

"More," Thalynder said and moved back against Bryn.

Bryn again kissed the left shoulder, the back of Thalynder's neck, and then her right shoulder. She spoke into Thalynder's ear. "If you want more, we will have to leave the bath."

"Don't forget my tunics," Thalynder replied. She moved toward the door and exited the little bathing room, walking quickly down the hall to her bedchamber. Bryn was right behind her carrying Thalynder's clothing, belt, and sword. The princess walked into the room and stood in the shaft of sunlight that came in through the high window.

Bryn placed Thalynder's things on the small, narrow table along the wall. She closed the door and stared at Thalynder standing in the sunlight and smiled.

"Even with the simple robe of that sheet, you are beautiful. You tease me with your beauty."

"I used to. I used to want to goad you into saying something, or to notice me. It was a game at first."

Bryn took a step toward Thalynder, stopping out of reach. "What has changed?"

"*I* have," Thalynder said and dropped the sheet. "It is no longer a game, Bryn. I want your love."

Bryn did not know how to respond. Her body ached to touch Thalynder and her heart sang loudly in her ears, but her mind cautioned her. She did not close the gap between them. Instead she walked over to the bed and sat down on the edge. She patted the section next to her, gesturing Thalynder to sit with her. "Lynder, we need to talk about this."

Thalynder reached down and lifted the sheet to cover herself. She walked to the bed with her head hanging slightly and a pout on her lips. She sat next to Bryn but did not touch her. "Have I said the wrong thing?"

Bryn pulled the edge of the sheet toward her so she could begin to dry off Thalynder's arms. She was silent for a moment. "No, Lynder. You have said nothing wrong. We simply need to speak of your feelings before I allow either of us to take a step one of us might regret."

"How could I regret your loving me?" Thalynder turned to face Bryn. The sheet fell off her arms, exposing the tops of her breasts.

"Lynder, it is your love for *me* that has me concerned." Bryn ran the cloth over Thalynder's shoulders. "You have not yet said you love me."

"But," Thalynder started, only to be silenced by Bryn's fingers on her mouth.

"You said you want my love and that you would not regret me loving you," Bryn said, her voice gentle and calm. "You never said you were prepared to love me."

Thalynder looked at Bryn for a long silent moment. Tears welled in her eyes and as she blinked they fell to her cheeks. "Bryn, I am a princess. I have to marry. If I allowed myself to love you with everything I have inside, how could I claim a husband and produce an heir? My whole life up to now has prepared me to be a mother for a throne-sitter," she spat out the words. "You can love me and not be under the duress of the throne. You don't know the pressure I am under."

"Do I not?" Bryn asked. "Do I not share each day, each thought, each struggle with you? Do you believe that I have merely stumbled upon this love for you? How dare you suggest that I could love any less than you." Bryn stood up and paced the room.

Thalynder was silent. She shook her head and looked at Bryn. She took a deep breath. "You are stronger than I, Bryn of the Brae. I have always known that. I have kept my heart securely locked behind a thick iron door." She stood up and walked over to Bryn. "I knew that if I opened that door, you would be the first to find my heart. As much as I hoped my father would sire another heir, I know he will not. I am to rule a kingdom, and I am to be a wife and mother. Even if my heart belongs to you, I would have to give you up." She let the sheet fall so she could put her arms around Bryn's neck. "I don't want to give you up, my Bryn."

Bryn wrapped her arms around Thalynder's waist and held her close.

"I cannot bring myself to admit to this love. It disrupts all I have been taught since I was born into the life of a princess. Not only is loving someone other than a prospective royal partner forbidden, but loving another of the same gender, outside childhood, is not allowed in my father's realm. Since youth I have been primed to marry a male, a prince or a king."

Bryn could see that the princess was struggling. She sighed against Thalynder's shoulder. Breaking the embrace, Bryn leaned down to pick up the sheet. She took Thalynder's hand and said, "Sit down, Lynder."

Thalynder sat on the edge of the bed.

Bryn began to dry Thalynder's body, beginning with her feet. She ran the sheet lightly over one foot at a time, drying first the heel and sole, then moving to each toe. She moved to dry each shin, each calf. When she reached the knees, she looked up at Thalynder and spoke softly, "Move back on the bed."

Thalynder moved back onto the bed so that her entire body was prone upon the feathered coverlet. The coolness of the cover caused her skin to react with little bumps.

"Are you cold, Lynder?"

"A little."

Bryn stood where Thalynder could watch her. She removed her boots first and untied the ribbons that held her hose in place. She removed her hose, dropping them to the floor. She unlaced her bodice and kept her eyes on Thalynder.

Thalynder watched Bryn undress and the little bumps became more pronounced. She grabbed the sheet that was at her knees and covered her exposed chest and stomach, but continued to watch Bryn.

Bryn removed her bodice and pulled the first tunic over her head. She stood in her second tunic, her nipples erect against the cloth, and reached down and pulled the sheet out of Thalynder's hands, dropping it to the floor. She untied the laces on her undertunic and let it drop off her shoulders, down her arms, and off her body to land on the small pile of clothing. She stood naked before Thalynder and tried to control her breathing. She realized she was shaking but she did not feel cold. She sat on the bed and started to dry Thalynder's body, beginning at the knees where she had left off, only now she used her hands.

Bryn moved her hands slowly over the tops of Thalynder's knees, then up to her thighs, one hand on each. She straddled her legs and eased her hands higher to the tops of the thighs. Only her hands touched her body. She slid her hands to Thalynder's hips, and Thalynder let out a little moan. Bryn moved up to her waist—more slender now that they had been riding and walking—and ran her hands over Thalynder's stomach.

Thalynder's breathing began to deepen and her pulse quickened. She placed one arm under her head to raise up and watch Bryn, captivated by the slow deliberate movements.

Bryn stopped and looked at the princess, who was now watching her every move. "Are you comfortable with what I'm doing?"

"Yes."

Bryn moved higher over Thalynder's body, placing her knees on either side of Thalynder's hips. Still, the only thing touching Thalynder was Bryn's hands. Bryn slowly moved her hands up the sides of Thalynder's chest until she reached her armpits. She pulled at the fine blond hair there and felt Thalynder squirm under her touch. She closed the gap between her knees and Thalynder's hips, resting her knees against Thalynder's cool skin. She then eased her hands up Thalynder's shoulders. With a hand on each side of her neck, Bryn tugged on Thalynder's earlobes and leaned down to kiss her chin.

"You are so soft, Lynder," Bryn cooed. "I love the way you feel under my fingers."

"What do you want me to do?" Thalynder asked.

"Nothing, my princess. Let me worship you." Bryn kissed Thalynder's mouth again. Kissing Thalynder was nothing new, but having her naked body so close was new, and Bryn intensified the kiss. Her own desire to consume Thalynder built inside her like a newly kindled fire—a spark to get it started and as more fuel was consumed, the fire blazed. Bryn was fed by the touch of Thalynder's skin under her hands, the touch of her lips, the exchange of breath. Bryn parted Thalynder's lips with her tongue and sought the soft, wet inside of Thalynder's mouth. She felt Thalynder moan on her tongue.

Thalynder eagerly accepted Bryn's kiss. She brought her hands up to find Bryn's breasts and cupped them softly.

Bryn pushed her breasts into Thalynder's hands and sank her body on top of Thalynder. She placed her hands on either side of Thalynder's chest and used the leverage to move her breasts against Thalynder. Breast to breast, nipple to nipple, Bryn continued to explore Thalynder's mouth with her tongue while she kept time with her breasts. Circling with her tongue and her nipples. She could feel Thalynder reacting, feel her lift her chest to press her hardened nipples against Bryn's skin. Bryn moved her legs to lie on top of Thalynder's legs and used her knee to part Thalynder's legs. Thalynder opened like a flower to rain, and it was Bryn's turn to moan. She moved her hand to cup Thalynder's breast and pulled softly on Thalynder's nipple.

"More," Thalynder breathed. "Harder, Bryn."

Bryn grasped Thalynder's nipple between her thumb and forefinger and pulled. Thalynder arched her back and thrust her head back. Bryn kissed Thalynder's exposed neck and slid down and kissed her other breast. With a hand on one breast and her mouth on the other, Bryn pulled and kissed Thalynder's erect nipples. She could feel Thalynder's hips move beneath her.

"Lynder, I want to taste you."

"Oh," Thalynder moaned.

Bryn slid down Thalynder's body, kissing her skin down to her navel and to her mound of soft blond curls. She lay between

Thalynder's legs and pushed them further apart, kissing the insides of Thalynder's thighs. Gently, with careful fingers, Bryn opened Thalynder and ran her tongue against the soft, warm, and very wet skin.

Thalynder responded with a low, animal-like growl that rose from the depths of her belly. She moved her hips and pushed against Bryn's mouth.

Bryn pushed her tongue over and around, licking all of Thalynder's sex. She brought her fingers up to join her tongue. She started slowly, but when Thalynder's breathing became a pant, she knew she could not stop. She took the gem that pulsed under her touch into her mouth and sucked softly while her fingers pulled on the outer lips that covered the velvet.

Thalynder's hips moved with the rhythm of the sucking, her head tilted back and her back arched. Her hands held Bryn's head gently but firmly and her legs stiffened. She held her breath and as the shudders that began deep inside reached the surface, she exhaled softly, "Oh, Bryn," and her body surrendered to the convulsive ecstasy.

Bryn kept up the gentle sucking until Thalynder's body relaxed. She kissed the outer lips softly and moved back to the insides of her thighs. She kissed up to Thalynder's navel and back up to her darkened nipples. When she reached Thalynder's neck, the princess stopped her.

"Bryn, my Bryn, what can I do for you?"

Bryn rolled off Thalynder, careful not to roll on her arm, which had begun to throb with the exertion, and lay back on the bed. She turned her head to Thalynder. "How do you pleasure yourself?"

"With my fingers," Thalynder replied. "Should I do that to you?"

Bryn blushed at the thought of Thalynder's slender fingers on her sex, which made her giggle. "I don't know why I am embarrassed to ask it of you, but I am."

"Oh, silly Bryn, let me touch you."

Bryn took Thalynder's hand and guided it to her mound. It too was warm and wet from the erotic play. She guided

Thalynder's fingers to her hard and wanting pearl. "There. Just there," she breathed.

Thalynder began a slow circle around Bryn's yielding flesh, increasing the pressure with each pass. She leaned down and took Bryn's nipple in her mouth. She suckled at Bryn's breast with the same increasing pressure. Bryn's hips joined the rhythm and Lynder sucked hard against her nipple. Bryn let out a moan, then another and her breathing came in short deep pants. Thalynder pinched Bryn's nipple with her teeth and with another stroke of her fingers, Bryn's body pulsed against her.

Bryn released the passion that threatened to consume her and arched her body hard against Thalynder's hand. She pulled Thalynder to her mouth and sucked on her tongue, while waves of unchecked pleasure rocked her body. When at last the tide ebbed, she grabbed Thalynder's hand and said, "Lynder, dearest, sweet Lynder, what now are we to do?"

Thalynder was quiet the following morning, which caused Bryn to be concerned. She approached Thalynder, who sat at Anethar's table, playing with the frayed edge of the blanket that lay upon her knees, and sat beside her on the bench. Thalynder looked at Bryn and gave a weak smile. Bryn feared the worst and hoped Lynder was not now having regrets about the passionate night they had spent wrapped in each other's arms. She took a deep breath and moved to face Thalynder.

"You are pensive this morning," Bryn said. She waited for Thalynder to speak and felt her heart beat fast in her chest. "Are you concerned about last night?"

Thalynder looked at Bryn and at first frowned. Then she smiled. "Dearest Bryn, no. Last night will never be forgotten nor regretted. I was trying to work something out in my head."

"What do you need to work out, Lynder?" Bryn took Thalynder's hand in hers. She was glad that their night together had not caused Thalynder distress, though seeing the princess so quiet troubled her. "Tell me, upon what have you been thinking?"

Thalynder got up from the table, took the book off the mantelpiece, and set it down in front of Bryn. "I cannot read the words of your native tongue, but the pictures tell many stories of devastation by the raiders from over the North Sea," Thalynder said as she sat back down next to Bryn. "Why did I not learn the history of these raiders? If I am to rule, why have I not been taught about them and the death they have brought to the clans and the Picts?"

Bryn ran her hands over the cover. She opened the book to the beginning pages. "I will tell you what I know."

"It had long been believed that the Druids were a race of elves that chose to live in the world with the race of men, forsaking longevity for broader knowledge. The Druids settled the lowlands and the forests first, and brought with them their companions, the dragons. They were envied by the race of men that was only beginning to learn the ways of the world. At first they were feared, revered as powerful beings who held sway over life and death. As time passed, men came to understand what the Druids had been trying to teach them, and their reverence of the race was tempered with the knowledge that the Druids were not powerful beings, but rather caretakers who understood the finer points of life.

"From the Druids, men learned to care for animals, domesticating them for various reasons. They learned about growth cycles in plants, and some men became farmers. After a time, they took the seed of knowledge their ancestors had planted in them and traveled to other lands. Lands that could only be reached on the backs of dragons or in sturdy boats. They traveled the short distance east and began to populate the new lands. They moved overland, taking their dragons with them. They met other races and began to marry into those different races and clans. There were some elves, who held themselves in higher regard and did not wish to marry into the clans. Those elves distanced themselves from the men, and for as far as anyone could see, they had disappeared altogether.

"We know there are elves still on Alban," Thalynder said.

"True, and someday I hope you meet them," Bryn said.

"Continue the story."

Bryn touched Thalynder's cheek and smiled.

"The original Druids and their offspring remained clustered in clanns. Remaining in the north of those lands where the soil was rich and open. The Druids loved the open sky and chose to live where they could see the stars at night and follow the sun during the day."

"The dragon stars," the princess said. "Yes, you've told me about those. Go on."

"Over time men began to forget the knowledge they learned from the Druids and became jealous of all that the Druids could accomplish, believing the Druids were hiding something from them. They began to seek out the Druids and forced them to provide for men. The Druids wished only to coexist peacefully with them, so they again tried to teach. This time the men did not want to know how to accomplish something, they only wanted it done.

"Some of the Druid clanns managed to live alongside men, becoming less and less like their ancestors and more and more like the men. There were among the clanns some Druids that followed the old ways and who decided they would leave the men. With their dragons they moved to remote lands surrounded on all sides by great seas—the great northern islands. Their seclusion lasted many generations and the Druids flourished. The men who did eventually find the islands were strong men looking for a home where they could live free of tyranny or oppression. They got on well with the Druids and again came to regard the Druids as teachers and lawgivers.

"The men that inhabited the lands east and over the North Sea did not seek out the Druids for their skills, but coveted the Druids' knowledge and what they thought was Druid magic. The crusade began to seek out the Druids and their clanns and enslave or destroy them.

"The wars," Thalynder said.

"Yes, the wars began and the kingdoms split so that a defense could be made more readily.

"As the raiders discovered new lands where Druids were revered, they killed all in their path, including livestock, stopping at nothing to find the clanns. They burned crops and houses. My ancestors found they could build sturdy defensible structures of rock. The insides could be burned out, so they began to craft simple platforms out of stone to use as tables and beds, creating soft cushions for the stone beds from moss and feathers, sheep's wool and sea grass."

"Over thousands of years?" Thalynder asked. "Some of those villages were constructed a very long time ago."

"Yes, over thousands of years. The wars remained in the north until only recently. I believe now that the Druids are not the only prey, but that anyone the raiders meet will fall victim. Now it is a matter of suppression for the raiders. They can control their own by subjecting other defenseless peoples to the horrors of death and destruction. Enhancing their prowess, taking spoils back to their homeland. This will continue for future generations until someone stands up to them. They will continue to raid, pillage and kill, so long as we remain docile."

Thalynder sat quiet for several moments. She got up and replaced the book on the mantel. She stood behind Bryn and placed her hands on Bryn's shoulders. She gently pulled Bryn back and kissed the top of Bryn's head. "That is why you wanted to send a message to the jarl's people," she said. "You want to start another war."

"Not a war, Lynder. A rebellion. I want the raiders to understand that we will not sit idly by and let this continue to happen." Bryn placed her hands over Thalynder's and looked up at her. "If we do not do this now, your people will suffer as mine have. This island will not merely be raided but invaded and conquered, and our way of life destroyed."

"What do you propose to do?"

Bryn frowned and shook her head slightly. "I do not know. I am only a waiting lady with a sword and a shield."

"What about Wessex and Britannia? Surely, Prince Malcolm could bring aid." Thalynder let go of Bryn and sat back down beside her on the bench.

"No, Britannia is increasingly under Roman influence and may succumb to Roman rule at any time. Besides, the wall makes it difficult for us to expect aid would come quickly. No, we have to deal with the raiders ourselves. We have to stop the clanns from fighting amongst themselves and find a way to unite them. If that were achieved we would have the resources to help ourselves."

"We could gather the dragons and ask them to fight for us," Thalynder said.

"We cannot ask that of them," Bryn replied and frowned at the implication of fighting dragons.

"The need is great to find someone to lead the clanns, and not another head of state or king. Alban needs a high ruler. Someone the clanns can believe in and follow."

"Yes. Someone the clanns can follow."

"Arryn, perhaps," Thalynder said. "There is strength in him."

"Strength and loyalty. Yes, Arryn could lead the clanns."

CHAPTER TWELVE

Bryn sat on her horse and smiled down at Anethar. "Remember," Bryn said. "You promised to wait at least a week before sending word to my father. I want to be across the firth and be on the island long before he hears I have been injured. I am sure King Thamen will insist we return once he has word of the raiders."

"I will not send word," Anethar said. "Though I will venture that Lothan has already given word to Betony, and she will have sent word to King Thamen as well as to King Heli."

"That being so, we must be off," Thalynder said. "Quickly, before the hoards of my father's guard descend upon us and remove me from this company." Thalynder nodded at Anethar. "I am forever in your debt, Elder Anethar. To have lost Bryn would indeed have been a loss to many."

Anethar bowed her head low to the princess in return. She looked up at Arryn. "Wear your symbols proudly, Epidii. The clanns rejoice at your return."

Arryn bowed his head and touched his fist to his chest.

"Bryn of the Brae," Anethar said and reached up to touch Bryn's hand. "Return to your people."

"If at all possible, I will," Bryn said and urged her horse forward. She rode point with Thalynder behind her and Arryn bringing up the rear. The sky overhead held three dragons, IronHeart, Caraid and Meydra, like geese in a formation with Meydra leading. The journey to the small hamlet of Theòrsa that held the ferry would take three days. Between Skiel and Theòrsa there was nothing but heather moorland and bogs, and the going would be slow. Bryn looked up and sent out a thought to Meydra, *My fate is in your hands.*

Meydra glanced down at Bryn. She wanted to tell Bryn that her fate had been decided long before she was born, but she could not reveal that this soon. Nevertheless, she was right: Meydra did have a part to play in Bryn's fate. She sighed and replied to Bryn, *I will be there for you, little sister.*

The first day's ride was quiet and uneventful. Bryn could not guess how soon the jarl would be missed in his country, but she and Arryn believed it would be days, maybe weeks, before they saw a return attack. The summer was nearing its zenith and the North Sea was encased in fog.

Bryn studied the map and knew where she wished to rest for the night. She led the group forward, stopping occasionally to rest her arm and give the horses a chance to graze. The dragons, along with Prince Malcolm and Kenna, would alight whenever Bryn stopped.

Arryn got off his horse and offered his hand to Thalynder. Once the princess was off her mount, Arryn looked at Bryn, who was still mounted and looking out across the open moor. Bryn had stopped at a small densely wooded area at the river's edge to spend the night, and the dragons had set their riders down before heading to a rocky creag on which they would perch and keep watch. Bryn was looking at the marsh on the other side of the trees.

"What do you see, Bryn?" Arryn asked.

"Tonight's meal," she replied but did not look down at him. "I will return." She urged Pymmar out of the trees and took off across the open marsh, bringing her bow in front of her.

"Wait!" Arryn started back to his mount in time to see Kenna leap onto his horse's back and take off toward Bryn.

"I will go with her," Kenna said as she passed Arryn.

Thalynder was chuckling behind Arryn. "Have you still not learned?" she said and touched his sleeve. "She knows her limits, Arryn. She would not have gone had she sensed danger. As it is, we will have game for supper. Perhaps we should have a fire ready when they return."

Arryn shook his head, but did manage a smile. He took Thalynder's arm and led her to a spot where they could build a good hot fire.

Bryn heard the horse behind her and half expected to hear Arryn scolding her, but she did not look back. She had the red stag in her sights and it had not detected her. She held up her hand so that whoever was following knew not to approach or pass. She raised her bow and still moving forward, notched and loosed her arrow, giving a little grunt when she did so. The grunt caused the deer to raise its head in her direction and, her aim true, the arrow found its throat. Bryn checked her horse and slowed the pace to approach the deer from the other direction. She'd hoped for a clean kill, but if it was not, the wounded stag could still kick and hurt the horse. As she swung in a wide arc, she saw that it was Kenna who was behind her. She pointed in the opposite direction and Kenna moved to flank the stag from the other side. Bryn notched another arrow and Kenna drew her bow.

Bryn came around and saw that the deer was not moving. She still had to be careful of the stag's antlers. She got off her horse and approached the downed animal. She nodded at Kenna, who had also dismounted and had her arrow trained on the deer's chest. Bryn set her bow down and took her sword from her belt. She approached the deer noiselessly and stood behind it, checking its breathing. It was dead. Bryn put her sword in the scabbard and took the knife from her belt. Kneeling behind the deer, she cut the end of the arrow so that she could pull the shaft cleanly through the animal's throat. Once done, she placed her hand over the stag's heart and bowed her head.

Kenna lowered her bow and knelt beside Bryn. She placed her hands on the horns and bowed her head as well.

"I am your servant," Bryn began.

"I am your guardian," Kenna said.

"I am she that breathes the same air, feels the same wind, embraces the same earth. I am your servant," Bryn and Kenna said together.

From across the moorland came a soft, low song, soughing through the heather and the trees on the outer edge of the marsh. To Kenna it was faint like a gentle breeze, but to Bryn it was a strong melody of rebirth and renewal, loud in her heart. She had heard it every time she was a witness to death. It was the soul of the dead rising to meet those who would guide it to a new life. She began to sing the words.

I am bowing my head before you
In the eye of the Mother who gave me birth
In the eye of the Maid who loves me
In the eye of those that guide me
In friendship and affection
Through thy gift of nature, O Goddess
Bestow upon us fullness in our need
As the ageless ones ask
Every shade and light
Every day and night
Each moment in kindness

Kenna joined in the last stanza:
Am gáeth tar na bhfarraige,
Am tuile os chinn maighe.
Am dord na daíthbhe,
Am damh seacht mbeann.

"I am a wind across the sea, I am a flood across the plain, I am the roar of the tides, I am a stag of seven tines," Bryn repeated. She kissed the forehead of the dead stag and turned to Kenna. "We will gut him here and leave the entrails for the fox and the marten and maybe a dragon or two."

The stag provided plenty of meat for all, including the dragons, who preferred it raw. Arryn and Prince Malcolm had taken the legs and head to the dragons while Bryn and Kenna cut up the rest of the meat. Some would be eaten right away, the rest cooked and saved for the journey.

Thalynder was crushing the herbs as Bryn instructed her. Bryn made a brine of the crushed herbs and the air was filled with the scent of richly spiced and roasted meat. As a precaution, Thalynder, Malcolm and Kenna charged their dragons with extra vigilance.

Bryn sat at the edge of the fire basting the meat with the herb brine. Thalynder was behind Bryn braiding her hair. The two had turned a page in their relationship and it showed on their faces and in their attitudes toward the others. Both women were friendlier and it did not go unnoticed.

"They will outgrow it," Malcolm said to Arryn, who sat watching his two friends.

Arryn turned to Malcolm and frowned. "Why would you say that?"

"Because they will, I've seen it over and over again with waiting ladies. They adore their mistresses until some man comes and takes things in hand."

"I remind you, Prince, you are speaking about a princess who will most probably marry your brother, not to mention, she is King Thamen's daughter," Arryn said and stood up. "The other is a lady in her own right. Mind your tongue."

Arryn left the prince sitting red-faced and walked over to Bryn and Thalynder. He sat down next to Bryn and watched Thalynder finish with her hair. "You two have been glowing brighter than this fire since we left Skiel," he said, keeping his voice low.

Thalynder giggled.

Bryn kept her head straight and her eyes on the stag over the fire. She pushed against the meat with the end of her spoon to judge the firmness of the meat. "We are well rested," she said after a moment's thought. "Besides, you know we flourish in the wild."

"You flourish, on that I will agree, and it is the wild side of which I am speaking," Arryn said.

Thalynder leaned over Bryn's shoulder. "Where is the ribbon for your braid?" she asked.

"I used it on the stag's horns," Bryn replied. "I would say it is lying on the ground at the feet of a dragon."

"Do you have another?"

"I do, in the small bag on Pymmar." Thalynder rose to get another ribbon to tie off Bryn's braid.

Arryn took the opportunity to whisper to Bryn. "Your heart will break, Lady Bryn."

"Arryn, why do you feel the need to protect my heart, and *why* do you continue to call me Lady Bryn?" Bryn had noticed that Arryn's demeanor toward her had changed after the incident with the raiders. He was beginning to treat her as he did Thalynder and that was making Bryn uncomfortable. "We are friends, are we not? Please call me Bryn and do not use the term *Lady*."

"What I know about you, about my own ancestors, and what Anethar has told me, I should be calling you much more."

"You will do no such thing, Arryn of the Epidii. I know you have chosen to give up your captain's cloak for your clann's symbols but do not think for a moment that you are released from the vow you gave King Thamen. I am Princess Thalynder's waiting lady and Shieldmaiden. Here in the wild, you may call me Bryn. Bryn and nothing more."

"As you wish, Bryn. I was only trying to say that I do not want to see you hurt, in body or in spirit. We both know the princess must marry."

"Yes, and Thalynder and I have discussed that issue many times, Arryn." Bryn watched for Thalynder's return. "We will take each day as it dawns."

Arryn laid his hand on Bryn's arm. "I would love to see you happy, Bryn."

Thalynder came back with a piece of cloth and knelt behind Bryn. She tied the cloth around the end of Bryn's braid. "Tomorrow we will be in Theòrsa?" she asked.

"No," Arryn answered. "We have one more night before we reach the coast. You mentioned needing to find a way across to the island, Bryn. Do you believe we will not find a ferry?"

The news that the coastal towns on the north end of the country had been sacked time and time again by the raiders had caused Bryn some concern.

"The means to get across to the islands has been all but wiped out each time the raiders invade the town. New ferries are reestablished, only to be burned or severed anew. It is clear the raiders do not want anyone returning to the island." The best way over would be on the backs of the dragons, but that meant they would be on foot once on the island, and neither she nor Arryn thought that was a good idea.

"We know the raiders have not returned, and when they do come looking for the jarl, they will start at the mouth of the Nis, so there is the possibility a ferry has been reestablished," Bryn said.

"You still think we may have to use the dragons," Prince Malcolm said as he came over to the fire. "That meat smells good."

"I do think we will have to be prepared to use them, yes," Bryn said. "Unless we find the ferry or some other boat that will take the horses across. I do not mind leaving them behind and walking, but that would mean foraging for our meals."

"We have been fortunate thus far with the food we have found," Thalynder said from behind Bryn. She had finished Bryn's hair but continued to sit behind her, her arms around Bryn's waist. "Perhaps, we should consider leaving the horses and walking. I would be willing to give it a try."

Both Bryn and Arryn turned to look at Thalynder.

"Why do you look at me thus?" she asked. "Surely, you have seen that I am quite capable in the forest."

"True," Arryn replied. "When we have had to walk the horses through the denser forest, you have been quite capable."

"Why do you doubt I could walk from Staenis to Skerrabrae? If we forage for food on the island, and we are not climbing mountains, then I don't see why we can't walk."

Bryn listened to Thalynder and realized what she was asking. She was asking for more time. If they took the horses, they would reach Staenis sooner, all in a matter of a few days. Thalynder wanted to slow things down now that they approached the midpoint of their journey, and Bryn felt the same. Time was moving too fast—soon they would be on their way back to King Thamen, and to Thalynder's marriage.

"The meat is cooked. We may eat now," Bryn said. "We can discuss what supplies we can carry over to the island, should we find we must leave the horses and travel the island on foot."

✦

Bryn watched as clouds moved across the night sky. Her back was against Meydra and Thalynder lay snuggled against her chest.

"Sleep warm tonight, Lynder," Bryn said against Thalynder's neck. "It will be wet tomorrow and we will ride hard across the moors. Tomorrow night we sleep under an open sky."

"The rain will clear the fog on the coast," Thalynder said, yawning.

Bryn had been considering the same thing. It would be the perfect time for the raiders to return to look for the jarl.

"Yes." She kissed Thalynder's neck. "Sleep now."

In a few moments, Thalynder's breathing changed and she was asleep. Bryn waited another moment, then gently pushed back against Meydra. She released her hold on Thalynder, stood up and rubbed her arm. It was stiff from the ride and the butchering of the stag. She kissed Meydra's chest and walked out of the circle, past Malcolm and the fire, past Caraid and

Kenna. She lifted her head and saw IronHeart looking down at her. She touched her heart and he returned his gaze toward the east, ever watchful of the sea. Bryn walked for a short while around the camp and stopped to look at the moon as it struggled to shine through the clouds. She knew she had been followed and was glad Arryn was not asleep. She waited and when sure he was within the sound of her voice, she said, "The moon will be full by the time we reach the Stones."

"It will," Arryn replied and approached her side. "You are concerned about something."

"I can see that you are leaving more and more of the captain behind. That you now embrace your heritage without hesitation. Arryn, you have returned to the clann ways."

"Anethar said the same thing."

"What else did Anethar tell you?"

"That I should now be watchful of you along with my charge to watch over the princess. And that you will come to a crossroads at the Stones."

"When you were a child, were you taught the ways of your clann?" Bryn turned to look at Arryn. "I speak of the ancient ways of your elder fathers and mothers."

"No," Arryn replied. "I was given many things that belonged to my elder fathers: my sword, my jerkin, my map. I was never told why they were important, simply that they were."

"I sometimes wish I had been spared the ancient knowledge. I feel as if I am caught between two worlds. One, the courtly manners and duty to a royal house. The other, the world of my ancestors and a duty to my people. The crossroads will be a test for more than me, Arryn."

"That is what Anethar told me," he said, placing his hand on Bryn's shoulder. "It will be a test for all but one. For you it will not be a test. For you it will be a choice between two paths."

Bryn moved into Arryn's arms. She let the tears of frustration spill from her eyes and cried silently against his chest. She stood against him and let all that she was afraid of, all the choices she had made over the past few weeks—all the pain—fall with the tears. She knew already what path she would take, and convincing Thalynder that it was the right path was the only obstacle in her way. As the tears slowed and she felt better, the moon came out from behind the clouds, illuminating the moor. It was still and quiet, empty of movement and sound. She released her hold on Arryn and stepped back to look at him.

"What lies ahead has already been decided for me," she said.

"Yes, I know that, Bryn. As I said, it will be a test for all but one."

Thalynder woke and turned in Bryn's arms.

"How long have you been awake?"

"Not long. Are you ready for a wet ride?" Bryn asked.

Thalynder looked around and saw the rain falling in sheets. She looked up to see Meydra's wing opened above her head. "Well, thank you, Meydra," she said. "What a nice gesture."

Meydra smiled at the two women. "I would keep you safe and warm all day if possible. IronHeart has not returned."

Earlier, Bryn had awoken to the sound of IronHeart as he lifted into the air. She had not fully slept since coming out of the deep induced sleep when in Anethar's home, and she had spent many nights listening to the thoughts of the other dragons. IronHeart said he had seen something out toward the North Sea and had called to the other dragons. Bryn heard him mention elves and his thoughts were restless. Meydra was standing now and had both wings fully extended, something she did when need called for vigilance. Thalynder might believe Meydra did it to shield them from the rain, but the dragon was also in a heightened state of awareness. Bryn and Meydra waited for word from the other dragon.

"I will speak with Malcolm," Bryn said and rose to stand against Meydra. "Lynder, I need you to be ready to leave without a full breakfast. We will stop at Srath Nabhir for a meal but that will be well after midday."

"I will be ready," Thalynder said and raised her hand to Bryn. Bryn pulled her up to stand. "I will bring you something to eat as well."

Bryn gave Thalynder a quick kiss before walking out from under the shelter of Meydra's wing and into the driving rain. She pulled the hood of her cloak over her head and made her way to Malcolm. She found him with Kenna under Caraid's wing, speaking with Arryn.

"What is it?" Bryn asked as she approached the others.

"Elves," Arryn replied.

"This far north?" Bryn asked as she stepped under Caraid's wing. She could not reveal the fact that she could hear IronHeart's thoughts and knew elves approached from the south.

"They were spotted early this morning entering Galliabh. They appear to be headed for Theòrsa, what you call Ceann Dùnaid," Malcolm replied. "I have asked Coeur de Fer to confirm this and return. He should arrive without much delay."

Bryn looked at Arryn. "Ceann Dùnaid—coincidence, do you think?"

"No," he said and smiled. "I think we may have others joining our little company."

Bryn sighed. She knew her mother had sent them. There was still a small band of elves that remained on the island, and their ties to the Druids were strong.

"Once Coeur de Fer returns, we leave for Srath Nabhir," she said. She pulled her hood back over her head and walked back into the rain.

⟐

The rain fell in torrents and the company was thoroughly soaked upon arriving at Srath Nabhir. Even the dragon riders were wet and pensive when they set down at the foot of the loch. As promised, Bryn started to prepare a meal and was joined by Kenna. Both women were quiet as they retrieved the cooked meat from Bryn's saddlebag.

"Meat, and the last of the bread?" Kenna asked.

"Yes, and it may be helpful to get the mead from Arryn," Bryn replied. "I want to put some herbs in it to help keep a chill from setting in."

"The weather is fair and not too cold," Kenna said. "The mead will help, I'll find Arryn."

"Wait a moment, Kenna. There is something I have been meaning to ask you, and well, we never seem to be alone."

"What is that, Lady Bryn?"

"Do you speak with your dragon? With words and thoughts?" Bryn asked.

Kenna studied Bryn's face and smiled faintly. "I know few words to say to her, but I hear none in my mind or heart, though I can sometimes sense what Caraid is thinking. I have been meaning to ask you what happened to your dragon. You did have one once, did you not?"

"My family has always had a Companion."

"Did you have a Companion?" Kenna said and touched Bryn's hand. "Was she killed?"

"I may have had a Companion. I do not now," Bryn replied. "Please bring the mead."

"As you wish, Lady Bryn." Kenna started to leave but turned back to Bryn.

"I suspect, given the clarity with which you understand dragons, that you will again have a Companion at your side," she said and walked back into the rain.

The meal was short and after being assured that each of the company had drunk the herb-laden mead, Bryn got back onto her horse. She leaned over and spoke into her mount's ear. "Steady again, my Pymmar. We ride hard for another few hours, after which you will rest the night and well into the next morning." Pymmar nodded and stamped her foot against the wet ground. Bryn turned to look at Arryn and Thalynder. She nodded at them and urged Pymmar into a run. It was midsummer in the highlands and there was plenty of light, but the rain made for poor visibility. Bryn relied on Pymmar to take her over or around any obstacles on the ground, and she relied on Meydra to keep her eye on the terrain ahead.

The ride gave Bryn plenty of time to think over the recent events—meeting the other dragons, the death of the High Dragon, the raiders, killing a jarl, her growing awareness of other dragons' thoughts, and drifting in and out of the dreams of her youth—all flashed before her as she rode in the rain. She pondered why Kenna and Prince Malcolm remained with her company. Surely there was nothing for Malcolm in Arcaibh, other than Thalynder, but they had warned him that his brother was the prospective suitor. Perhaps he ventured north out of curiosity to see the Stones. Kenna, on the other hand, a Bridei clann member whose own clann had been sent from their homes because of the raiders, might herself be on a personal pilgrimage to the Stones to learn more about her ancestors. On top of all that, Bryn thought about the elves. "Why had her Mother sent them?"

Elder Anethar did not send word to Brymender or Arlendyl, but she did send word with Lothan to Queen Betony. Betony's lands had been under siege many times, and the death of the jarl would no doubt draw raiders again to her realm. Anethar knew that Betony and Bryn were like-minded when it came to dealing with marauders and sending messages. Betony's people were used to hiding store, and themselves, from the raiders and had over the years adopted the same stone-building practices of the clanns of the far north. The raiders could do nothing about the stone buildings in a quick raid and when finding nothing to loot or destroy, would quickly move out of the area. Anethar sent word to Betony to warn her, but she also sent word that Bryn of the Brae was on her pilgrimage. Betony would want to know that the Jewel might at last be found and released.

Arlendyl received word from Queen Betony that Bryn had reached Skiel and was nearing the ferry at Ceann Dùnaid. She did mention that Bryn had been injured in a small raid by a jarl, but that the company continued north, Bryn's injury being small.

Arlendyl in turn contacted the one person who would be most interested in Bryn's progress—the one other remaining High Elf sister—the Lady Adhar. Arlendyl, Anethar and Adhar were sister cousins, descended from the same elder mother and sister lines that went back millennia. The future of the clanns lay with these three women and two others: Anestar of the Bridei, mother of Kenna, currently living on the Isle of Skye, and Albistan, who had moved her clann west across the sea to another large island. It had been many years since any of the other sister cousins had heard from Albistan, but Arlendyl knew where she had moved her clann to distance them from the marauders. Arlendyl sent word to the Emerald Isle, Eire, that Bryn of the Brae would reach Staenis before the end of summer. Soon, the clanns may once again have the Jewel to unite them… so long as all went well.

That was the reason two elves, Neulta and Leus, traveled now to meet Bryn and her company at the northernmost point of the country—to accompany them to Staenis on behalf of the last remaining elves and the Lady Adhar—and be witness to whatever transpired.

❖

The company reached the stopping point for the night and after a quick meal, they retired to sleep. The long hard ride in the rain had tired not only the horses but also their riders. No one spoke more than a few grunts, as they left the fire and found places on the ground to fall down upon. No questions were asked and no decisions made other than to wake before midday and ride to Ceann Dùnaid, where they held out hope that the ferry was still intact. Bryn lay with her back to Meydra, Thalynder pulled close to her chest. The princess fell asleep a few short moments after she laid her head down. Bryn fell asleep, but her mind did not want to stop. It filled her dreams with questions about the Stones and what she would find written by the hands of her ancestors.

There in the dreams, Bryn heard Meydra assure her that all would be well, that changes would take place, but the result would bring hope to the thousands who had been waiting for this one moment. Bryn stirred against Thalynder.

As promised, Bryn did not rouse the others early the following morning, nor did she urge any of them to hurry along as the sun climbed in the sky. The dawn sky was clear, and Ceann Dùnaid was a short three hours north. She did not want to arrive until well after noon, allowing the sun time to lift the fog so she could see across the firth to Arcaibh. Several smaller islands dotted the outer waters that circled the main island, and it would aid them to see their destination before setting out across the open water. They still did not know if they would find the ferry intact or if they would have to take to dragon backs. She considered sending one of the dragons forward to scout the ferry landings. The best suited would be Meydra since she carried no rider.

Bryn moved away from the still-sleeping Thalynder and stood up. The subdued sounds of sleep drifted around her as she walked out past the rest of the company. Even the horses were quiet. She walked out into a small clearing and knelt in the damp grass. With her palms out, she raised her hands north toward Skerrabrae. She recited a small prayer of respect for her ancient family—those who had passed on and became reborn— and the thought of their spirits remaining near comforted her. In her heart she heard many voices, all encouraging, all hopeful. She completed the prayer and stood and faced the east, from whence came the marauders. She watched a few birds as they flew out toward the sea and wondered if they flew as far as the homes of the raiders. She looked up at the birds and said to them, "Take my promise, gulls of the air. Tell the Norsemen that I will do all in my power to quell their invasion into my country."

"Tell me, how do you plan to do that?" Arryn asked, as he came to stand beside her.

Bryn smiled a wry smile at Arryn. "By souring the milk."

CHAPTER THIRTEEN

The ride to Ceann Dùnaid was kept to a leisurely pace. The weather was cool after the previous day of relentless rain, but it was clear and bright and the sky a brilliant blue. Kenna and Malcolm rode their dragons and were winging over the small hamlet long before the others arrived. The two of them maintained a distance from the hamlet and set down in a field to wait for their company's arrival.

From Meydra came the report to Bryn: *The ferry is intact, little sister.*

That is good news, thank you, Bryn replied. *Did you see the elves?*

They are not visible, came the reply, but it was from IronHeart and not Meydra.

Bryn checked her horse as they neared the dragons in the open field. She dismounted and went to Thalynder.

"I want all of us to enter on horseback. I think it best to keep the dragons out of sight. I need to ask something of Meydra," she said as Thalynder slid off her horse. Bryn noted that Thalynder no longer waited to be helped off her horse.

There were other things about Thalynder that had changed as well. She was more confident, yet she was more reserved. Gone was the loud, insecure princess, and in her place was a quiet, stronger Thalynder. It made Bryn a little sad. She liked the nonstop chatter of the princess when she herself was feeling low.

"Bryn will speak with you," Thalynder said to Meydra. "You know, Bryn, you do not have to ask. I know you and Meydra speak when I am asleep."

"She is your Companion," Bryn said. "I respect that."

"Oh, I know you do. It is just that after all these years together, Meydra is as much yours as she is mine. From now on you need not ask for me to act as intermediary."

"If that is your wish."

"It is. Meydra, you will answer to both Bryn and I."

"Yes, Princess," Meydra replied.

Bryn gave Thalynder's hand a squeeze and turned to Meydra.

"We will approach the hamlet on horseback. I would ask that you and the other dragons keep watch on the eastern shores. I do not wish to put the good people of this hamlet in jeopardy with our presence. At the first sight of any who approach from over the sea, tell us immediately. I know your vision is keen, but can you see their coast?"

"No, they are below the horizon," Meydra replied. "Once above it, I will inform you."

"That is all I can ask," Bryn said, and she rubbed Meydra's foreleg. She turned back to Thalynder. "We will have to ride double on the horses. May I ride with you?"

"It would be my pleasure," Thalynder said.

They walked back to the others and Bryn stepped forward and looked at the company. "Prince Malcolm, would do you me the honor of riding my horse, Pymmar, into Ceann Dùnaid? Kenna, you have your choice of mounts."

Kenna looked from Malcolm to Arryn. She looked at the two horses and said, "If I may, I will ride with Arryn."

"Mount up, my friends," Bryn said. "We will enter Ceann Dùnaid and ask for the ferry to take us to Hoy. I will need to stop at a small stall near the ferry to speak with a kinsman. I will meet you at the ferry."

"Will you be taking the princess with you?" Arryn asked.

"I will."

"I'm afraid I will have to accompany you," he said.

Bryn had momentarily forgotten her and Arryn's vow to always flank the princess when in the presence of strangers. She frowned but knew he was right.

"A change of plans is in order." She kissed Thalynder's cheek and spoke to her in a whisper, "This is best, Lynder. Will you ride with the prince?"

"I will, but do not tarry," Thalynder replied.

Bryn looked at the prince. "Would you be so kind as to join Princess Thalynder on her mount, Your Highness?"

"It would be my honor," Prince Malcolm said. He bowed slightly before Thalynder.

"Arryn, please accompany Their Majesties. Kenna, would you please ride with me on Pymmar?" Bryn asked and turned back to Arryn. "Once we enter the hamlet, Kenna and I will meet up with you at the ferry. It would be best if we did not linger." Bryn changed mounts with Malcolm.

"Keep to her back," Arryn said to Kenna.

"I will," Kenna replied and took Bryn's offered hand to mount the horse. Bryn patted Kenna's hand and said, "Thank you for friendship, Kenna. Ready to ride?"

"I have not been this far north," Kenna said. "What can I expect?"

"We go to Ceann Dùnaid, Theòrsa in the common language, which is the northernmost hamlet on the mainland. It has survived many raids by man and many acts of nature. It is cooler and the nights will be cold. The sun will shine longer each day until the summer solstice, when it will shine nearly all day and night." Bryn replied.

"That will be something to see," Kenna said. "Tell me more."

"The water between the mainland and the small islands was once a solid mass, and my ancestors told of land between the islands existing before the ice came. Some of the old stories were that the ice carved the land away, and the islands were left to provide home to the few animals that did not leave during the bitter cold years."

"My clann does not speak much about these old homes," Kenna said. "How did the inhabitants survive?"

"A small band of men and elves ventured over the ice to the islands and found them rich in fertile land, with an abundance of fish and seals that were easily accessible in the little firths and lochs." Bryn patted Kenna's hand, clinging to her waist.

"Clanns established homes on the islands and eventually the Stones of Staenis were carved and erected. The Ring of Stones was made, and Skerrabrae became the gathering point of the northern clanns. There the Clann Brae became the High Clann of the north, with all other clanns united under the gentle leadership of the Brae elders."

"Why did the clanns leave?"

Bryn shook her head. "You do not know these stories?"

"My mother does not like telling the old stories. I believe she is too sad to want to remember her home up here," Kenna said above the wind. "I want to know more than she will tell."

Bryn sighed and continued. "When the men from over the North Sea came and the raids began, the clanns remained on the islands, rebuilding after each raid, wishing to preserve their way of life. Eventually, the clanns could no longer stay the raiders and moved from island to island, to return at last to the mainland.

"The Stones lay abandoned, with only the Arch Druids making the pilgrimage to the Stones to carve new words and symbols, recording important events that took place. The younger clann members all heard the same stories about the Stones and the significance to their ancestors. Some braved the seas and made pilgrimages of their own, thus forging a new tradition and making the pilgrimage to the Stones a rite of passage."

"And that is why you go to register for the pilgrimage?"

"Yes, all Druids, at least those of my clann, are now encouraged to make a pilgrimage to the Stones before the thirtieth anniversary of their birth. Most wait until their children are old enough to be left in the care of others before making the long journey. Others take family with them. That is why, in the hamlet of Ceann Dùnaid, the clanns set up a house where those traveling to the Stones on pilgrimage could stop and register their names with the elders. It is something I must do. You too should register if you intend on making the trek to Staenis."

"I do," Kenna said. "Thank you for taking me with you. I too wish to put down my name, though I do not know much about the pilgrimage."

"It is time you change that," Bryn said. "The young would be better able to understand why the elders are so passionate about our heritage if they made the journey themselves."

"True. That was my thought when I decided to accompany you after the death of the High Dragon. That, and I love taking Caraid flying."

Bryn thought about the other dragon and Kenna. "How is it that you have your own dragon?"

"I was wondering when you would ask about her," Kenna replied. "I am the daughter of Anestar. She is the leader of our clann and the Queen of Skye. My father chose her from a Druid clann and she was given permission to marry into his house."

Bryn chuckled. She placed her hand over Kenna's and gave it a squeeze. "My mother is Arlendyl. Kenna, you and I are sister cousins."

Kenna laughed. "I knew there was much to like about you. So my being drawn to you was because we are family."

"Family, Druids, women of like mind," Bryn said. "All things to admire about each other. What do you hope to find at Staenis?"

"Insight. That and perhaps the Jewel."

The Jewel, Bryn thought. She had heard that bedtime story so many times, always believing the Jewel was a metaphor. A spiritual symbol that gave the elders something to describe to the young clann members, something the younger ones could see in their minds. It made no sense to her that the Jewel would be something you could hold in your hand.

"What do you think the Jewel is?" Bryn asked Kenna. They had reached the outer houses of the hamlet, and Bryn had slowed her horse to walk.

"A deep green stone that when lit by the sun sends a rainbow of colors into the sky, and all the clanns see the colors and know the Jewel calls them. What do you think it is?"

"A symbol," Bryn said. "A token that symbolizes the coming together of the clanns. Not a real gem."

"What is not a real gem?" Prince Malcolm asked as he checked his horse next to Pymmar.

"The Jewel the clanns speak of in our lore," Kenna replied.

"What do you think it is?" Kenna asked Arryn. His horse was on the far side of the three, and he was dismounting.

"The Jewel?" Arryn asked. "A leader. A rare and precious someone who will find the passion to unite the clanns for one purpose."

Bryn looked at Arryn. His answer spoke to her heart. A leader. That was exactly what the Jewel had to be, she thought. The clanns were waiting for someone to lead them again. Arryn could be that leader. He *is* a warrior, she thought. And he is just. Or Kenna, whose mother was after all the queen of a clann. Bryn mulled over the others in the company and thought any of them could be a leader, including Thalynder.

The rest of the company dismounted and walked their horses into the hamlet. The little noises of daily life greeted and cheered them. There were no signs of recent raids, and as the group entered the center of the small village, the inhabitants came out to meet them. They were warm and friendly and seemed to expect the company. At the center of the hamlet was a well with a single structure of stone, simple in design with circles carved around the bottom, beautiful in its simplicity. The people of the hamlet began to gather at the well, and as the company approached, an older man stepped forward and held his hands out in a gesture of welcome. He approached Prince Malcolm first and embraced him. "I have word from your father," the man said.

"He knows I am here?" Prince Malcolm raised his eyebrows in amazement. "I did not know he was even aware I had left Britannia."

"He sends greetings and urges you to continue your quest. He awaits word."

Next, the older man greeted Thalynder. "Your father is encouraged by the presence of Prince Lludd's brother, Prince Malcolm. He sends his love and wishes to assure you that all is well at home."

Thalynder embraced the man but did not speak. He had not addressed her as a princess.

The man approached Arryn next and after a moment embraced him warmly. "It has been many years since we saw the Epidii this far north. You are most welcome. Your liege wishes you to know he is grateful for your service and understands your need for this quest. Greetings have also come from the clann at Islay. They extend their greatest pleasure at your presence here."

"It has been far too long since the Epidii ventured anywhere beyond their own homes," Arryn replied. "I intend to change that situation. Islay will again walk this path."

The man smiled at Arryn and patted his back. He approached Bryn and Kenna next, and stopped in front of Kenna. He took Kenna's hand in his, leaned over, and kissed her cheek. "The Bridei have also been too long away from this part of the country. Your father and mother send word as well. They wish you to know they are glad you have decided to make this pilgrimage. Your mother especially wishes to see you find that which is hidden."

Kenna embraced the gentleman and said, "Like the Epidii, I too intend to change the minds of the Bridei and be not so long in returning." He smiled at her.

When he turned to face Bryn, the man bowed his head and waited. Bryn reached out to touch his chin. "You bow to the wrong woman," she whispered as she embraced him.

"No, Brae," he said in her ear. "I know to whom I owe this privileged meeting."

They released each other, and Bryn noticed the people were watching, a collective breath being held, waiting. The man held her hand.

"Welcome, Bryn of the Brae, we have waited long for you to make this pilgrimage. I am Gement, elder of Ceann Dùnaid."

"Thank you, Elder," Bryn replied. "The friendly greeting from so many warms my heart." Bryn smiled at the townspeople and turned back to Gement. "My friends and I wish to use the ferry to reach Hoy."

"It is at your disposal. Your mother sends one wish."

"What wish does my mother send?"

"That you return to your people." Gement bowed his head again.

Bryn looked at Gement for a long moment. Each day, each step that brought her closer to the Stones and to Skerrabrae had been forged long before she was born. All the preparations, all the instruction from her parents, it all led to this journey. She was being tasked with something she was unsure of how to accomplish. Everyone wanted the Jewel to be found. Was that something she was meant to do, or was she leading someone else to find it? Arryn, perhaps? Thalynder. Yes, it could be Thalynder. All those years in her court meant to bring her here now. Or it could be one of the others. Malcolm? Kenna? Either could be the one to discover the Jewel. Bryn's own knowledge of the country, her ties to the island, had led this company north. In her heart she knew it was not a coincidence.

Bryn looked at the people around her—they were all waiting for something or someone. They looked at her the same way the subjects back in the Realm that Touches Two Seas looked to the king when he was about to speak, their lives dependent upon the king's words.

She smiled and gently touched Gement's cheek with her palm. "Now, what daughter could go against her mother's wish?"

The small house at the end of the hamlet was as unremarkable on the outside as all of the other houses there. Sturdily built of stone and thatch, with a wide door and several windows, it could have been home to anyone. Inside the home, though, was where the difference lay. The mantel over the fireplace looked like all Druid homes. A symbol of each element, earth, sea and sky, sat on the right side of the mantelpiece—the governing side. A stone, carved with never-ending circles in different sizes and shapes, sat at the left side of the mantelpiece—the spiritual side. In the center sat the *book*—the heart of the family, the lifeblood of the clann. In this house the book was joined by another book, one in which were recorded the names of all those who came to register their pilgrimage.

Inside, a woman waited quietly while Gement, Kenna and Bryn entered through the wide door. A fire crackled in the hearth and the room was warm and inviting. The woman rose from the table in the center of the room and approached Kenna and Bryn. Gement took the smaller of the two books from the mantelpiece and placed it on the table. Then he stepped back to warm his hands by the fire. The woman, cloaked in gray cloth, appeared to be old by the telling of years, but her eyes shone with a youthful light. She silently embraced Kenna first. After giving Bryn a quick but warm hug, she led them to the table and sat down opposite them. On the table was a narrow stick, a small knife, and a quill feather.

"Can you write your name, Bridei?" the woman asked.

"I can leave my mark," Kenna replied proudly.

"Place your mark here." The woman opened the book to a section near the back and pointed to other marks and names. "Here is where the Bridei, those who have come before you, have left their marks."

The woman handed Kenna the stick, which was a piece of charred wood that had been sharpened to a fine point. Kenna made her mark on the top of the page where the woman indicated. She looked at the page opposite. "Are these my kin?"

"Yes," the woman replied. "This one here is the name Anestar."

"That is my mother," Kenna said. "That is my mother's mark."

"That is her name spelled in letters. I will write your name next to your mark."

The woman wrote Kenna's name next to her mark and that pleased her. "Thank you," she said.

The woman laid the stick on the table. She looked at Bryn and held out her hand. Bryn placed her left hand in the woman's leathery palm. The older woman took up the small knife and said, "You understand the ritual?"

"I do," Bryn replied. "You may have my blood."

Kenna watched as the woman took the knife and pierced the thick pad of skin on the thumb side of Bryn's palm. The woman took the quill and dipped the tip in the blood. She opened the book to a section near the front and handed the quill to Bryn. "Place your name there." She pointed to a space above several other names.

Bryn took the quill and wrote Bryn~Brae on the book's thick parchment page. She saw the names of those she knew below her own. Her name now joined those of her mother, her father, and two of her brothers. She was very pleased.

"Did you bring your mother's book?" the woman asked.

"Yes," Bryn replied. "It is on my horse outside." The woman looked at Gement, and he left to fetch the book. The women were silent while he was gone. When Gement returned, he set the book in front of Bryn.

"Open to a page near the front that resembles this page," the woman said.

Bryn opened the book and found the page the woman wanted. She saw the names of her family, going back many generations, written on the page. The woman turned Bryn's palm up again and dipped the quill into the blood. She did not hand the quill to Bryn, but instead turned the book to face her direction. She wrote Bryn's name in the book, the script matching all the names written above hers. It then occurred to Bryn that this woman had witnessed several generations of Brae that came through the hamlet. This would make her quite old indeed.

"Yes," the woman said with a smile. "As old as the dragons."

Immediately Bryn knew who the woman was and gave a short bow of her head. "Elder Mother Adhar, I am humbled by your presence." Bryn knew the Lady Adhar, Elven Queen, and one-time Druid elder—daughter of Ahndulyl, Elf Queen of the first race of elves that populated the land—had been born long before the ice cut the lands apart. Bryn's mother had told her that Adhar had been born under the wings of a dragon and was one of the first to be separated from her dragon for reasons known only to her and her husband, the Elf King Lionin. Adhar rarely left the cool forests located at the heart of Britannia, and her presence, though unexpected, was neither unwanted nor uninvited. "Are the others with you?" Bryn asked.

"They are," Lady Adhar replied. She stood up and removed her outer cloak, revealing a tunic of deep forest green. Upon it the Tree of Life was embroidered in gold thread. There was no dragon on her tree; instead the tree had silver threads fashioned into the likeness of stars with long tails that resembled dragon tails.

Gement placed a small cloth bundle on the table before Lady Adhar. She opened it and removed a small headpiece of gold. She placed it on her head where it rested on her forehead. In the center was a small emerald held by gold threads that were fashioned to look like leaves.

She stood up and Bryn and Kenna followed. Lady Adhar embraced Kenna. "Find the others and tell them Bryn will be along momentarily. I wish a word alone with my daughter before you send the Epidii."

Kenna bowed her head and left the house, leaving Bryn alone with the Elf Queen.

Lady Adhar embraced Bryn and held her tightly for several long seconds. When she released Bryn, she pointed to the benches near the fire. "Please sit, Bryn," Lady Adhar said. "Gement, will you ask the other two guests to join us now."

Bryn sat down and waited as Gement left the room. She looked at Lady Adhar and struggled with how to form her question.

"I can see by your frown that you are concerned," Lady Adhar said. "There is good reason for concern and you will find things written on the Stones that will not make sense to you. You will have Meydra to aid you in those things. There will be other things that Meydra may not be able to explain. That is where my kin, Neulta and Leus, may be of assistance to you. It is important that you understand fully the words and the meaning behind the Standing Stones."

"Why is it so important? Do the elves accompany everyone on pilgrimage?"

"No, Bryn. they do not. When Brymeldan, father of your father, brought the clann south, there were only a few new members of your clann, babies and small children, who had not seen the Stones. Those few had no need to understand the meaning behind the words, as their parents would tell them the stories in time, so they went to the Stones unaccompanied by elves."

"Were the members of my family accompanied?"

"No, Bryn. Your mother and father had already been to the Stones. Your mother had already been given the knowledge long before she wed your father. She and your father took your two older brothers when they too reached the age of consent. I was sad to hear of your third brother's passing before he had seen the Stones." Adhar touched Bryn's hand.

"Your parents knew that you were capable of making this journey alone, and given the request of King Thamen that his daughter accompany you, your mother and father decided not to accompany you."

"How do you come to know all of this?" Bryn asked.

"Your mother and I are always in each other's thoughts."

A curtain moved at the back of the house and Gement came back into the room, followed by two richly robed elves. Bryn watched them enter the room. The female, Neulta, was dressed in a gray-colored tunic of gossamer-like fabric that covered her arms to the wrists and rose up to cover her throat. The wisps of fabric resembled the morning mist as it came in quietly and covered the fields. She wore a darker gray bodice upon which the Tree of Life was embroidered in silver thread, much like Bryn's own. The male, Leus, was dressed in hose and a tunic the color of robin's eggs. He wore a jerkin the color of a fawn's coat, and it too was embroidered with the Tree of Life, his tree in gold thread. Neither bodice nor jerkin had a dragon with the Tree. Bryn started to stand, but Adhar placed a hand over hers and said, "They come to see you, Bryn."

Both Neulta and Leus approached Bryn and knelt before her and Lady Adhar. They bowed their heads and waited. Lady Adhar placed her hand on the head of each elf. "Raise your faces and greet your cousin, Bryn of the Skerrabrae."

First, to suggest that Neulta and Leus were cousins to Bryn would mean that they were Adhar's children. Bryn knew the elves lived long lives, but something didn't fit. Second, it would mean Bryn too was elf-kind. Yes, she knew her mother came from the half elven, but Bryn did not believe it possible for herself to be so favored, so she dismissed the idea from her mind. She looked at the two as they raised their faces toward her.

"I am honored to meet you," Bryn said. "I welcome your company."

Neulta blushed and touched the hem of Bryn's tunic. "It is my honor, Bryn of the Brae. Long have we waited to witness this pilgrimage."

Bryn inwardly frowned. What could she mean? Surely they had not been waiting all their lives to go to the Stones at Staenis.

Leus touched the hem of Bryn's tunic and said, "It is my honor, Bryn of the Brae. This is a great gift."

Bryn shook her head slightly. She was confused by the way these two addressed her. I should be the one bowing before them, she thought. They are, after all, elves. Ancients in a world still in its infancy. She needed to clear her head. "I need to find my companions and advise them that we will be two more. Will you be ready to join us soon? Arryn of the Epidii has need to register as well."

"We are ready now, Lady Bryn," Neulta replied. "We will go with you to the others." With that, both Neulta and Leus rose before Lady Adhar. Neulta held out her hand, palm up, and Lady Adhar placed her hand in it.

Leus held his hand out for Bryn, and she followed Lady Adhar's lead, placing her hand in Leus's hand. The two women stood up, and the four of them walked toward the open door. Lady Adhar stopped and turned to Gement. "Remember this day, Gement. Do not let it pass without writing it down."

More riddles, Bryn thought, as the old man bowed low at the words.

Adhar turned to Bryn. "Send the Epidii to me."

The company stood at the ferry and with them were seven horses. Bryn was glad to see that Kenna and Malcolm had decided to ride the horses and not the dragons as they traveled the smaller islands to reach the Stones. Having to wait at each stopping point with the dragons for the rest of the company to catch up had begun to wear on them.

Bryn smiled at the childlike awe the elves evoked in the others. She herself was in awe of them, but on a different level. What she found most wonderful was the way they hid their fierce nature. Taking great pains to remain hidden in the glens and vales had given them the reputation of being secretive and magic. Bryn knew the other side of the elves. The one as told by her mother and grandmother, the one that told of great battles with great beasts and terrible monsters that ruled the land before men and dragons appeared. The elves waged war on all that threatened to control the earth, sea and sky. It was those elves that Bryn had grown up knowing and not the secret, magic elves of children's stories.

Arryn was not long with Lady Adhar, but when the two returned, Bryn noticed the deep frown he wore. Bryn saw that Arryn watched Leus, who was at Bryn's arm. Kenna was watching Lady Adhar and Neulta. Prince Malcolm, standing next to Thalynder, was watching the latter two women, and Thalynder had her eyes on Bryn. Their eyes met and Bryn smiled as the princess took a step forward and bowed her head to Lady Adhar.

"Your presence honors us, Queen Adhar," Thalynder said in her most mature princess voice. "The company and I extend our greetings." Thalynder used the formal greeting for Lady Adhar. A title the elves did not use, nor did the clanns, but the others, those of King Thamen's ilk, chose to pin the title "Queen" on her so as to set her apart from the others. Adhar bristled only enough for Bryn to notice. Thalynder did not.

"Thank you, Princess Thalynder," Lady Adhar said. "This is Neulta. She and her brother, Leus, have been granted permission to join your company to Staenis."

Thalynder introduced the rest of the company with a gracious and practiced manner. She was ever the royal daughter, and her demeanor welcomed the newcomers as if they were new subjects to her realm. Bryn chuckled inside at Thalynder's behavior. When the introductions were complete, Thalynder turned to Bryn.

"Lady Bryn, we await your instruction. We have taken a meal, and if you have not, we will wait until you do so. Otherwise, we are prepared to take the ferry at your command."

"I will take a small meal before we ask the ferryman to take us across." Bryn turned to Lady Adhar. "Have you the time to join us, Elder Mother?"

"No, Daughter. I must leave now." Lady Adhar embraced Bryn and held her tight for a long moment. When the elder woman stepped back, there was the shine of tears in her eyes. "Be careful, Bryn of Skerrabrae. Not only is the knowledge you seek filled with unexpected implications but the road too is filled with surprise threats. The raiders from over the North Sea are, even as we speak, leaving their shores to look for the jarl." As the lady spoke, a group of seven elves approached on horseback. They dismounted and waited for Adhar.

"We will be vigilant," Bryn replied. "Will you take word to my parents?"

"I will tell them that you are well, that the princess is protected and that you are nearing the last leg of your journey north."

"Tell my mother this too." Bryn touched Adhar's hand. "I will return to my people."

Lady Adhar looked at Bryn, her gray eyes burning into Bryn's blue ones. She bowed her head, as did all the elves, including Neulta and Leus, as well as those folk gathered to watch the company's parting. Lady Adhar lifted her head and kissed Bryn lightly on the mouth. "I ask your leave, Lady Bryn," she said and turned to the elves. She gracefully leapt up onto the back of her horse, and with one last smile, she waved at Bryn. She turned her horse and left the ferry dock, followed by the seven elves.

Thalynder watched Adhar and the elves depart. "Well," she said. "Eat something and let us get across before night falls. Where do you have us sleeping tonight, Lady Bryn?"

Bryn took Thalynder's hand and approached Arryn and the others. "I will not be long. We will travel across Hoy and will stop for the night at the foot of the hill overlooking Grimr's Island." Bryn closed the gap between her and Arryn and said, "I do not know what provisions the others have with them; could you see if they need to secure more while I find a meal?"

"I will take care of it, Bryn," Arryn said. "You two go, but do not squander the daylight."

Thalynder laughed and pulled Bryn along. "Come, I know exactly what you shall have to eat."

CHAPTER FOURTEEN

The ferry ride to the island of Hoy was not long, but by the time the horses were taken off and the company ready to get underway, the sun was beginning to tip toward the west. The group would have to ride hard if they wished to make the other side of the small island before nightfall. Even in the early days of summer the sun still set and Bryn wanted them far inland before it did. Although Staenis was only two days' journey from Hoy, Bryn felt the need to reach the Stones before too much time passed. The thought of the raiders coming and catching them exposed weighed heavily on her, and she was tempted to send Thalynder home on Meydra's back.

Bryn pulled her horse up alongside Arryn. "I'm feeling caged," she said. "Being on the smaller island has me rethinking my plans. Do you think I could persuade Thalynder to go home or at least wait for us back in Skiel?"

Arryn chuckled. "No, Bryn, I don't think you could persuade her to do anything that would take her away from you. Do you believe we are in danger on the island?"

"Not on this smaller one. There is no reason to think the raiders will come here until they have made Nis and find the jarl dead. After that they will try to track us. We should be on Arcaibh and in Staenis, or even Skerrabrae, by then. No, it is just being this far north without an army to back us that has me concerned."

"Bryn, if it helps to ease your worry, an army is behind us," Arryn said. "Prince Malcolm sent word to his father about the death of the jarl and possible retaliation, and I would bet my life that a legion of Thamen's own guard is already waiting as far north as Skiel by the time we reach Staenis. The fact that the elves were in Ceann Dùnaid tells me that King Thamen and the other lesser kings know of the raiding party and the jarl's demise. We will not be alone for long."

"Any returning raiding party should be a small contingent at first. A scouting party to find the jarl, followed by a massive return with an army of Norsemen. I do believe we have some time, but I don't want to linger any longer than necessary. There is still the matter of Thalynder's true love to be found."

Arryn laughed. It had been a while since Bryn had heard him laugh so openly, and she waited for him to catch his breath. "You need not play that game any longer, Bryn. Do you not see? She has found her true love. She clings to you like a leech to bare skin."

"She is in love with love," Bryn replied. "You were one to warn me, remember? To be my true love, she would have to give up the throne, children, all those things she would have back in the realm. No, she is happy for the moment only."

"Why do you doubt yourself, Bryn? Many of us love you. Thalynder has the one thing we can't have, and that is your love in return. She'd be a fool to let that go."

"You also have my love, Arryn, as a trusted friend. But Thalynder would be a bigger fool to give up the realm. I won't let her do that." Bryn moved her horse away from Arryn and rode back out to point. The sun sunk further into the west and would soon be below the horizon. Bryn saw a stand of trees in the distance and turned to signal Kenna to join her.

"Ask Caraid to scout that stand of trees," Bryn said. "I'd like to stay there for the night."

"Yes, Bryn," Kenna replied.

Bryn went back to Thalynder. "Lynder, ask Meydra to be a second pair of eyes on that stand of trees. We will sleep there tonight." *Done*, Meydra's voice called in her head.

"Yes, Bryn," Thalynder replied. "Will you sleep with me?"

"If we can get Meydra on the ground nearby. I don't want you sleeping in the open."

"Yes, Bryn."

Bryn smiled at Thalynder. She missed the bossy Thalynder, princess of the realm, but she liked the submissive Thalynder as well. A softer side to Thalynder made Bryn all the more protective of her, and she liked being Thalynder's protector.

The stand of trees was thick and left little room for the dragons to set down and provide shelter. Bryn instructed the dragon riders to ask their dragons to stay as close to the trees as possible and to keep their eyes and ears turned to the east.

"Prince Malcolm, will you ask your dragon to move high and keep an eye on the ferry crossing?"

"I will," Malcolm replied.

Bryn saw Meydra take up a spot east, and Caraid stayed to the north. Bryn feared no reprisal from the western realm, as there were many clannsmen and many hamlets to the west, and they would provide her the defense she needed from that direction.

"Thalynder, you and Kenna should sleep with your backs to the trees," Bryn said. "Arryn, would you and Malcolm take up positions in front of the princess?"

Thalynder started to balk until Bryn took her hand and patted it gently. "I need answers from the elves, but I will join you soon."

The princess, Kenna, and Malcolm prepared a cold supper, while Bryn, Arryn, and the elves sat in conference.

"Our disadvantage is that we cannot control the dragons," Leus said. "If we had the air power, we could be sure of safe passage to Staenis. This pilgrimage must not be forfeited due to the riders' lack of skill."

"That is a callous way to speak about the riders," Arryn said.

Bryn placed her hand on Arryn's arm to calm him before he went too far with Leus. She knew the minds of the elves. What appeared as the elves' cold dismissal of the others was the logical side of their minds coming to the only conclusion possible with the facts laid before them. She understood their warrior side and knew that if Arryn thought about it, he would also understand.

"The dragon riders have been quite helpful," Bryn said. "I have not met with any resistance from them or their dragons. And you forget, cousin, the dragons cannot fight. It is against the most ancient and most sacred pact between the dragons and the Companions."

"Arryn of the Epidii," Neulta said. "My brother and I mean no disrespect. However, he is right. This pilgrimage is too important to the clanns to be left in the hands of others. As a clannsman, you must feel the importance that stirs the very air you breathe." Neulta turned to look at Bryn. She spoke in a voice full of sadness and concern.

"My brother and I were asked by our mother, Lady Adhar, to accompany you on your pilgrimage. She stated that the journey may be dangerous, but that we were to help ensure the journey to Staenis was not altered nor interfered with by outsiders. There will come a time in the next few days when we will all know the true nature of this pilgrimage. From that point forward, you, Arryn of the Epidii, and you, Bryn of the Skerrabrae, will be faced with decisions that will affect many others, and not only those who accompany you now. You will have to choose, Lady Bryn. My brother and I are here to witness the choice. We cannot help you with your decision. We cannot ask anything of you, nor guide your steps in any way. We can only witness. As for the others, they too will be made to understand what lies at the heart of the words carved on the Stones, and they may wish to influence your decision. Neither of you can hear their words. You must decide for yourself what the Stones mean to you and how you will be moved by them."

Bryn's pulse quickened. There was a decision waiting for her and Arryn at the Stones. The clues she had stumbled upon during their journey thus far had led her to that one conclusion: the journey had always been meant for her and not for Thalynder. Her mother and father knew it, even the king knew it. Arryn may have suspected it, but never said a word about it. She had, from the beginning, believed something long in the coming awaited her at Staenis. On impulse, Bryn removed her sword from its scabbard at her belt and held it in the dim twilight. The sword sparkled as if lit from within with moonlight. Cool silver flashes of light danced across the blade. She turned it so that the words engraved on the steel could be clearly read.

Leus held out his hand to touch the blade. In a soft singsong manner, he read the words, "*Till gu talamh, leug camhanaich.*"

"What does that mean?" Arryn asked.

"Return it to us, precious Jewel of the dawn," Neulta replied.

Bryn had never heard it translated that way. It had always been read to her by her Druid teachers as *Precious Jewel of the dawn, return to earth*, and she had always believed that it meant something was lost and needed to be found. Listening to Neulta speak the words anew, Bryn felt a thrill run through her blood. The Jewel was *not* lost, it needed only to show itself. She inhaled sharply and looked at Arryn. "I think I know where to find the Jewel."

Thalynder looked out over the others as they slept on the ground in front of her. She rose quietly and walked out toward the opening of the little stand of trees. She could see Bryn silhouetted in the moonlight, her sword drawn and flashing in the clear light. As she stepped toward Bryn, Meydra set down on the ground near Bryn. Thalynder moved out of the trees to stand next to Bryn and face Meydra.

"The night is clear," Thalynder said.

"It is," Bryn said. "Why are you awake, Lynder?"

"I do not sleep well when you are away." Thalynder took Bryn's free hand in hers. "Your sword sparkles as if it is full of the moon's own light."

Bryn held the sword aloft and watched the light dance off the blade. "It was forged at night under a full moon, and legend tells that the moon lent her rays to temper the steel. Lynder, I have asked Meydra for a report on the raiders. I did not take the time to wake you to ask this request of your dragon."

"Bryn, Bryn, how many times have I seen you and Meydra chattering among yourselves? I know you and Meydra are friends. And I've told you not to wait to speak with her. As this journey has become more dangerous and more secretive, I appreciate your attention to detail and fully expect you to ask things of her when I am not available."

"Thank you Lynder." Bryn raised Thalynder's hand to her lips and placed a soft kiss on the palm of her hand. Bryn released her grip and turned to Meydra. "What have you seen?" Bryn asked, spoken aloud for Thalynder's benefit, as Meydra had already reported to Bryn several minutes before Thalynder had joined them in the open.

"The coast remains clear of enemies," Meydra stated. "Caraid has also seen nothing coming in from the north. You remain alone on the island."

"Thank you, Meydra," Thalynder said. "You are a loyal and dutiful Companion."

"It is my pleasure to serve," Meydra said.

"Are you planning to sleep, Bryn?" Thalynder asked, and dismissed Meydra.

"No," Bryn replied. "I have need to speak with Neulta and Leus. You should sleep, Lynder. Tomorrow will be a long day and some of it will be spent on foot."

"I leave you to the secrets of the elves, my Bryn. Do not forget, you are not an elf and you *do* need your sleep. I miss your scent next to me, Bryn of the Brae."

"I will be with you again soon. Once we are in Staenis, we will be where we can sleep with Meydra again. Go now, I'll not be long with the elves."

Bryn watched Thalynder until she was again resting with her back against the tree. Bryn looked at the others and accepted a nod from Arryn. He must feel the same anxiousness in the air. She walked over to where Neulta and Leus sat in quiet conversation, well away from the others. She replaced her sword in its scabbard and sat across from the two elves.

"You are troubled, cousin," Leus said.

"I am only concerned about the welfare of my friends," Bryn replied. "Had I known that this seemingly innocent journey would turn out to be fraught with great peril, I would never have suggested the pilgrimage."

"Lady Bryn, you were destined to make this pilgrimage this year," Neulta said. She looked over at Arryn and the others. "The Epidii does not sleep so long as you are awake. I admire his loyalty."

"He is my friend," Bryn said. "He has also been charged with protecting the Princess Thalynder. I am lucky to have both the Epidii and the Bridei with me."

"Yes," Leus said, "though you should have your own company of guardsmen, Lady Bryn."

"Your allusions to my station confound me," Bryn said. "I know my mother is regarded highly in the clann, as is my father, but I am simply their daughter. I am nothing more."

"You are the daughter of Arlendyl, that is enough," Neulta said. "The daughter of a high clann, with ties to the first dragons, you are a dragon Companion as well. It is known to us that you were chosen by a dragon and that the dragon was given to another to pay a debt."

"It is why you do not tell the others that you can speak with the dragons," Leus said. "You do not wish to draw attention to this ability. It is a wise position you take with this gift."

"Surely, there are others who hear the dragons as I do."

"The Bridei, Kenna, has limited communication with Caraid," Neulta said. "She can understand some of the words and that allows them a tenuous bond."

"What do you mean, she understands some of the words?"

"The Bridei does not understand the language of the dragons," Leus said. "She learned a few words from her mother, Anestar. She does not have the knowledge that you have, nor was she schooled as you were in the lore and languages."

"I was schooled in the lore, yes, but I do not remember learning words to use with a dragon."

"You were, by Arlendyl. Your gift of languages aids you in many other ways," Neulta said. "We have spoken with you in our own language since we first met you, Lady Bryn. Except when the need for the others to understand us was great, you have been speaking to us in our tongue."

Bryn chuckled. "So that is why the princess said we were secretive."

Neulta smiled. "We understood you to be schooled in the old languages, yet still expected to be speaking with you in the new tongue. I must say, though, I am glad we do not have to resort to that language often, as it hurts my throat. It is enough to speak with the Epidii in the new tongue." She reached out and held her palm up toward Bryn. "You may not need the dragon to explain the words on the Stones, Bryn of the Brae. I believe you will have no trouble reading or comprehending the words on your own."

"I may be able to read them and understand their use. I am not sure I will understand their meaning."

"As you read the words on the Stones, you will begin to understand their meaning. Your instruction over the years was meant to bring you to this moment," Leus said. "We know this already: it is what you do with the knowledge that lies in the balance. Your decision must be entirely your own. For that to happen, the others must not speak to what they see at the Stones."

"That would not be fair to the Epidii or to the Bridei," Bryn replied. "They have as much right to the Stones as I do."

"True," Neulta said. "Though they will not see what you see. They will not understand the words or symbols as you will. They will only see those things that pertain to their clann. You will see many other things. They will begin to understand the true depth of your knowledge once they hear the Stones begin to whisper. It is at that time that they will want to have their say."

"They may need my knowledge," Bryn said. "If I am here to shed light, to be the one who holds the door open, then surely they must have their say."

"Whatever must be, will be," Leus said. "The Stones will reveal all."

"I will be mindful of the whispers," Bryn said. "For now, I must sleep."

Leus and Neulta stood up and watched as Bryn left them and walked toward the others. They waited until she was again in the dark under the trees before turning toward the north to sit and watch the sky.

Bryn did not go directly to the others. She walked through the trees and back out to the open ground, where she waited for Meydra to join her. Meydra descended silently in front of Bryn, her scales shimmering in the moonlight.

"What keeps you awake, little sister?" Meydra asked, her voice soft and low.

"The sound of my own heartbeat."

"That is not what is keeping you awake."

"No." Bryn took a step toward Meydra. "I have been lonely for so long. My brothers killed by the raiders. Spending all my years in the shadow of all the other men and women of the court. For so long I have held Thalynder in my heart, believing it was she who stilled the wild beating and calmed my thoughts. I know now that was not the case. It was you that stilled my wild heart, you that calmed my distress, and you that sang me to sleep. This I feel is truth. Now I question my reasons for bringing Thalynder on this journey, for it has grown far too dangerous."

"Perhaps you should send her home," Meydra said. "It may be best for her to give her father a firsthand account of what has happened with the raiders."

"Yes, King Thamen deserves an accurate accounting. You know it will not be easy to send Thalynder home. She was on her own quest for true love. I know she believes she loves me, but we both know her heart. She will do as her father wishes and marry a prince. She is a loyal subject of her realm."

"Allow her to continue to the Stones. From there she may make her own decision to return to her father. There is much knowledge there she will need to think over and decide how to address." Meydra bowed her head and allowed Bryn to place her forehead against her brow. Bryn reached out and placed a hand on each of Meydra's cheeks, and Meydra moved her tail to rest against Bryn's back. They stood that way, human to dragon, for many long minutes.

Keeping watch over the Standing Stones of Staenis, a lone dragon felt his heart glow with a peaceful warmth. He began to sing, and the song lifted into the air and made its way south toward the heather moors of the island of Hoy. His song was heard by IronHeart, Prince Malcolm's FireBreather, and IronHeart opened his heart to hear the soft melody. It spoke to him of the now lost pleasures of flying without purpose, and his heart filled with glee. He glanced out across the open plain and saw Caraid look down from her perch on a high hill in the north. Her gaze was fixed on the grove where the dragon riders slept. She raised her head and her voice joined that of the distant dragon. Together they filled the night with a soothing melody, a dragon song of peace that filled all who heard with contentment.

In the moonlight, Meydra and Bryn let the dragon song wash over them as they stood obscured by their own light…one that rivaled the moon herself.

Malcolm and Arryn were deep in conversation when Bryn approached them at dawn. She waited until she sensed a break and offered each a small round bread roll. "May I offer you gentlemen some warm bread?"

"Thank you," Malcolm said and bowed his head slightly. "Lady Bryn, I have something I feel I need to say to you."

Bryn hesitated a moment, then smiled at the prince. "Yes, Prince Malcolm?"

The prince stood holding the bread roll, passing it from one hand to the other. He started to speak but paused. Bryn knew he was finding it difficult to frame the right words.

"What is it that concerns you, Prince Malcolm? Something I can shed light on perhaps?"

"As is your gift, Lady Bryn, you see through the mist. I need to know what it is you think you will find at the Stones. I need to understand if this will affect my own people."

Bryn looked at Arryn. She knew that Prince Malcolm was beginning to piece things together and had tried to get information from Arryn. To his credit, Arryn did not elaborate on the true nature of the journey.

"I expect to find a record of my ancestors," Bryn replied.

"There is more," Malcolm said. "You have been met by the Elf Queen, and you have elves traveling with you now. Leus tells me that my father has sent troops toward Northumbria and Queen Betony. Princess Thalynder's father has sent his own troops north and they are approaching Skiel. There is more to this journey than the pilgrimage of a Druid."

"You say that word as if it carries the taste of rotting fruit in your mouth," Arryn said as he stood up and placed a hand on Malcolm's shoulder. "Lady Bryn is a Druid, yes, but she is also a Lady, as I have reminded you in the past. And you forget, I am also a Druid."

"Please, Arryn," Bryn said. "I am sure it is because the prince is not accustomed to the presence of a Druid. He is unaware of our meaning of the pilgrimage." Bryn bristled inwardly at the way Malcolm referenced her ancestors with his manner, but she needed allies and not enemies.

"You are right, Your Highness. There is more to this journey now than there was when it first began. The killing of the jarl has changed the journey considerably. What started out as a simple pilgrimage to honor my ancestors, something you do as well in Britannia, has now become a quest to find the Jewel of legend before the raiders destroy the entire island looking for it.

I am now truly convinced that this is why they are here. The jarl told me he has had Druids in his country. Thus, the legend must be known to him and his king. The time has come for all the peoples of Alban to come together to decide how we are to live with these raiding Norsemen. Do we allow them to continue to plunder, rape and murder our kinsmen?" Bryn absently touched the Tree of Life on her tunic.

"Believe me, the raiders will return, their numbers will be great, and their anger will consume them. The island we all share, with Alban in the north, Northumbria at her midpoint, and Britannia in the south, will soon be overrun by men determined to raze every village. Destroy every crop. Kill all living creatures, including our children. Men who will stop only when nothing under the stars moves between here and the sea at your father's back." Bryn turned and saw that the rest of the company stood listening to her speak. She took a breath.

"It began as a simple pilgrimage for a simple Druid. A pilgrimage to see the Standing Stones of Staenis before I am to become waiting lady to a queen." Bryn looked out through the trees, her eyes fixed on some distant object. She continued but her voice was quiet and carried a note of sadness. "Princess Thalynder will return to the Realm that Touches Two Seas and will someday rule as queen, Sir Arryn may return to captain a legion, and I will fade into the tapestry of my sovereign. This was our last chance at a summer of no responsibility except that which we held for ourselves. It has since been altered by circumstance out of our control. The death of the High Dragon brought us together, but how much of that was coincidence? And what about the jarl and his party still on our island long after the winter thaw?

"So much has happened that I now believe this was our destiny: to meet here and now to lend aid to one another. None of us embarked on this journey believing we would meet with raiders and face death. And no one thought there would be anything more at the Stones than relics of a long-lost community. Sadly, this is no longer a simple pilgrimage." Bryn turned back to face the others. "Now it is a quest to find the one thing that will unite all the peoples of this great island in defense of our lives. We go to the Stones to find the means to unite the clanns. We go to the Stones to find the Jewel of legend. And whether you find it, Prince Malcolm, or Arryn finds it, or Thalynder, Kenna or I find it, is not the issue. It matters not *who* wields that symbol that may unite the peoples of this land. What matters is that we *are* united."

Bryn held her breath as she tried to read the emotions that held the others in a tight embrace. She looked at Thalynder.

Thalynder took a step toward her. "We could turn back and leave you and the elves to finish this journey," Thalynder said. "That would be the easy way out. If I am any judge of character, I would say that all who stand here now will choose to follow you to Staenis. They have met with the enemy once and know his ruthless heart. They have seen wondrous things—like elves that appear for no reason—that to some may seem mystical and otherworldly, and yet they remain. For myself, I choose to remain at your side. If there is the chance that something may be found there that would aid my realm, my people and yours, then that is where I *must* be. To be elsewhere would be folly for a ruler."

Arryn stepped forward. "It is true. At first I believed I was being sent on a fool's errand: to watch two women play in the forest for a few weeks. I know better now. Princess Thalynder is a brave and trustworthly royal. Protecting her is a privilege." He raised his fist to his heart. "Lady Bryn, I have seen you scout, kill, and skin game. I have seen you devise cunning and carefully thought-out battle strategy. I have also seen you take a blow that would have had many a man take to their bed for months. Even if this were a simple pilgrimage for a simple Druid, I would follow you until you no longer drew breath. I believe the Jewel will be found, Bryn of the Brae. I believe we will bring it back for the clanns to see and it will unite us. I *am* a captain of a legion, but I am also a Druid. I am a sworn guardian of this island."

Kenna drew an arrow from her quiver and drew her sword. She walked over to Bryn and placed both on the ground at her feet. "Though I am a dragon rider of another realm and could easily leave you and the others to finish your journey, or even go out on my own quest for the Jewel, I will not. My clann has long since deserted the notion of unity with the other clanns. My mother holds her tongue because she can find nothing good to say. I too believe *we* will find the Jewel."

Neulta and Leus stepped forward. Neulta placed her hand, palm out, on her forehead. She spoke first in her own tongue, followed by the common tongue of the company: "My brother and I, your cousins, can make no pledge, offer no alternatives. We are here to witness a pilgrimage, we will stay the course."

Bryn looked at each of those who had stepped forward and nodded her head in admiration. She stopped at Malcolm and met his gaze. She waited.

Prince Malcolm, heir to the throne of Britannia, captain of the King's Army and dragon rider, bowed his head for a moment. When he raised it, he looked at Bryn. "Though I still do not understand the lore behind the legend or the need to find the Jewel, it would be my honor to accompany you and your company, Lady Bryn, Druid daughter of Skerrabrae, to the Stones of Staenis."

CHAPTER FIFTEEN

The route that led to the other side of the island was not as long as first judged, but it was slow going on foot. The horses had to be led through the thick heather and wet marshes that took the company to where they could cross to the main island of Arcaibh. The sea had risen and tides now covered sections of Hoy that had once been higher and drier. When the company did reach a point where they could see across to the main island, they could also see that crossing was not going to be easy. There was no ferry from Hoy to Grimr—a small island between Hoy and the main island of Arcaibh—and therefore no way for the horses to cross. Bryn dismounted at a small stretch of beach and waited until the others did the same before she spoke.

"Any suggestions?" she asked.

"We could leave the horses, take the dragons, and fly right to Staenis," Malcolm said.

"Yes, and I would ask that someone stay to watch the horses and our store," Arryn said. "That would have one of us not reaching the Stones."

"Why leave someone with the horses? There are no inhabitants on this island and we have had no word on the return of the Norsemen," Thalynder said.

"Horses wander, birds pick at food sacks, fox, marten, all would want what little store we carry," Arryn replied.

"As there are three dragons, three dragon riders and seven in the company, we could double up on the backs of the dragons, and still leave one behind with the horses," Kenna said.

"It would be difficult to choose who would stay behind," Thalynder said. She walked over to Bryn, placed her hand on Bryn's arm, and gave her a warm smile. "You look tired."

"I am a bit," Bryn replied. "As I see it, if we take to the dragons, one of us is left behind to stay with the horses. True, we need them to be tended, and we need the store to be available to us when we return. However, we cannot use the dragons to get from here to Staenis, then Staenis to Skerrabrae and expect to be back before sunset. That would mean taking supplies with us. And there is the question of whom do we leave with the horses?" Bryn looked at the company. She proposed a solution to Meydra. *Could we harness the horses so that two of you could carry them over to the main island?*

Yes, came the answer. *Yet there is no need. If you wait until twilight, the tide will be low enough for you to cross. It is in your book, Bryn.*

Bryn opened the sack that hung from Pymmar's saddle. She took out the book and thumbed through the pages. "There may be something about the crossing in here." She found the passages Meydra referred to and read aloud from the diary of her mother:

The way north was blocked by the sea. With no ferry to cross, our only thought was how those before us had managed to make the crossing? We decided to wait until morning before trying another route. As the day drew to a close, the tide began to recede, and we saw that the way across to Arcaibh could be made on horseback. The water level dropped considerably between Grimr and Hoy, and we knew we could manage the horses in the low tide. It is midsummer and the weather is mild enough for the animals to be in the water. The horses

*will not suffer. If all goes well, we will be on Arcaibh before the sun
has fully set.*

Bryn placed the book back into the sack. "I suggest we
ready ourselves to make the crossing. We will ride hard once we
make land, reaching the section we need to cross from Grimr
to Arcaibh before the sun has set. Prepare yourself for a little
water."

"How do you know that is still the way of things?" Thalynder
asked.

"Meydra has confirmed it," Bryn replied without thinking.

The company stared at Bryn.

"When did Meydra confirm this for you, Bryn?" Thalynder
asked.

Bryn led Thalynder aside and took her hands. She kissed the
princess on each cheek.

"I meant to tell you sooner."

"Go on, Bryn. What has happened between you and my
Companion?"

"I seem to be able to hear some of her thoughts." Bryn held
Thalynder's hands and stared into her leaf-green eyes.

"Another Druid trick," Thalynder said and smiled. "I guess
I'll believe you when we make the crossing and all is well."

"All will be well," Bryn said and kissed Thalynder's cheek.

"What was that for? Not that I want to question you when
you are so sweet, but you have been so busy of late, taking care
that the company is safe. Why now the display?"

"I miss you. I miss your laugh, I miss your scent. I miss the
way you breathe when you sleep. I wanted you to know that I
will always miss you."

"This sounds like goodbye. You aren't planning to leave me,
are you?"

"No, Lynder. I am not planning to leave you or the company.
I am thinking about the future. Your future and mine. We both
know our futures will not always be side by side."

"I know this, Bryn. We will marry someday."

"No, Lynder. I will not marry." Bryn felt her heart grow
heavy. "I have another path before me."

"You will find someone, Bryn of the Brae. How else will you make little Braes? You are the last of your line, you must think of the future of the Brae clann." Thalynder kissed Bryn's nose.

Bryn had been thinking about that fact for several days. She was the only child left to her parents, as Thalynder was her father's only child. Their fates were already in someone else's hands. Bryn knew there would come a time when a new Brae would have to come into the world. For the moment, she did not want to think of that twist of fate. Today, she wanted Thalynder near her, to breathe her scent, to feel the softness of her skin, to hold her close and feel her shudder as their bodies moved against each other. She held Thalynder's hands to her lips and placed a soft kiss on each palm.

"Tonight, we sleep on Arcaibh, in each other's arms."

The tide receded, just as Arlendyl had written. The company mounted the horses and rode slowly across the narrow channel to the small island of Grimr, where they reached the shore with plenty of daylight remaining. Bryn was grateful to her mother and to Meydra.

First time Meydra has revealed anything regarding my parents, Bryn thought. *There is still so much to learn.*

Bryn led the company swiftly across the small island to the other side and found the tide still out far enough to risk a crossing to Arcaibh. She paused only a moment before urging Pymmar back into the water. The others followed and were soon upon the southern shore of Arcaibh, the main island in the family of northern islands. The embankment led up into the heather moors.

"The heather is only on the shore," Bryn said to the company. "Once out of the heather, we should find sure footing and grassy plains. There are a few stands of trees, but those are too far inland for us tonight. We do need to move toward them, as there can be large tidal surges in this area after the earth shakes."

As they came out of the heather and up a gentle slope, the company could see far out across the moors. Bryn resumed point and led the group to its last stop for the night. She knew the Stones were a short ride away, but she did not want to reach them in the dark. She brought Pymmar to a stop at the edge of a small loch and dismounted.

"We have reached the loch of Staenis. Tomorrow we will reach the Stones. Let us stop now, prepare a hot meal and discuss our plans for tomorrow." She offered her hand to Thalynder and waited until the princess was off her mount. She pulled Thalynder to her and kissed her cheek. "We will sleep with Meydra at my back, you against my chest and my breath on your neck."

"Let us not worry about a meal, and go now to slumber in the shelter of Meydra's wing," Thalynder said. Her smile was wide as she held Bryn.

"We must eat, Lynder. We must also discuss tomorrow's plans before drifting off to sleep in each other's arms."

"As you wish, Lady Bryn. I will do as you bid, but I warn you, you may have a sleepless night."

"I am forewarned," Bryn said and lifted Thalynder off her feet. They were laughing as they turned to assist the others with the meal preparation.

"It is good to hear the two of you laughing again," Arryn said. He was busy taking his bags off his horse's back and tossing things to the ground. "We are safe enough to have a fire. I'll get one started."

"Thank you, Arryn," Bryn replied. "You know what I'd like? A bath."

"Oh!" Thalynder and Kenna replied at the same time.

"Seems you are not the only one wishing to rid yourself of some dust and dirt," Arryn laughed. "Perhaps the loch would serve."

Bryn looked at Thalynder and Kenna. "Ask your dragons to scout the loch. If all is well, we will bathe while Arryn and the prince set up our camp. Neulta, would you like to join us?"

The elf looked at her hands and back at Bryn. A smile touched her lips for a brief moment but disappeared quickly.

Bryn could see Neulta's indecision. She walked over and spoke quietly to the elf. "Would you prefer to bathe alone? I can arrange for that as well."

"No, Lady Bryn," Neulta replied. "I was trying to form the correct words for you and your companions. I would love to join the women. It has been a long time since I stepped into a pool of water. I usually bathe under falling water."

"You shall join us." Bryn took Neulta's arm and led her to the other women. "We will wait for word from the dragons." Caraid and Meydra had still been in the air when Bryn had suggested the bath. Kenna and Thalynder called to their dragons and the two set down in front of the women. Thalynder walked to Meydra and touched her forehead.

"Sweet dragon," Thalynder said. "We wish to bathe. Will you scout the loch and report back to me, and please do try to say all is well. I smell of horses and dirt."

"I will do my best, Princess." Meydra rose into the air, followed quickly by Caraid, and the two moved out over the loch. Meydra had already scouted the loch when Bryn had told her that was her destination for the night. She had scoured the land around the clearing and had passed her eyes over the loch for several miles. This pass would be to appease Thalynder and the others, but Meydra had already told Bryn where they could bathe.

When the dragons returned and alit before the company, Meydra bowed her head and waited for Thalynder.

"You have good news?" Thalynder asked.

"I do, Princess. You may rid yourself of the horse scent and the dirt."

Thalynder gave a yelp and kissed Meydra's cheek. "You have earned a reward. How would you like to accompany us to the water, and after we have eaten you can cuddle up with Bryn and me?"

"It would be my pleasure, Princess.

"Come, ladies, let us wash the dirt from our limbs. We will sleep one more night before we make our last leg of the journey to the Stones. Tomorrow will be a day of discovery."

Thalynder backed up against Bryn. She took Bryn's arm and pulled it across her waist. "It is good to be back in your arms."

Bryn pulled Thalynder close and held her tightly against her breast. She kissed the back of Thalynder's neck and gently nibbled on her earlobe. She pushed herself back against Meydra and felt the peace of being surrounded by the two creatures that held her heart. Bryn was acutely aware that in a few short hours all that she had believed to be in her future might change and be lost. She had these few hours to hold and cherish her Lynder.

"You are my heart's delight, Lynder," she whispered into Thalynder's ear. "I want to see you."

"In this night of eternal sun, you can do little else," Thalynder replied. "I am before you, my Bryn. Look at me."

Bryn let her eyes move from Thalynder's green eyes to her soft pink lips. Down her throat to the rise of her tunic that suggested two soft breasts. Bryn knew the color of Thalynder's nipples and their texture. She could see them again as they had been when they were bathing earlier in the loch. She looked further down to the flat of Thalynder's belly and her softly rounded hips. She let her eyes trace the shape of Thalynder's mound, her thighs, legs, and feet.

"You are so beautiful," Bryn said.

"We will sleep now."

"Yes, Lynder."

Bryn pulled Thalynder back against her chest and rested her arm over Thalynder's shoulder. "Sleep now. Tomorrow we see the Stones."

"I have not forgotten that promise, cousin," Leus said to Bryn. "I fear the world is changing enough to realize that the ancient ways may no longer be the best ways. Do you speak with all the dragons?"

Arryn looked at Bryn and saw her reaction to the statement. He frowned and took her hand in his. "What troubles you, Lady Bryn?"

Bryn knew she would have to disclose more about her ties with the dragons, but she had hoped to do so at the Stones and not before. The need to assure the elves and Arryn that the royals had become unexpected assets, and not to be dismissed, changed her timing. She squeezed Arryn's hand. She leaned in closer to the elves and lowered her voice. Arryn moved in to hear her.

"I *am* in contact with the dragons. Though I do not wish for this knowledge to be known by the dragon riders, for reasons that should be obvious. We can ill afford jealousy on this journey, especially now that I have put the lives of the royals at risk."

"What do you mean, you are in contact with the dragons?" Arryn asked, his voice barely above a whisper. He had long expected that Bryn and Meydra conversed behind Thalynder's back, but now he was unsure of what Bryn implied.

"She can speak with *all* the dragons with her heart and mind without the use of words," Leus replied. His voice betrayed his own awe at the fact that Bryn had said *dragons* and not *dragon*.

"All of them?" Arryn asked.

"Yes," Bryn replied. "Please, I beg you, do not tell the others. The dragons have been my eyes since the death of the High Dragon. It was there at the loch that they revealed themselves to me."

Neulta bowed her head slightly at Bryn and waited. Bryn touched Neulta's chin with her hand and said, "You must not do that in front of the others, Neulta. It may cause a curiosity I cannot explain."

"They are not aware of who you are?" Leus asked.

"I do not even know who I am," Bryn replied. "There is much information I need from the Stones."

The Stones were visible in the distance, and the company slowed as they approached from the southeast corner of the loch. The circle stood in a natural cauldron, even so, the tall Stones of the circle could be seen on the horizon. On the southernmost point of the entrance to the circle stood a solitary monolith.

Bryn checked Pymmar before reaching the monolith and waited for the others to reach her. One by one the company approached Bryn and waited. She turned Pymmar to face the others.

"This is the Gathering Stone, the first Stone for any traveler coming from the south or east. Each traveler must decide how they will enter the sacred area. Some come as a visitor, seeking a glimpse at an ancient knowledge. Some, a warrior seeking protection from the gods for whom some believe the Stones were erected. Some come not knowing what to expect, but are drawn in nonetheless. Still others come to find a treasure of ancient legend, not completely sure what it is they seek. Those with ties to the area, descendants of those ancient peoples who first placed these Stones, come to offer their respect to those ancestors. All are hoping to leave with a better understanding of their place in this world.

"What started out for me as a simple summer journey with two trusted friends has blossomed into a journey of discovery. I left the Realm that Touches Two Seas in the company of a princess and a knight. We have since become true friends. Staunch companions who would each give their own life for the life of the other. Along the way we experienced the death of a High Dragon with those of her own kin. We have met new friends along the way, and hope they will remain our friends. We have met with fierce enemies and sent them to their deaths. We have been joined by elves from the most revered race to yet walk this earth. For me, this journey has brought me full circle. I was born on this island. I approach this area not as a visitor, a warrior, or a treasure hunter. I come to discover the nature of myself in these Stones."

Bryn looked out toward the circle for a moment and then back to the company.

"As you approach this first Stone, you may wish to leave your mark. The Stone will guide you as to how to do that. If you do not wish to go any further, I ask that you wait for the rest of us here at this Stone. I do not know what awaits us at the circle, and the journey has not ended now that we are here. From this Stone, the journey begins. Dragon riders, I wish to address your dragons."

Prince Malcolm nodded at Bryn. "I come as a visitor, Lady Bryn. If you will be so kind as to answer questions along the way, I will go without hesitation or reservation. You may call to Coeur de Fer, or IronHeart, as you call him."

Bryn looked up and called out, "IronHeart." At once IronHeart alit on the plain north of the Stone, inside the ancient area.

Kenna looked at Bryn and over to Arryn. "I will follow you as another seeker, but I cannot read the runes either. I will not understand what I see. I will have to rely on you, Lady Bryn, to answer my questions. Caraid is yours to command."

"I will give answers to the best of my ability," Bryn replied. She looked up and called to Caraid. The small and delicate Angelwing descended and came to rest next to IronHeart.

The two elves only nodded at Bryn, and Bryn bowed her head briefly.

Arryn watched and listened to the others. The other dragon rider, Thalynder, had yet to speak.

Thalynder called to Meydra, and the Twayling came to rest at Bryn's side.

"Princess."

"Until I again call for you, you will respond to Bryn," Thalynder said.

"Yes, Princess Thalynder," Meydra replied and turned to look at Bryn. "Have you a request, Lady Bryn?"

"If you would, please join the other dragons. We will join the rest of you shortly," Bryn said. Meydra lifted up and over to where the other two dragons waited. As she set down, IronHeart touched her tail with his. Meydra took a small step toward the FireBreather and settled her tail to curl up under his. Bryn noticed the last touch as she turned back to face the others.

"If it be your wish to go with me to Skerrabrae, please approach the Stone and leave your mark. I will be the last to enter."

Prince Malcolm led the way and approached the Stone slowly. The Stone was covered in runes and symbols he did not recognize. There were several areas on the Stone that were covered in thumb prints. Dark prints. Blood, he thought. Next to the Stone was a mound of rocks, a cairn of sorts. Malcolm dismounted and looked at the ground for a rock to add to the cairn. He walked several meters out from the Stone to a little rise of earth and picked up a small rock. He placed it on the cairn and got back onto his horse. He passed the Stone to stop on the other side to wait for the rest of the company. Glancing at the back side of the monolith, he saw the now-familiar Tree of Life, the Stone circle and a dragon inside the circle. He noted that the forehead of the dragon was etched to show a small orb in the center that appeared to have rays of light extending out from it. He waited while the others approached the monolith one by one.

Kenna was next to approach the Stone. Getting down from her horse, she ran her hand over the face of the Stone, then circled over to its west side. She traced some of the runes with her fingers and then took her sword from its scabbard. She ran her left thumb lightly over the edge of the blade before bending down toward the bottom of the Stone. There the symbol of a star resting upon a hill could be seen with a few old and faded thumbprints below it. She knew that symbol as the one that represented her clann. She had seen it in the book she had signed back in Ceann Dùnaid. Squeezing her thumb to get the blood to flow, Kenna pressed her right thumb into the blood. Then she pressed her thumb against the Stone and left her print beside the others that ringed the bottom of the symbol. Wiping her thumb on her tunic, she led her horse over to Malcolm and tried to will her heart to beat slower. She watched the others and waited.

"Do you see the circle on the back of the Stone?"

"Yes, and the Tree and the Dragon," Kenna replied.

"Do you understand the drawings?"

"No. I am not schooled in the lore or the language. From the stories I have heard, the dragon came before the clanns."

"When did the Druids arrive?" Malcolm asked.

"I am not sure. It was after the elves, but around the time the dragons first appeared."

"Hmmm." Malcolm turned his attention back to the company.

The elves dismounted and walked their horses toward the Stone. As they approached, Neulta reached up her long, slender arm and ran her hand over a rune near the center of the Stone. She looked back at Bryn and smiled. She and Leus did not leave a rock on the cairn, nor did they leave a thumbprint as Kenna had. Instead, they continued out to the plain where the dragons and the others waited. Leus passed his hand over the back of the Stone without looking at it.

Arryn nodded at Bryn and urged his horse forward. He dismounted in front of the Stone and stared at the spot where Neulta had placed her hand. In the center of the Stone was the carved symbol of what resembled a crown. It was a single large circle with a set of three smaller circles stacked one on top of the other at what would be the front. In the middle of the three smaller circles was the rune symbol for the sun, with its rays moving out behind the circles. Arryn recognized it as the legend symbol for the Jewel that Unites. It resembled the headpiece that Bryn carried in her pack, and though he had been prepared for its appearance on the Stones by Lady Anethar in Skiel, he felt giddy knowing Bryn carried an ancient relic. He traced the Stone with his eyes and hands, searching for his symbol, the Fish Circle of the Epidii Clann of the West. He searched the front of the Stone and followed the runes around to the back. There he found his clann symbol in several places around the Tree of Life as if guarding it. There was one word etched under his clann symbol—*dideanach*—guardian. His clann was tied to the Brae clann. Protector and guardian of the high clann. He heaved a heavy sigh. He ran his fingers over the symbol and the word, then took the knife from his belt and pricked the thick pad of his palm. He rubbed his right thumb in the blood and pressed it against the Stone under the Fish Circle at the bottom of the Tree. He leaned in and placed a kiss on the symbol. Placing his knife in his belt, Arryn stepped back to look at the Tree of Life. He looked at the sun symbol in the center of the dragon's forehead and smiled. *The dragons* are *tied to the Druids*, he thought. *I think I am beginning to finally understand.* "There is one question in my mind," he said to the Stone. "Why would my clann disown such a heritage?"

The answer came to him in an unfamiliar voice: *To protect and guard that which unites.*

Arryn glanced across the plain to the Stone circle. Turning back to the monolith, he lifted his chin and nodded once back at Bryn. He touched his clann symbol again, then walked his horse away from the Stone where he mounted and rode out to the dragons.

"You are smiling a knowing smile, Sir Arryn," Malcolm said when Arryn stopped beside him. "What is it that you know?"

"You are so full of questions," Kenna remarked to Malcolm. "Can you not wait for the princess and the Lady Bryn?"

"I have questions," Malcolm said. "I want answers."

"You will have answers soon, Prince Malcolm," Arryn said. "I do not know if you will like those answers, but you will have them." Arryn turned his attention back to Thalynder and Bryn.

Thalynder looked at Bryn. She did not speak but bowed her head slightly. When she raised her head, she smiled and turned her horse. Out where Prince Malcolm had found his loose rock, Thalynder dismounted to find her own. Carefully turning over several, she picked up a palm-sized, rounded stone of pale gray-green. She turned her horse around and mounted it to return to Bryn and saw that Bryn had dismounted and stood at the base of the monolith. Thalynder slowly walked her horse toward Bryn.

"I cannot leave my blood on your Stone," Thalynder said as she neared Bryn. "I am not a Druid or a clann member."

"I understand," Bryn replied. "I am glad you understood that without my having to tell you."

"I have known all my life that I am not a Druid," Thalynder said and looked at the cairn. "Watching you trot off for lessons in things I would never learn was a source of great anger when we were younger. My father explained it to me one day when I threatened to have you replaced."

Bryn chuckled. "Was that when I bested you the first time with the bow?"

"Yes. I was sure it was because you used some magic spell to win the contest. I was a terrible loser." Thalynder got off her horse and stood next to Bryn.

"You still are, Lynder. I am glad you did not have me replaced."

"As am I, my Bryn." Thalynder placed the rock on top of Malcolm's. "I am still competitive as you can see. Will you be leaving your blood?"

"No," Bryn replied. "Here look at this." Bryn pointed to the center of the Stone on the south-facing side. "This is the headpiece of my clann, the High House that first placed these Stones. On the other side you will see the Tree of Life." She walked around to the north side of the Stone to look at the Tree. "No, I will not leave my blood. My ancestors did that for me when they struggled to place these here."

Thalynder looked up at the center symbol and stared at the headpiece. "I have seen that before somewhere."

"In my mother's house," Bryn replied. "It is on the carved stone ball that sits on the mantelpiece."

"No, elsewhere," Thalynder said. "Yes! It was at the home of Lady Anethar. You were dead to the world in a drugged sleep. Anethar asked for the pouch I used to make the dressing for your arm. I brought back the entire sack from your horse since I forgot which pouch had the right herbs. There was a headpiece in one of the bundles and Anethar would not tell me what it was, though she did tell Arryn. I was angry for several hours for being left out of the conversation."

"And you did not think to mention this before now?"

"There was no reason to. Arryn and Anethar were tight-lipped. By the time you came to, I was so relieved you were awake that I did not think about the headpiece."

Bryn glanced over at Arryn who held her gaze.

"Tell me about it, Bryn."

"It is as it appears," Bryn said walking back to the south side and Thalynder. Reaching out, she touched the circle in the Stone. "It is a crown and in the center at the front are three smaller circles connected one to the other. Inside the three circles is where a Jewel could rest."

"*The* Jewel?" Thalynder asked.

"According to legend, yes."

"And Anethar believes your headpiece is this crown? What else about the legend?"

"Lady Anethar, like the others of her family, does believe the headpiece is a crown. It is an ancient heirloom."

"Bryn! You have a crown!"

"I did not know it was a crown," Bryn replied shyly. "I had always thought it was simply a headpiece. Something my mother had me wear for special Druid occasions."

"Do you think we will find the Jewel that fits inside?" Thalynder asked.

"I don't know. It is a legend told over many millennia. I do not know if the Jewel ever existed. For all I know, the crown has always been empty."

"Why do you say that?"

"The circles do not have a bottom or a top. The crown can be worn one way, or turned upside down and worn another way. A jewel would fall out."

"Hmmm," Thalynder replied. "Still, you have the crown. Will you wear it?"

"I am not a queen, nor an elder, Thalynder. I am a simple Druid. I would not feel right wearing it now."

"Then why did your mother give it to you for this journey?"

"I have no idea."

"You are a princess, Bryn of the Brae. Adhar the Elf-Queen told us your mother is half eleven and a princess in her own right. You are also the daughter of a high-ranking Druid. Perhaps you are meant to wear the crown while you are here. You said we would know what to do when we approached the Stone. Read the Stone. What are you supposed to do?"

Bryn ran her hands over the Stone and read the runes surrounding the crown. Thalynder's instincts were good. Bryn looked at Thalynder.

"I am to wear the headpiece, as it is called here, when I reach the Stone Circle," she said. "It is there that I will need to be aware of the voices from the past."

"The voices from the past? Whispers in the wind. Like the story you once told me of the man and his daughter, lost in the woods," Thalynder said.

Bryn laughed. "Yes, Lynder. Whispers in the wind, like the story. The father told the daughter to listen to the whispers in the wind, and the voices from the past would guide her steps."

"Well, Princess High Druid Daughter of the Jewel, or whatever you should be called, let us join the others. Are we near the circle?" Thalynder walked her horse to the back side of the Stone and saw the Tree of Life carved into it.

"Arryn's clann symbol surrounds the Tree," she said and ran her hand over the Tree. "Where is the dragon, like the one on your tunic?"

"It is the one that sits in the center of this circle, the one with the symbol of the sun on its forehead," Bryn replied. "I must do one thing before I join the others. Will you wait a moment?"

"I will wait for you, Bryn."

Bryn took from her belt the small knife that had been made by her brother. She located the section on the Stone near the Tree that held the runes placed by her family. With the knife she etched a small sun rune, and next to it, a symbol that represented her name. She stood back and looked at the markings. Her eyes widened.

"Look, Lynder. The rune for my name closely resembles the three circles on the front of the headpiece." *A question*, she said with her heart.

Yes, came Meydra's answer.

Am I tied to this crown?

Yes, came the answer, but it was not Meydra's voice.

The wind touched Bryn's face as she lifted it to the sun. The breeze had pushed the clouds away and she felt the sun warm her face.

Bryn walked away from the Stone and mounted Pymmar. As she and Thalynder rode away with their backs to the monolith, the sun caught Bryn's etchings and for a moment they glowed.

"Did you see that?" Arryn asked.

"The Stone catching fire with the sun's rays? I did," Kenna said.

"A trick of the light," Malcolm said.

"I wonder," Arryn replied and in the wind that was rising, he heard the sound of many voices.

Bryn rode point again toward the Stone Circle that lay on the north side of the loch. The Circle was visible from the monolith and grew larger in the landscape as the company drew nigh. Bryn led the company up a gentle rise, and at the top, the full Circle and its grandeur caught the company by surprise. All, that is, except Bryn.

"These have been here how long?" Malcolm asked.

"Millennia," Arryn replied.

"I never guessed they would be so imposing," Thalynder said.

"Much like the stories my parents and the elders have been telling me for as long as I can remember," Bryn said. "Come, let's have a closer look."

Bryn began the descent toward the Circle when she stopped short and checked Pymmar. *Someone is coming*, she thought. Bryn waited until Meydra, IronHeart and Caraid set down around the party. From the sky came a call that the company could feel all the way to their toes. Meydra turned to look back at Bryn and Thalynder.

"It is the High Dragon," Bryn said to the company.

Why would Meylarn be here at the Stones? Bryn wondered.

To greet you, came the reply in the same voice Bryn had heard earlier. Turning her attention skyward, Bryn saw a speck high above their heads. The speck became several specks and soon she realized that High Dragon had brought her own company. Meydra, IronHeart and Caraid moved out onto the plain and waited, bowing their heads and folding their wings back behind them. Bryn dismounted and left Pymmar and the others to join the dragons. Arryn started after her, but Thalynder reached out to grab his arm to stop him.

"This is her domain," Thalynder said. "Here we bow to her."

Arryn touched Thalynder's hand and nodded. "You have learned the truth."

"I have seen the suspicion become the truth. Bryn commands the dragons."

"How were any of us to know?"

"We were not meant to know," Thalynder said and removed her hand from Arryn's arm. "Her parents did not want anyone to know. It was their way of protecting her from those who wish her race wiped from the face of the earth. You know all too well what has happened to the Druids in the recent past here in Alban and other countries. You, Bryn and Kenna coming together in one place at this time was meant for something. We still do not know the breadth of the path, only the length. I for one believe Bryn not only to be a princess in her own right but a dragon Companion as well."

Arryn smiled at Thalynder. "I believe you may be right."

"Perhaps, with the presence of the new High Dragon, we will learn the full truth at last."

With that, seven dragons descended and stood on the open plain. In the center of the seven, one dragon held her head a little higher than the others. The High Dragon stepped forward and the others bowed low behind her. Meydra, IronHeart, and Caraid continued to keep their own heads bowed before their liege. Bryn removed her sword from its scabbard and placed it upon the ground at her feet. She sank to the earth on her knees, her hands in her lap, her head bowed. Behind her, those of the company who were still on a horse dismounted. Arryn and Kenna knelt. Malcolm and Thalynder bowed their heads but remained standing. Neulta and Leus raised their hands, palms out, and placed them on their foreheads in the tradition of the elves. All waited quietly.

"Rise, our daughter," Meylarn said. Her voice was firm, but gentle; the sound was much like cool water after a long drought and it filled the companions with ease. She spoke in the tongue of humans, yet in Bryn's heart she sang in a dragon language, the same one Meydra had taught Bryn when she was a baby.

Bryn stood, and the others lifted their heads.

"Come to me, Daughter."

Bryn stood up and approached Meylarn. She remained back far enough for Meylarn to see her clearly. Meylarn was a Twayling dragon of the same size and color as Meydra. The only difference was the color of her eyes. Where Meydra's were deep blue, as dark as the night sky, much like Bryn's, Meylarn's eyes were the color of a storm. Deep gray eyes that sparkled with bits of silver. Her eyes smiled at Bryn as they looked her over.

"We have waited long for your coming."

"As have I."

"Your story awaits you in the Circle. Are you ready to hear it?"

"I am." Bryn took out a bit of cloth from her tunic pocket. She unwrapped the cloth to expose the items it held. She took one of the objects and held it out for Meylarn to see.

"My father sends this." Bryn held up the piece of stone that Brymender had slipped into her tunic the night of their parting. It was a piece of the Gathering Stone that had been worn smooth by all the hands that had caressed it over the years. Bryn had recognized its likeness carved on the monolith when she first approached it. The pattern was carved in the runes that surrounded the headpiece symbol.

Meylarn smiled at Bryn. "Your father is a faithful follower." Meylarn blew a small breath onto the stone. The stone glowed and when the light subsided a second rune joined the clann symbol. It was the dragon rune. Bryn put the stone back into her pocket.

Next, Bryn held up the circle of silver her mother had packed away for her: the headpiece of the Brae. The silver glinted in the sunlight and looked like rays of light were emanating from the smaller circles that adorned the front of the headpiece.

"Your mother is a wise woman," Meylarn said. "You will want to wear that later."

Behind Bryn, Prince Malcolm and Thalynder watched with an understanding the others did not fully have. Bryn was holding a crown. Both royals knew the significance, and their silent suspicion regarding Bryn and her ancestry was finally being made public. Malcolm looked at Thalynder and nodded. Thalynder returned the nod, and as she looked back at Bryn, tears welled in her eyes. Her childhood friend and court attendant carried hidden inside her ties to the ancients of this world. Ties that neither she, her father nor any other royal now living could boast of—a bond with all the creatures of the earth, sea, and sky that no one could sever. It made the princess proud, and it made her sad. Her Bryn, the girl she had played with, the youth she competed against and the woman she grew to love, was moving out of her reach. Until now, Thalynder believed it would be she who had to leave Bryn behind for royal duties. Now, she knew it was she herself who would be left behind, and unless she could find a way to stay with her love, she would be forever on the outside looking in.

Arryn watched as Bryn held up the headpiece for the High Dragon to examine. He saw the sparkle of the silver, the intricate twisting to the metal that caught the sun and held it. He saw the three smaller circles form a spire and watched as they seemed to catch fire and blaze brightly. He glanced at Kenna and saw tears falling on her cheeks. He reached over and took her hand.

Meylarn looked at Meydra. *My kin*, she said in dragon song. *You have waited long for this; soon it will be as it should be.*

Meydra raised her head to look at Bryn.

Bryn stood silently and held the headpiece aloft. She listened to the exchange between Meylarn and Meydra and was confused. Although she believed she understood that Meydra had once been her dragon, and that all the other dragons knew it as well, Bryn still did not understand all the reasons for their sadness at that thought. For it was sadness and great loss that they all felt whenever Meydra and Bryn's connection was discussed among them.

Meylarn bowed her head and spoke to Bryn's heart. *Come to me, Daughter, come let me feel your touch.*

Bryn wrapped the headpiece back in the cloth and put it in her tunic pocket. She approached Meylarn. Bryn did not know if protocol meant she should touch the High Dragon with her hand or her forehead. Her heart told her to touch Meylarn as she did Meydra. Bryn held out both hands, placing them on Meylarn's cheeks. She moved her forehead to rest between Meylarn's eyes. She felt her heartbeat slow to match that of the High Dragon and her breath deepen with the dragon's. She felt a sweet peace wash over her body.

Meydra watched the two together and she too felt her heart beat with theirs, her breathing slow to theirs. She felt the same sweet, peaceful sensation course through her body. She lifted her head and her heart began the song.

Caraid, IronHeart and the six other dragons joined Meydra in a song of ethereal beauty. It called out to every living soul, including those of the immovable elves. The birds that flew overhead perched to listen and the sheep that grazed raised their heads. The fox and the marten were quiet in their dens. Off the coast in the shallows of the sea, an orca slapped her tail hard on the water's surface. All who heard the song knew something wonderful was happening. All who heard the song knew that change was in the wind.

CHAPTER SIXTEEN

The silent Stone Circle stood waiting for them. Bryn led the others down into the Circle, accompanied now by seven more dragons. All were quiet, the company more so because of the peace that had rested in them with the dragon song.

Bryn spoke to Meydra with her heart. The two, joined now and again by Meylarn or one of the other dragons, discussed the dragon riders among them. How things had changed since the first dragons arrived, and how they wanted to bring the old days of dragons choosing their Companions back to the few remaining dragons of the world.

What do you mean, few remaining dragons? Bryn asked Meydra.

There are very few of us left, Meydra replied. *We have been hunted in some lands, or else kept on display. We have been destroyed in other lands, out of fear we would turn on humans. It is only here in the west that we are still regarded as dragons and not as pets or showpieces, though that is also changing. As you can see by the law of this land, which forbids any human but a royal to bond as a Companion to a dragon. We are becoming possessions and not Companions.*

"We cannot let that happen," Bryn said.

"Cannot let what happen?" Thalynder asked, riding her horse up next to Bryn.

"We cannot let the raiders invade and take our land from us," Bryn stammered. She had not realized she had spoken aloud. "Meylarn has told me that men across the East Sea are loading their boats with many weapons. We must not linger at the Stones longer than necessary."

"Perhaps we should be returning now to my father," Prince Malcolm said from behind Bryn. "His army could be at our backs before the raiders make the north shores."

"Yes," Bryn replied. "It is time we discussed that." She stopped at the rise of ground that lay before the Standing Stone Circle. In the center of the circle was a smaller configuration of blocks. "Ride to the center. We will stop there and further discuss the need for haste." She leaned down and spoke into Pymmar's ear. Her horse neighed and took off down the embankment at a furious gallop. Bryn's hair flowed out from her braid like water from a pitcher and streamed behind her. Seeing the sight from afar, it would appear that she had unfurled a flag and rode like the wind with it heralding her arrival.

"Tell me about the Circle," Malcolm said as they slowed their horses.

Arryn checked his horse next to Bryn. "I know very little about the Circle. Could you tell us a little more?"

Bryn raised her hand and drew a circle in the air.

"For millennia, the Stones had been the gathering place of the Druids. It served as a meeting hall, a joining chapel, a place to celebrate birth and death. It was once a place to celebrate the changing seasons, the sun setting and the moon rising. Here many elders learned their craft from the words of their ancestors. The Circle was a place for warriors to strategize and for elders to think. The shape, a circle, holds special meaning to the Druids. A circle has no beginning and no end. From anywhere in the circle, you would know that you were covered by—and enclosed in—a never-ending ring of protection."

"It does make good battle sense," Malcolm said.

"It is why the coasts are doted with circular stone buildings," Kenna said. "That much I do know. The land where my clann lives has many circular towers."

They approached an inner circle in which stood several blocks of stone.

Bryn slowed Pymmar as she neared the center blocks. "These blocks, laid out to resemble a table, are known by the clanns as the Decision Stones. It is here that decisions—those that would affect the entire clann—were made and debated." She approached the stone table, dismounted, and left Pymmar to graze on the sweet grass that grew between the stones. Remembering stories that her mother had told her of the knights and warriors, she drew her sword and placed it on the stone block as a show of trust. Immediately, a soft glow filled the blade as it rested in the niche on the table. The rest of the company kept their distance and did not approach the Decision Stones. The sword sat in the niche as if the stone had been hollowed precisely for that particular sword. The light surrounding the blade began to intensify and caused Bryn to shield her eyes with her hand. As she stood mesmerized by the growing light, the sun moved out from behind the clouds and touched the Stones on the outer Circle. One by one the Stones came alive with the sun's light. The light filled the spaces between the Stones of the inner circle, closing the gaps.

Thalynder, Malcolm, Arryn, and Kenna checked their horses before entering the inner Circle. The light that was coming from inside, where Bryn stood, startled them and they hesitated. IronHeart and Caraid set down next to their Companions and waited with them, unsure of entering the Circle on their own. Meydra and Meylarn continued to the inner Circle and Bryn. Thalynder started to follow Meydra, but at that moment Meydra turned to face her.

"Do not enter yet, Your Highness," Meydra said. "It is not safe for you or the others to enter this Circle at this time."

Thalynder nodded at Meydra and remained behind with the others. Thalynder's mount was spooked by the light and began to stamp his hooves. Arryn grabbed the horse's bit and held him steady. The light inside the Circle began to change color.

"What is happening?" Malcolm asked.

"The sword has opened the way," Neulta said.

"The way for what?" Kenna whispered.

"The way for the Jewel to be seen," Arryn replied.

Thalynder looked at Arryn and frowned. She looked back at Bryn and the dragons. Meydra and Meylarn were perched on top of two of the ten stones. They stood as sentinels looking down upon Bryn. As the light changed from brilliant white to a softer blue-white hue, other dragons came in and began to take up stations on the remaining Stones of the outer Circle. These were not the dragons that had accompanied Meylarn earlier that morning, but new ones that Thalynder and the others had not seen before. They were older by the look of their bodies, and they did not look at the Companions on the outside of the Circle. They kept their gaze on the center stone and Bryn. Thalynder looked back at Bryn and there on her tunic, the Tree of Life and the dragon began to sparkle and shine with their own light. Thalynder felt the soft rumble of the earth beneath her and shivered.

Bryn lowered her hand from her brow, and stood still and waited. As a new dragon came to perch on each Standing Stone, she could hear their greetings in her heart. She greeted each as they came to rest on top of a Stone. Bryn heard Meylarn greet each dragon by name, and as she heard the names, she realized she was meeting the dragons of the Druid stories of her youth: FairHeart, StarGazer, NightShade, RimWalker and others. Once the last dragon had set down on top of the final Standing Stone, Meylarn spoke to the company. The words, melodious and soft, filled the air with dragon song.

"Listen now to the whispers of the Stones," Meylarn sang. "A tale of lost lands, lost kin and lost treasures will fill your heart. Can you hear the words?"

Bryn inhaled sharply as the words touched her ears and swirled about her head. The warm rush of blood coursed through her veins. Her arms and legs grew light as if suspended in air. She heard every word that Meylarn sang as if each were its own symphony. Her heart began to beat slower and slower until all time stopped.

Thalynder gasped. Bryn was covered in light and it appeared as if she would disappear altogether in a flash of brilliance. Arryn dismounted and stood silent as a sentinel, his hand on the hilt of his sword. The others dismounted and stood on the trembling ground.

Meydra spoke now. Her voice, calm and reassuring, lifted above the Stones and touched the company.

"Long before dragons came to these lands, elves held this ground to be sacred," she began. As one, the company sat down upon the soft grass and listened. The earth stopped trembling.

"The elves used these islands to see the stars as they passed through the night skies. The elves tracked time and seasons for many thousands of years. They witnessed the birth of new stars and the death of old ones. They witnessed many celestial events and began to record them by way of spoken stories. They recorded the cycles of the stars, and in time had developed a calendar of the stars' movements. They began to predict events by the movements of the stars. One cold and clear night, the sky lit up and something unpredicted happened. A star fell from the sky and landed here where we now gather."

The company looked around at the hollow. Meydra waited until they turned their attention back to her.

"The High Elf, the beautiful Queen Athyl with eyes the color of the twilight sky, led her kin to see the fallen star. Upon finding the still-smoldering hollow, the very curious Queen descended into the hollow amid cries of distress from her kin. Queen Athyl did not heed their cries, and she disappeared into the smoke and ash.

"The elves waited many long hours for their queen to come back out of the hollow, but she did not come. The elves could not leave without knowing what happened to her, so they waited. They waited silently, unmoving, for days on end. Until one year later, on the anniversary of the star's fall to earth, a light began to grow at the bottom of the hollow. The elves watched and waited, hoping beyond all hope that their beloved queen was at last returning to them."

Arryn looked at Bryn. The light inside the Circle had now surrounded her completely, and she was bathed in its brilliance. His heart leapt at how beautiful she appeared. He reached over and took Thalynder's hand.

Thalynder sat enraptured by Meydra's words and the sight of Bryn glowing in light. Her heart raced with each spark that flew from the Stones to Bryn.

Meydra continued. "In the center of the hollow, the light began to take form among the wisps of mist that rose up from the ground. The mist and light mingled and grew taller and taller, until it surpassed even the tallest of elves. It continued to grow and when the light stopped moving and the mist hung in the air, the form was as tall as the oldest trees. The form shifted in the light and the light began to dim. The mist dissipated and there before the elves stood the first dragon."

Kenna looked from Neulta to Leus and back to Meydra. She pulled her knees up to her chest and rested her chin there.

"Created in stardust to fall to earth—to join with the earth—the dragon had physically bonded with the first thing it encountered, Queen Athyl. The dragon and Athyl had become one. The crown that had sat upon Queen Athyl's brow was now embedded in the forehead of the dragon. The elves were stunned by the size of the dragon and immediately began to shrink from its presence. They were certain that the beast had devoured their queen and they were afraid.

"The dragon spoke to the elves. *Do not fear, my children*, she said. *I am Athyl, your queen. Do you not know me?* The elves looked up at the beast. They approached the great head and looked into the dragon's eyes. Shining back at them was the twilight blue of Athyl's eyes, and in those eyes the elves saw their queen.

"*How can this be?*" the elves asked. The dragon shook her head slightly and smiled at them. *I came to the fallen star and discovered an egg. When I touched the egg, all things stopped. At the next moment, I was rising from the earth, back into the light of day. I am now as you see me*, Queen Athyl said to the elves.

She explained that more stars had fallen, and that there were other eggs in other lands that would hatch to produce dragons. She told the elves that the dragons would seek others to bond with, but because they did not bond before birth, they could only bond with hearts and minds and not their bodies. The elves were repulsed by the thought."

Neulta looked at Leus. She took his hand in hers, looked at Meylarn, and said, "I am sorry."

"Do not worry, little cousin," Meylarn said. "It was a beginning, and beginnings are often made on unsteady feet."

Meydra smiled at Meylarn and looked down at Neulta. "You are here now, and that is a good thing," Meydra said. She raised her head and began again.

"Queen Athyl explained that if the elves did not wish to bond with the dragons, they would eventually perish from the earth. The elves, though they themselves did not wish to bond with the dragons, felt sad that any creature would have to leave the earth. They lamented and cried that they could not bond with beasts, but they could not endure the suffering of having been the source of pain for the dragons. Queen Athyl was quiet for a long time. When next she spoke, she spoke from the dragon's heart. *They will bond with the humans*, she said. The elves again were repulsed. They cried 'No!' The first dragon stood up and spread her wings. She held her head high and cried out over the land with such a wail as to break the heart of every living soul that heard the sorrow. The elves cowered but did not flee. At long last, Arstender, daughter of Queen Athyl, who had assumed the royal mantel and was now Queen of the Elves, stood and spoke to the other elves. *We have long known that we would need to coexist with humankind. We have long known that, left to their own ways, humans would not grow in heart and mind for ages. We claim to be the earth's caretakers, yet we shy away from humankind, which sprang from the earth as did we. Can we now say they are worth less than other creatures?*

"The elves debated long among themselves and at last they were decided. Arstender approached her mother. *What would you have us do?* The dragon shed a single tear and let it fall to the ground at Arstender's feet. *Elves and humans must come together and bear children,* the dragon told them. *Those children, half elf, half human, will be the Companions to the dragons. From there life will take its own course.*

"Arstender reached down to pick up the tear. It was hard as stone but clear as water. She held it up to the sun and the colors of the world blinked from inside the crystal tear. She looked at the dragon. *Mother, what beauty is this?* The dragon sighed and said, *It is the promise that dragons will not harm human Companions. It is all I have to give. Hold it to your heart and it will live there forever.*

"Arstender held the gem to her heart and in a flash of light the gem attached itself to her skin. Watching in awe of the spectacle, the elves were speechless. The gem dissolved into Arstender's skin and found a home in her heart. Arstender called out to the dragon, *Mother, I have you with me!* The dragon smiled and assured Arstender that her descendants would be linked with all dragons until the last of her kind were long gone from this world."

Bryn heard the words Meydra was speaking, but heard them in the language of the dragon in her heart and felt too the pain that went with them. The first dragons were meant to physically bond with their earthbound charges. The loss of that capability forever saddened the dragons and left them unfulfilled. Bryn's heart cried out to Meydra and the others.

Meydra glanced at Bryn before continuing. Bathed in the clear light of truth, Bryn was the exact image of her ancestor Queen Athyl. For millennia the dragons had waited for Athyl to be reborn. That time was nearing.

"Arstender accepted the gift of the dragon and agreed to help the dragons bond with humans. She pledged the elves' assistance, and for several hundred years the elves and humans interacted. The elves began teaching the humans about the earth, sea, and sky. A small group of humans understood the elves' ideas with greater personal depth than did the other humans. The elves gravitated toward that small group of humans and in time found they had much in common. The elves and those humans chose to live together and as had been requested by the first dragon, children were born of the union. Those children became the chosen Companions to the dragons, and the dragon bond tradition was born."

"But I am not half elven," Prince Malcolm said.

"Nor am I," Thalynder echoed.

"No. You are not," Meylarn replied. "The story continues."

Meydra glanced at Thalynder. She knew the truth would hurt a little, but it had to be told.

"As time passed," Meydra continued. "The elf and human communities grew. They maintained a High House near this sacred spot, in Skerrabrae. From there the direct descendants of the first union of elf and man presided over the other clanns. That first union was the star that fell from the sky with Queen Athyl at the dragon's birth. After Athyl came Arstender. Arstender joined with a human male. Their female descendants carry the link to the dragons, the dragon tear filtering its light to the hearts of the female child. All of their female descendants are held in high esteem by the dragons. It is these descendants that the dragons seek out as Companions. It is these descendants that eventually hold sway over the lives of the dragons. We, the dragons, are on this earth because those descendants allow us to be, and we will leave only when the last of Queen Athyl's descendants draws her final breath."

Bryn heard the words and knew that the last days of the dragons were coming. It was why the dragons were sad whenever her name was mentioned. They were seeing their last days on earth. *No*, she thought. *I cannot let this happen. I cannot be the last, there must be another.*

"Generation after generation of the half elf, half humans witnessed bonds with dragons. A single chance out of many and the bond is nearly the same true union that was the first between the stardust and Queen Athyl. Though circumstance may separate the Companions, that bond cannot be broken and will keep them alive." Meydra paused and looked down at the two royals.

"Before you two were born, Prince Malcolm and Princess Thalynder, dragons only bonded with those that *they* heard call to them from the wombs of their mothers. But a time came when a decision had to be made. The decision to give up the bond or give up life was laid before one dragon. She chose to give up her bond to save the life of the Companion she had yet to meet. This dragon, Companion to the High House of Skerrabrae, took an oath and made a vow to keep that oath or die."

"You are talking about the rule that royals can only Companion dragons," Arryn said. "That dragon pledged to make that happen? Why?"

"These lands you see before you lay long in peace," Meydra continued. "The elves moved south to the woods, and the half elf, half human communities remained in the north. The humans that followed the elves south began to refer to those who remained in the north as Dryws or Seers. The term has evolved to Druid as you know it now. The Druids remained in the north with the other human communities of Picts and Gaels. Raised in lore steeped in elf and human tradition, the Druids remained friends of every creature, where the elves in the south eventually lost all touch with humans. To the dragons, the Druids were the true children of the earth, and since it was the first dragon's request that elves and humans mate and bear children, the dragons felt more like parents to the Druids, and as such held them close to their hearts."

"Why, then, did they allow non-Druids to have Companions?" Malcolm asked.

"The lands over the eastern sea often went through terribly harsh seasons. A drought, a famine, a winter of bitter cold would drive the men from those lands west to these islands. Here they found seals, whales, fish and deer thriving in the milder climate. At first these men were content to fish and hunt and return to their homes across the sea. Eventually, they began to rout the communities, taking women and children back with them across the sea to be slaves. The Druids and other peaceful communities came together to protect themselves from the raiders. They developed brochs, tall buildings of stone used for defense against fire. They built underground caches for their grain. They even devised stone buildings underground where the villagers could retreat and hide from the raiders.

"But the raiders grew angrier. When the time came that the Druids, Picts and Gaels could no longer defend themselves, they turned to the men and kingdoms of the south for protection. The kings of these southern realms agreed to aid the northern clanns, but there was a price. The Druid elder who took it upon himself to seek aid from the kings was a dragon Companion. His dragon went with him to seek the king's aid, and when terms of payment could not be agreed upon, the dragon proposed a solution."

"Oh no," Thalynder whispered.

"If the king sent his army to help defend the northern communities, the dragon would, upon the Druid elder's death, wait to find a Companion. This would give the king time to produce an heir the dragon would consider as a Companion. The king liked the idea. The Druid elder, on the other hand, was not pleased by the thought of giving up his Companion so he added one thing. The dragon would only leave the Druids if the need for the king's defense was the last recourse to the clann's survival."

Thalynder turned to Arryn. She knew the story. She buried her face in her hands.

"The king, a good man with a good heart, agreed and made the dragon swear an oath to abide by the terms. The dragon shed a single tear and left her pledge at the king's feet. For the pledge, the king released the dragon to stay with the old Druid, but as a final thought, because he coveted the dragon so, he decreed that no one may Companion a dragon in his lands unless they were of royal blood. If he couldn't have the dragon now, no one else would. The decree spread to all the other kingdoms and became the law of the land.

"The Druid elder and his dragon left the kingdom with a small contingent of the king's army and returned to their home in the north by the sea. In time the old Druid died and his son became leader of the High House, chosen so because his wife was as near a full elf as any of his generation had known. The dragon, now without a Companion, remembered her oath. She did not choose a new Companion right away, but remained with the new Druid elder and his family until a new Companion was found.

"In a particularly hard winter, the raiders came and stayed on the islands, routing, pillaging, killing all living creatures they met. The Druid elder asked for help from the king and it was again granted. But the king's small army was no match for the number of raiders. Clannsmen took up arms and joined the army. It was still not enough. It was a difficult decision, but it had to be made—the clans disbanded and fled the coastlands."

Bryn tried to reach out to Thalynder but could not break through the light that held her in the middle of the Circle. She knew the truth would hurt her Lynder, and she desperately wanted to hold her in her arms.

Meydra felt Bryn's plea. *It must come out,* she said to Bryn.

No, Bryn replied. *I cannot hurt her.*

You were warned that this would happen, Meylarn said to Bryn. *Will you listen to your heart, or hers?*

Bryn closed her eyes and did not reply. She reached out with her heart and held Thalynder close. When she opened her eyes, she saw Thalynder looking at her. She held Thalynder's gaze while Meydra continued.

"For three winters Brymender waited to see if he could stave off the raiders long enough to avoid needing the king's aid. On the winter solstice of the third year, a daughter was born to Brymender and Arlendyl. The dragon had known long before the child was born that she was her next Companion. No royal edict or oath could break this bond. Six months after her birth, when it was time for her naming, Brymender called together all the remaining clans' men and women and all the children who had been born within the last six months. He would ask as he always did on naming days whether the dragon had found her new Companion. What worried him most was that also on this naming day, a royal daughter was born to the king. Brymender looked first at the children gathered and then at the dragon. He asked the dragon to name her Companion."

"I did not know!" Thalynder cried. "How was I to know?"

Arryn moved to sit close to Thalynder and pulled her to his chest.

"I chose Bryn over the newborn princess," Meydra said. "I could not break the bond that already existed. Brymender, Arlendyl and I agreed not to tell the king until it was absolutely necessary. There was always the chance that the oath would not need to be honored.

"That following winter, the raiders returned and were bent on destroying everything in their path. Bryn's last brother was killed, as were nearly all the men of the village. Bryn's father and mother went to see King Thafyn, only to find that the old king had died two years earlier and his son, King Thamen, now sat on the throne. King Thamen was gracious and offered his entire army to go and bring the Druids to the realm. Accepting them into his kingdom and thereby offering them protection for as long as they wished to stay. It was then that he also claimed the promise."

"You are Bryn's dragon?" Malcolm asked.

"I am," Meydra replied.

"How could you go to a royal if you were already bonded?"

"I was bonded to Bryn, yes, but the lives of those I had watched from my own infancy—the clann Brae—those lives were in danger. I kept the promise. Yet, King Thamen took pity on Bryn. He offered that she become an attendant to the court, a waiting lady to the princess, so that she would always be near her dragon. He allowed Bryn to be schooled in the lore and language of her clann, so that should a time ever come that I had to chose between the two women's lives, Bryn would understand what was at stake and make the right decision herself."

"I don't understand," Thalynder said, wiping tears from her face.

"The choice of which life to save, yours or Bryn's, could not be left to Meydra," Arryn said. "Meydra would choose Bryn. In order for you to live, Bryn had to understand dragons and be allowed to hear Meydra in her heart. Bryn was schooled to die in your stead."

Malcolm looked at Bryn. He passed his hands over his eyes and they came away wet with tears. He reached over and put his hand on Arryn's arm.

"How long have you known this?"

"Though I have suspected it since Skiel, it is only now becoming clear to me," Arryn said.

"You have been protecting Thalynder to keep Bryn alive," Kenna said.

"Yes. I suspect that my clann followed the Brae. When the Brae came under the protection of the king, our duty was to guard the Druids. How or why I came to be in the king's guard is not relevant. Being charged with protecting the princess would also keep Bryn safe." Arryn replied and looked up at Meydra. "You could have told me."

Meydra looked at Arryn and tried to convey her feelings to him. She had wanted to bring him into the inner circle long before now, but many things had restricted her efforts.

"She could not!" Meylarn said and her voice startled the company. She stood up and held out her wings. "You must listen to the rest of the story. It involves all of us gathered here. Hold your tongues."

The company went quiet and sat very still.

"There is only one way to keep the raiders from these lands," Meydra said. "The clanns must unite, and they must unite with the realms in the south. To do so, they must have a leader. The potential exists in Bryn. She is a direct descendant of Queen Athyl by her daughter, Arstender. She carries the stardust of the first dragon. As do I."

Thalynder looked from Meydra to Bryn and gasped. "You mean to *join* with her? That will kill her!"

Malcolm lunged to his feet but was smacked down by the tail of the dragon on the Stone above him.

"Be still!" Meylarn slapped her tail hard upon the ground.

"Sadly, that is no longer possible, as I said before. Athyl was the first and only to physically join with a dragon," Meydra replied to Thalynder. "There is a way though for Bryn to understand all the knowledge of her ancestors and apply it to uniting the clanns, but it is still dangerous."

"To whom?" Malcolm asked.

"To you, the company and to Bryn," Meylarn replied. "You must do as you are told, you must not enter the inner Circle, you must be still and listen."

Meydra looked at the company and continued, "The elves did not raise the Stones as you see them now, but left them on the ground and in the earth from whence they originated. They proposed no monuments, no reminder of the loss of their queen. The Druids raised the Stones for this very event. They prepared for all possible futures including one that would need another joining. They did not know how long the Circle would need to stand, so they built the Circle of Stones with their sweat and their blood and their lives. They built it in hopes that their queen would again unite them and protect them and their way of life."

Meylarn lifted her head and began to sing. The other dragons joined in. As the song lifted above the Stones, the sky began to darken. High overhead the stars began to shine in the blackness.

"Stars in the daytime?" Kenna whispered.

"All dragons, here on earth or resting in the empyrean regions, will bear witness," Meydra replied.

The song went out and touched the group, though none there could understand the words. Each member of the company felt the chorus in a different way, and it altered the way they saw both Bryn and the lights in the Circle. Meydra watched the company for signs of distress, knowing that in some the words could evoke a feeling of being trapped. Those were the ones who could cause harm to Bryn. Meydra believed that none of the company were capable of hurting Bryn intentionally, yet she remained watchful. Meylarn continued the dragon song, filling the air with somber melody, and Meydra watched as each member reacted to it.

Kenna began to laugh and cry at the same time. The song filled her heart and revealed to her that she was not alone.

Her clann could cease its shadowed existence and again join the other clanns where they would be welcomed as family. Her mother had been wrong to shun the other clanns and Kenna knew that she herself would lead her clann to Bryn. She removed her sword from its scabbard, held it aloft, and called out to the wind. "We will unite!" She lowered her sword and walked over to one of the Standing Stones at the inner Circle and placed her hand on the glowing Stone. Above her, one of the dragons in Meylarn's company, an old Angelwing, looked down and smiled. Kenna returned the dragon's smile and in an instant the Angelwing began to glow as brightly as the sun. Her lacy wings appeared to catch fire and disappear against the star-filled sky. The dragon's tail slapped the Stone and sparks hit the Stone, etching a rune on its face: the rune of the Bridei. Kenna watched as the Angelwing then stood up and became a pillar of light. The light lifted above the Stone and moved toward Bryn. In a flash of blue light, the Angelwing was gone. Kenna heard the beat of wings behind her and turned to see Caraid come and sit on the empty Stone.

"Welcome, dragon rider," Caraid said to Kenna.

Bryn watched as the older Angelwing dragon soared above the Stones and Caraid took her place. A single tear fell from the dragon's eye and landed on the hilt of her sword where it lay on the table stone. In an instant the tear became a deep blue sapphire and fused to the hilt of the sword, reflecting the dark blue of the sky overhead. The Angelwing opened her wings wide and lifted her chest and in an instant she was gone. Bryn felt the ache in the song the other dragons were singing, but it was not met with sadness. It was a last goodbye to the Angelwing and a welcome to Caraid, who now sat in the old dragon's place.

The changing of the guard had begun.

Arryn felt the pull of the dragon melody. His heart beat hard in his chest as he approached the Stones. He could see Bryn's figure among the brilliant light that filled the center of the Circle, and everything about the event told him he was witnessing the birth of a new life for Bryn. A new beginning for the clanns and especially for himself. He *would* captain a legion.

A legion of clannsman united under one banner. He removed the cloak that covered his own Fish Circle symbol embroidered on his jerkin, and approached the second Stone, placing his hand on it. On top of the Stone sat an old Talbern dragon. Arryn did not fear the dragon, and in his heart he reached out to it. The dragon greeted him with a smile and a quick wink. She slapped her tail on the stone, and again sparks etched a rune on the face: the rune of the Epidii. The dragon then stood up tall and spread her wings. Her immense size blocked out the starlit sky and for a moment all was dark where Arryn stood. The Talbern gave a short cry and sprang straight up, bursting into flame as she rose higher and higher. At the apex of her climb, the flame became a single point of deep emerald light that fell down into the center of the Circle.

Bryn's heart laughed at the Talbern's ascent. The dragon's heart sang to Bryn and said it was her joy to be on hand for this long-awaited day. Bryn's heart reached out to the Talbern and for a moment they held each other close in thought. Bryn watched the single tear fall and land upon her sword, becoming a clear emerald of brilliant green. It flowed like water to fill the small depressions that were engraved in the blade of the sword. A green field surrounded the silver leaves that swirled around the words etched into the sword. The Talbern continued her ascent toward the sky and soon was more light than substance. The other dragons called out to the creature with their final goodbye—and she was gone. In her place, a young fire-breathing Oslona came out of the sky and perched upon the Stone above Arryn. The young dragon looked at Arryn and bowed his head.

"Welcome, dragon rider," the Oslona said.

"Dragon rider?" Arryn asked. He glanced over at Bryn, still bathed in the brilliant light of the inner Circle. She smiled at him and in his heart he heard her call.

Welcome, dragon rider, she sang to him.

Prince Malcolm heard a much different song in his heart. The thrill of a battle cry quickened his blood. He felt the need to call to his armies and bring them to this place, serving with the others in the defense of the country. He stood up and looked back at his dragon, IronHeart, as he now called him. Malcolm hesitated, not knowing what he was supposed to do, and hoped his dragon would guide him.

IronHeart glanced down at the prince and nodded. He knew he must wait until the older Timon de Flamme left his post. It was the younger dragon's destiny, as it was the destiny of the Companions, to have come to this place at this time. He moved his head toward the older yellow and gray dragon that sat perched on the Stone to Kenna's right.

Prince Malcolm looked at the older dragon and smiled. He recognized the markings as those of his own dragon and knew that IronHeart would be taking that place. As he moved toward the Stone, the older creature dipped his neck down toward Malcolm. He inhaled deeply and Malcolm lifted his head to look directly at him. In a moment of inspiration, Malcolm bowed low before the older beast. The older dragon snorted (a dragon snicker of sorts) and a puff of smoke left his nostrils. He then flexed his wings and turned back to look toward the center of the circle and Bryn. His breath began to quicken and his whole body radiated heat. The gray of his outer wings darkened to black and the yellow markings along his body and at the wings tips turned to a bright gold. He spread his large wings and lifted effortlessly off the Stone. He raised his head high and released a long white trail of smoke from his mouth. The smoke arched and fell into the circle.

Bryn heard the call of the older dragon as his body changed into smoke. From the smoke fell a tear and it landed on the handle of the sword. The gold droplet filled the sun symbol at the top of the sword's handle and shone as brightly as the sun itself. Bryn thanked the Timon de Flamme as she felt his heart beat slow and stop. The wisp of smoke drifted higher and disappeared into the twinkling sky. As the smoke dissipated on the ground, IronHeart came over to sit upon the vacant Stone. He bowed his head before Malcolm.

"Are you to replace the elder dragon in this Circle and leave me behind?" Malcolm asked.

IronHeart smiled. "No, my prince. I am here to witness this event, as are you. We can, at your bidding, pledge our allegiance to the Brae. Here it will bind us, and we cannot go against this bond; to do so would mean our death. The other choice is to leave now and return to Wessex to wait. It is and always will be your choice."

Prince Malcolm looked up at his dragon and nodded, then looked over to the light that encircled Bryn. He did not fully understand what was happening, but he knew in his heart he could never leave this company. He nodded at Bryn and said, "I accept the bond. I pledge my life to this company."

Neulta and Leus spoke together. "What lies before us is not of our choosing."

Mcylarn smiled at them. "You must witness the joining. To do so you must choose."

Neulta looked at Leus. "Can we take this step?"

"We must or the joining does not take place," Leus replied.

Neulta turned back to Meylarn. "I need guidance."

"I can give none."

Neulta looked at the other dragons that sat around the Circle. Each one was sitting as if turned to stone and would not meet Neulta's gaze. Neulta moved her eyes over each dragon. She could not choose.

"We have never chosen dragons," she said, her voice full of remorse. "I know not how to choose."

Bryn heard the exchange and felt that she had to come to Neulta's aid. She could not move toward Neulta, but she could speak with her heart. *Cousin, what in your heart is most dear to you? The woods, the water, the earth, the sky?*

"All of these things I hold precious," Neulta and Leus replied together.

And you wish for them to remain safe from harm?

"We do."

I am your servant, Bryn began.

"I am your guardian," Neulta replied.

Bryn looked up at a Vent de Nuit. She knew that the breed had once been a friend of the woodland elves that lived in the lands over the southern seas. Bryn called to the deep blue dragon and she bowed her head. The dragon looked at Bryn and over to the elves.

"I cannot bond with these creatures," the dragon said. "Yet, I will remain with them so long as they are with you, dragon daughter. They will need to choose to stay with you or return to their own kind."

Bryn nodded her acknowledgement. She silently called back to Neulta and Leus.

Stand beside the deep blue dragon. His name is NightWatcher. He will remain with you so long as you are with the company. Do you accept?

Neulta looked at NightWatcher and went to stand at the Stone. She bowed her head once and turned her gaze toward Bryn and the center of the Circle. Leus hesitated a moment longer before joining his sister. He nodded at the dragon.

NightWatcher turned his attention back to Bryn.

I will remain, NightWatcher said to Bryn's heart.

"We have missed much," Leus said to his sister. "I would have liked to see these dragons long before now."

Neulta smiled at her brother. "It is why we are here now, little brother. It is why we were chosen to witness this event."

I am grateful to you, Bryn told Neulta and Leus.

"It is we who should thank you, Bryn of the Brae," Leus replied. "It is past the time for elves and humans to again dwell together."

On the ten Stones that created the arc of the Circle, three elder dragons had been replaced with three young dragons, and a young dragon had come to stand with the elves. The disappearance of the others did not feel like death to Bryn's heart, and she felt alive with their parting tears. There remained five dragons on the remaining five Stones, as well as Meydra and Meylarn, who sat on the last two Stones that closed the Circle. From far up in the sky, the company heard the call of more dragons. Looking up, Bryn saw the shapes of three new ones as they descended toward the Circle. A trio of Vermeil dragons—the flash of orange and gold from their wings gave away the breed—swooped down and hovered over the Stone Circle. They set down on the grass outside the Circle and stood with wings open wide. From the sky dropped two more, a Nomic Reaper and a large and beautiful Astrum, rarely seen in this part of the world. Bryn greeted the Astrum and thanked her for her company.

I have waited long for this, the Astrum replied in dragon song.

The two new dragons took up spots on the ground next to the Vermeils, with their wings held open wide. Bryn recognized the Nomic Reaper as the dragon that had Companioned Lothan and was at the loch for the death of the former High Dragon.

"Where is your rider?" she called to the Reaper.

"He prepares for war," the Reaper replied. "The menace prepares his revenge."

Bryn's heart sank. The raiders were coming and she had yet to reach Skerrabrae. She turned slowly to see all the dragons standing with their wings outstretched, and noticed that Thalynder had not yet approached the Stones.

Thalynder had sat quietly while the others moved to the Stones. She watched in awe as the older dragons were replaced with younger versions of themselves. So many dragons coming to one place and she felt overwhelmed. Those dragons she had met at the loch had all come now and had either replaced an older dragon, like Caraid and IronHeart, or had come to see Bryn, as was the case with Lothan's dragon. She did not see another Twayling dragon on the Stones except for Meylarn.

Thalynder's thoughts turned over and over. She fidgeted with the hem of her tunic to avoid looking directly at Meydra. In her heart she heard the song and it filled her with sadness. She felt as if her heart would break, and wanted to run to Bryn and feel Bryn's steady arms holding her against the deepening abyss in her heart. She did not know if Meydra would be replaced, she did not want Meydra to be replaced. She felt lost and did not know what to do. Looking down at her hands she saw the dirt on her fingernails, the calluses on her palms. I am no longer the pampered princess, she thought. Can I commit to being a warrior? Her head told her to run, that if she did not approach the Stone, Meydra would be safe. Yet her heart pulled her toward Bryn.

Bryn turned to see Thalynder still as death. She tried to hold her arms out toward Thalynder, but she could not move.

No, Meylarn said silently to Bryn. *You must not influence her decision.*

She is unsure, I must help her.

You cannot, Meydra said and turned to look at Thalynder. She could not speak to Thalynder, as it was Thalynder's decision, and neither she nor Bryn were permitted to make her mind up for her. Meydra saw the hesitation in Thalynder's shoulders. She felt the pull of Bryn on her, but she also felt the strong-headed childish stubbornness that had always guided Thalynder in the past.

The choice that lay before Thalynder would test her love. Meydra had known this all along. The choice for Thalynder was either life with Bryn or life with Meydra. If Thalynder chose Meydra, the dragon would not be with Bryn, and all that was hoped for would cease. If Thalynder chose Bryn, she also chose the path that would lead her away from Bryn and back to the Realm that Touches Two Seas. For if she chose Bryn, she was choosing to lead the army of her realm, even if she did not understand that was where her choice would take her. Meydra waited.

Meylarn sensed the hesitation in the princess. Though she was unable to provide guidance, Meylarn could facilitate things a bit by her suggestions. She looked at Bryn. *Place the crown on your head, Daughter.*

Bryn reached into her tunic and pulled the headpiece from her pocket. As she placed it on her forehead, the headpiece sparkled and began to glow. But then the glow began to fade. The front with the smaller circles began to darken, the silver dulled and became black as soot. The outer circle too began to turn black.

"What has happened to the crown?" Kenna asked.

Arryn looked over at Bryn and saw the crown losing its luster. He frowned. Something was wrong. "I do not know."

Thalynder looked at the crown and realized that her indecision was causing it to fade. She knew in her heart what she had to do, and that was to give up one love for the other. She could not give up her dragon, and she could not give up Bryn. She knew she would see Bryn over the years, as nothing could truly separate them, but could she give up riding her dragon, or having a dragon to protect her through the coming battles? She stood up and ran her hands over her tunic. She fingered the embroidery of her family crest and took a deep breath, releasing it slowly to gain strength. Finally, she took a tentative step forward. She looked up at Meydra. Slowly, she walked toward the Stone where Meydra sat and as she approached it, she held her palms out and up toward Meydra. "I do not wish to see you replaced, Meydra. You have been as a mother to me."

Meydra's heart skipped a beat, thinking Thalynder had chosen her and not Bryn. In her heart, she knew this was the decision that all the dragons feared.

Thalynder took another deep breath. "But I must choose Bryn."

Meydra's heart leapt with joy, and she lifted her head and began another song, deep and soulful. The dragons perched both on the Stones and on the ground joined her and sang in unison. Their voices filled the air. From high in the sky, other dragons began their descent, and in a matter of moments, the Stone Circle was surrounded by dragons. Meydra lifted off her Stone and went to stand next to Bryn.

Thalynder's heart began to ache. She knew Meydra was going to be replaced. She could not choose her new dragon, her dragon must choose her. But would she be chosen? She who had been the reason why Bryn did not have her dragon. She who did not understand until today the pain Meydra must have endured to uphold an oath. She wept as she waited to see which, if any, dragon would come to sit on the Stone.

Arryn understood now the words of Anethar back in Skiel. She had warned him that there would be a choice and it would be a difficult one for Bryn and Thalynder. Anethar had warned him to remain strong for Bryn's sake. He believed that Thalynder's choice to have Meydra replaced would crush Bryn's heart. He tried to speak but found he could not.

Bryn felt the wave of relief wash over her like mist on the heather moors. She was warmed and comforted by the beating of the dragons' hearts with her own. She felt their sadness too, but it was not the sadness of loss but of change. Sad to see one thing become another, but at the same time, elated by the prospect of the change itself. Bryn could feel the anticipation and the expectation that each dragon held inside. She also could feel the confusion among the Companions. Above all, she felt the most amazing feeling of unconditional love fill her with joy.

The Astrum, ancient dragon of the far eastern lands, lifted up from the ground and settled on the Stone that Meydra had vacated. She looked down at Thalynder. "I choose you, little Princess," she said in halting speech. "We have much to learn from each other."

Thalynder bowed to the Astrum. "I am honored. What name may I call you?"

"In your tongue, I am ApinYa."

Bryn thanked ApinYa with her heart and looked at Meydra. Bryn understood but knew the rest of the company did not. She spoke silently to Meylarn: *They need resolution.*

"It is my need as well," Meylarn said aloud.

Meylarn glanced at Thalynder and smiled. "We thank you for your decision. In time you will see the wisdom." Meylarn faced Meydra and Bryn. She bowed her head once very low to them.

"This day has been long in coming." Meylarn stood tall on the Stone, her wings spread and her head held high. She raised her voice in song:

> *There sits a Jewel waiting*
> *Hidden deep inside the breast*
> *When light is shone upon its face*
> *It will outshine the rest*
> *In the heart lies the desire*
> *To unite a troubled land*

To seek the hearts of noble kin
With open and outstretched hand
Under her spell of dragon song
And lit with an inner light
The Jewel will shine for all to see
And at last they will unite.

The company bowed their heads at the words and as the last note was sung, they felt the rumble of the earth beneath their feet. The Stones rocked gently and the Companions started to back away from the heavy monoliths. The dragons at their backs urged the company to step deeper into the Circle, near the wings of the dragons on the ground. As the company moved forward in the Circle, the shaking of the ground stopped and the Stones became still. The sky overhead darkened and the stars disappeared.

Meylarn lifted above the Circle with all eyes following her. Meydra lifted to join Meylarn, and Thalynder felt a tug at her heart. The two dragons lifted high into the sky, swirling around each other, turning to a white mist that rose above the Circle, glowing against the black sky. All was dark, except for the two dragons—and Bryn. The silver Tree of Life glowed on Bryn's tunic. Her sword shone with a blue-white light. Bryn herself was encased in a brilliant light, and at her forehead the headpiece began to shine again. As the mist that was the two dragons rose, it took the light of the Circle with it. The sword stopped glowing, as did Bryn's tunic. Bryn's body shimmered lightly, but the light receded as the dragons' light rose higher. The only light left below the disappearing dragons was the soft glow of the silver outer circle of the headpiece Bryn wore and the three smaller circles at the center.

The company had followed the wisp of light up with the two dragons. The dragons standing on the Stones also followed the two Twaylings up into the air with their heads lifted and their eyes turned skyward. As all continued to watch, the dragons vanished and the wisp dissipated. For a moment all was black; the earth trembled once, and a brilliant flash lit up the sky. An explosion of light and color overhead caused all to gasp at the sight.

"No!" Kenna and Arryn called out at the same time and bowed their heads in disbelief. Malcolm shielded his eyes, and Neulta and Leus clutched each other's hands and stood as still as stone. Thalynder bowed her head and began to weep.

From inside the Circle, Bryn called to her company.

"Do not lose heart my family, as this is only the beginning. Look to the sky!"

The company raised their heads and watched in awe as a light sparked and a star fell from the sky. It landed in the middle of the small circles on Bryn's headpiece. A single diamond of clear dragon tear formed to resemble a pointed star, its rays extending out from the three small circles. Bryn disappeared behind the brilliance of the tear. A second flash overhead caused the company to look up again. This time the shards of the explosion lifted high into the sky to join the stars that were beginning to show themselves again in the inky darkness. One small spark of light wavered and began a slow descent toward the Circle. As it came closer, the company could see that it was a dragon. A shimmering gray-white dragon they did not recognize. It descended slowly on a wisp of stardust sparkles. The sparkles fell before the dragon and landed on Bryn's tunic.

The sky began to lighten, and again it was day with a cloudless blue sky. Bryn stood in the Circle wearing a calf-length undertunic of storm gray, and a deep blue hip-length tunic with the embroidered Tree of Life and the silver dragon, only now the silver shone as if it were starlight itself. Her feet were bare and her long unbraided hair lay against her back. In her hand she held the sword with the three jewels glinting in the sun. On her head she wore the ancient crown, crafted by the first dragons and their first human-elf Companions. In the middle of the crown, the diamond dragon tear shone brightly.

Bryn held her sword over her head and called in dragon song to the creature above her.

I am your servant, she called.

The dragon was still high, slowly descending back to earth. As it neared the others, and the company, it sang a sweet, soft song of peace. It alighted on the Decision Stone and immediately the gray-white light dimmed. On the Stone, clad in a new color of gray and white, stood Meydra. Upon her forehead a single diamond twinkled. She bowed her head slightly at the other dragons, which in turn dropped their gazes and lowered their heads. She turned to Bryn and bowed.

Bryn sheathed her sword and stepped toward Meydra. She held out her hands to place them on each of Meydra's cheeks. She touched her forehead to the dragon's, and the two diamonds glinted in the sunlight as they came together. The gem in Bryn's crown flared in brilliance and in an instant was fused to her skin; the silver outer circle fused to her brow. Bryn kissed Meydra's cheek and turned to smile at the Companions.

"Meylarn has given herself to the stars so that this joining could take place. Her tear has taken its place in this crown. Meylarn was born for this purpose, to hold the position of High Dragon until the time Meydra could assume her rightful place. Meydra's place as High Dragon began over one thousand years ago and was set aside when the world changed and became a place of wars. Her brother took her place to allow her to protect the line that would someday produce the Jewel that Unites. When Meldred died, Meylarn took his place, again to protect the truth. The time has come to reveal the truth. Meydra and I will lead you to Skerrabrae, where questions will be asked and answers given."

"I thought we had lost you," Thalynder said to Meydra. "I did not know this would happen."

"Ah, Princess," Meydra cooed. "Did you not? You knew in your heart that you must choose Bryn."

"That I did," Thalynder replied. "But I thought that meant you had to be replaced."

"Have I not been replaced by the magnificent ApinYa?"

"You have. I am still a child and do not fully understand."

"You are learning the ways of the world, little princess. You will soon have another decision to make. Listen to your heart and you will know which path to take."

Thalynder bowed her head to Meydra.

Bryn looked at the company. "We must fight to keep the truth that is our heritage. The raiders from over the seas *will* come. They will come and continue to come. We will fight them for generations, until the last of the clanns draw breath and the last dragon takes to the stars. It is our destiny. You five have chosen to witness, now you must choose to follow. I need your strength, I need your armies." She looked at Malcolm and Kenna. "I need the realm you command, Prince Malcolm, and the clann you will lead, Kenna of the Bridei, to be my allies and my captains."

Prince Malcolm nodded and took a step toward Bryn. His dragon dropped his tail to come between Malcolm and Bryn. "You must not touch her," IronHeart said.

Malcolm cleared his throat. "I will advise my father, but you have my word. My armies will come to your aid."

"Do you accept, Kenna of the Bridei?"

"I do, Jewel of the Brae. My clann welcomes you with open arms."

Bryn nodded her head at Kenna. "It is we who welcome you, the Bridei, back to the arms of the clanns."

Bryn turned to Neulta and Leus. "Your kith and kin are not long for this world. Already the ways of man have driven the elves further and further from our tribulations. You were long in coming to the ways of the dragons, you were long in coming to the aid of man. I can ask nothing of you excect for your loyalty when it comes to the company. For myself, I ask that you, my cousins, remember we are of the same first peoples. My mother is sister to your mother. We descend from the same stock, and as such I ask that our common ancestry become our bond of trust."

Neulta and Leus spoke together. "We are your cousins, we are your right and left hands. We will follow you, and we will aid man in this fight against the tyrants from over the seas. You have our word. We need your strength as you need our loyalty." Leus took his sword from his belt and stuck it into the ground. "The earth as our witness."

Bryn nodded her head at the two elves. She then turned to Arryn.

"Trusted friend," she said and smiled. "You have known for many days now that this would be an end and a beginning. You replaced your coat of armor from the king with the jerkin of your clann. Will you lead your clann to join the others? You will give up much if you so decide to follow me. Though, in my heart, I see a light at the end of your dark journey. There is much ahead of you, Arryn of the Epidii. What is your desire?"

Arryn had already made up his mind to follow Bryn when he first put on his clann jerkin. He took a small object out of his pocket and placed it over his head to rest on his neck. It was the stone with the fish rune carved into the rock, strung on a piece of leather. As he adjusted it on his neck, Meydra blew a short breath on the stone. The stone glowed and as the light receded, a new rune appeared on the stone above the Epidii symbol. It was the rune symbol for the Brae clann. Meydra smiled at Arryn.

"It was your destiny to lead the clanns under the Brae," she said to him. "My heart is glad to see you have chosen this path as your own."

The Oslona dragon that sat upon the Stone above Arryn dropped its tail to brush Arryn's back. Arryn looked up and saw kindness in the dragon's eyes. He began to understand the bond a dragon has with its Companion. He now felt the beating of the Oslona's heart match his own, and it filled him with great joy.

Bryn turned to look at Thalynder. Her heart, though filled with the joy of all the dragons and the newly found trust of the Companion, still held a sliver of doubt as she looked at her love. Would Thalynder choose on her own to leave Bryn and return to her father's realm to assume the crown when it became hers, thus providing Bryn with the needed army? Or would she choose to stay with Bryn, forsaking her destiny as queen? Bryn wanted Thalynder beside her, but she knew that her own destiny no longer permitted her to dwell on personal need.

Do not worry, Sister, Meydra said to Bryn's heart. *You will feel Thalynder in your arms again.*

Thalynder understood her choice. It was made clear to her when Meydra descended from the sky and not Meylarn. The journey to the Stones was preordained. She weighed her options carefully. It was her choice to either stay with Bryn and fight at her side, living a nomadic life, sleeping in caves and under trees, curled up together when time allowed; or to return to her father, become queen of the realm upon her father's death, and send her army to aid Bryn. There has to be a center line, she thought.

"I cannot give you up," Thalynder began. "Yet, I cannot endure hurting my father. I too have the same sense of wanting to lead my people. We could do this together, could we not? Could you not choose the Realm that Touches Two Seas to be your home from where you command the clanns?"

Bryn looked up at Meydra. Meydra nodded and Bryn walked over to Thalynder.

As Thalynder watched Bryn approach her, Bryn appeared taller to Thalynder's eyes and softer around the edges, yet her eyes held a firm conviction. The crown with its jewel at her forehead was fused with her skin now. Bryn would not be able to remove that crown, Thalynder knew. She would be forever the Jewel that Unites. It saddened Thalynder a little.

"How can I decide to leave you?" Thalynder said as Bryn approached.

Bryn fingered the cowrie shell at Thalynder's throat. "How can I have you leave?" Bryn took Thalynder's hands in hers. "I must fight the invader. I can do it with you here at my side and risk your death, or I can do it with you safely behind the walls of your keep, where I could come to see you often."

"I will still have to marry."

Bryn chuckled. "We knew you would, that has always been your destiny. You will just have to marry a man who will turn his head when I come for a visit. Will you continue to wear this?"

"You said we would wear them until we found my true love and our quest was over," Thalynder replied. "The quest is not over."

"You still believe that true love awaits you?" Arryn asked.

"No, silly," Thalynder replied. "I said the quest was not over, I never said anything about not finding true love."

Bryn smiled at Thalynder. "Then wear it, my Lynder, until the quest is over."

Thalynder smiled and felt better. She kissed Bryn's cheeks and looked into her eyes.

"Your eyes are different."

"What do you see in them?"

"The color of twilight, I think. Your blue eyes have specks of deep lavender."

"You see Athyl," Meydra replied.

Thalynder nodded. "It may be hard to sleep with that jewel shining in my eyes." She looked closer at the jewel and noticed the runes that were carved into it. She started to reach up to touch them, when Bryn took her hand and shook her head slightly.

"It will burn you, my love."

"What are the words etched into the jewel?"

"It is my name."

"That is not Bryn," Thalynder said. "I have seen the rune that is your name. Yet, this rune too is familiar. Where have I seen it before?"

Meydra nudged Bryn's back, and Bryn stepped back to face the others. Meydra spoke quietly. "The rune is the symbol of the Daughter of the Ancients—Athebryn, Jewel of the Brae. It is carved into the stones that grace Arlendyl's mantelpiece. It is also written on all the Gathering Stones that lead to this Circle, and many of you saw it on the monolith out on the plain. Written long before Bryn was ever conceived was the story of the princess who would join with a dragon and become the leader of her people in a time when a leader was sorely needed. The name given to that princess was Athebryn and it means Born of Athyl. I gave Bryn that name knowing who she was long before her birth. Her mother, Arlendyl, asked me to name the child after I took her to be my Companion. Her true name was never revealed so as not to draw attention to the child.

"It was her song that called me to her. It was at that time that I knew the legend was no longer myth. The Jewel that would unite the clans was to be born among Arlendyl's Druids. Bryn's family shared stories with her that no other Druid child was told. Her path was set before her in hopes that she would come to choose what destiny already held for her."

Meydra turned and said to Bryn, "It is time. Your people await you."

Bryn drew her sword. The dragons spread their wings and lifted their heads toward the sky. Bryn raised her sword skyward and called with them.

"I never left my people," she said onto the wind. "I am Athebryn, Jewel of the Ancients, Dragon Daughter of the Brae. Follow me!"

King Heardred stood on the banks of the wide river and spoke to the gods. "I will have my revenge!" Word had not yet returned to him about his missing son, but in his heart he knew Helstun had died or been killed. Helstun, his true son and heir, would not now return to Götaland—leaving the realm to fall to his stepsons Hygid and Heoroth. King Heardred did not wish to wait for the boats to return with the sad news. Nevertheless, he knew if he went against the seers' recommendations and left without word, he would lose the faith of his subjects.

The boats were filled with supplies and the army kept at the ready, prepared to man the boats and launch at a moment's notice. Heardred would not waste one minute once he received news, good or ill. Even if his son were returned to him, he did not intend to wait for winter to begin anew his plan to take the northern islands from the squeamish painted Picts or the docile Druids. If he could not build an empire, he would take one.

So ends the first leg of our company's journey.